Dance Me to the End of Love

By

Theresa E. Liggins

ISBN: 1-4107-4027-7 (e-book)
ISBN: 1-4107-4026-9 (Paperback)
ISBN: 1-4107-4025-0 (Dust Jacket)

Library of Congress Control Number: 2003092287

This book is printed on acid free paper.

Printed in the United States of America
Bloomington, IN

1stBooks – rev. 04/04/03

Acknowledgements

My family and friends... You saw me through. Thank you!

"Within the embrace of family we discover the sharing of life's most precious legacy. It is here we learn to love and to be loved, and to understand the meaning of listening hearts, outstretched hands, and the song of joy and laughter. The beauty of family brings us cherished memories we wish to hold forever, for it is through our memories that our hearts find their way home." —Flavia

José, thanks for the dance! Te quiero.

"When those who know us best believe in us, they give hope to our hearts and strength to our dreams." —Flavia

Rhonda, thank you for the beautiful artwork for my cover. It has been my pleasure having the opportunity to work with you and to have your art adorn my book.

"Cast your dreams upon these pages and reach for the music that dances within your soul." —Flavia

Theresa

Original Artwork for Cover by Rhonda Polen Wernick,
Copyright 2003 DancingArtTM
More of Rhonda's art can be found at www.dancingart.com

Chapter One

It was five in the morning when the sound of someone entering the dark bedroom jolted Tyana awake from a deep sleep. She was having difficulty waking and clearing her head so she could make out the sounds that seemed to be approaching her in the quiet night. She wasn't able to completely focus her eyes on the figure coming toward her but she could see a silhouette of what appeared to be a tall man. She glanced over at the clock but couldn't make out the time. She could only hear the ticking sound it was making, which seemed to get louder the longer she stared at it. Her heart started pounding wildly as the tall figure got closer.

She sat straight up in bed in an attempt to focus her eyes better. Everything was so fuzzy, and she wasn't sure if she was still dreaming or not. A voice called out to her, "Tyana? Are you awake? Did I wake you?"

"Ellis? Is that you? What are you doing here—why are you here? I thought we had decided that you were not to return here." Tyana was confused and shocked by Ellis' presence.

"What are you talking about, I live here, and when did we have that discussion? I'm just getting in from my trip. Are you OK?" Ellis turned on the lamp next to the bed where she lay. He was confused. She wasn't making any sense.

Tyana realized then that she had been asleep, dreaming. However, she still wasn't absolutely sure that she could distinguish

1

between her dream-state and reality. As she pulled the sheets away from her body, she scanned the room, glanced over herself to see what she was wearing, then looked up at Ellis. "Yes. I'm OK. I guess I was dreaming when you came in. What time is it?" She continued to try to get her bearings, still very disoriented.

"It's a little after five a.m., honey. I'm sorry I woke you. The flight was delayed—it was a fiasco. It took us forever to get out of there. I didn't want to call you to tell you about the delay because I didn't want to wake you, but maybe I should have called. You still look confused about me being here. Did something happen? Are you sure you're all right?" Ellis sat down next to Tyana and put his hand on her face. He moved in closer to give her a kiss but she instantly leaned away. "What is it? Why did you pull away like that?"

She got up and began walking toward the bathroom, leaving Ellis still sitting on the bed. "Uh…I just have to go to the bathroom, that's all. Where was your trip? You're away so much I lose track sometimes. I must have too much going on and my brain is overloaded or something." She was stalling, as she still wasn't feeling completely coherent. She closed the bathroom door behind her and splashed some cold water on her face. She stared at herself in the mirror, wondering why she was so confused. She was thinking about the dream that she had been having before Ellis awakened her, and how incredibly real it seemed to her. She still wasn't convinced that it was only a dream. She was also thinking how bizarre and vivid the whole dream was and how she couldn't get it out of her head. It seemed to her that she had been asleep for a lifetime.

Tyana had been in the bathroom for quite a while before Ellis knocked on the door to check on her. He couldn't figure out why she was acting so strange. He'd come home during the night on several occasions and had never seen her behave in this manner. He was becoming a little concerned.

"What do you mean, where was the trip? I told you I was in San Diego and I called you several times while I was there. Tyana, is everything all right in there? You've been in there for quite a while now. Are you feeling OK? Do you need something?" He was doing his best to understand, but just figured she was a little disoriented from being awakened. Perhaps she had been in a deep sleep, he was thinking.

"Yeah, I'm fine. I'll be out in a minute."

Tyana immediately stiffened when she heard Ellis say he had been in San Diego. There was something about San Diego that got her attention. Why was San Diego so significant to her? She had so many questions scrambling about in her head. She appeared dazed when she returned from the bathroom, still looking at Ellis in a peculiar way, as if she wasn't sure who he was or why he was there. He just watched her as she returned to bed. Now he was beginning to worry about her. He thought that maybe she was sick or coming down with something. He wanted to check her for fever.

"Tyana, baby, are you feeling ill? You don't look too well. Should we take your temperature? Here, let me feel your head to see if you're warm at all. Do you think you caught a bug or something?" He approached her to feel her head, but she backed away from him

3

slightly. That was the second time she had done that to him and he wasn't going to let it go again. "Tyana, what is wrong with you? Why are you acting like this? I was just going to feel your forehead. What's with you?" he asked, growing impatient with her eccentric behavior. He was much too tired to play guessing games with her, especially if she was ill. He wanted to get her medical attention immediately if she needed it.

Tyana looked around the room again with a puzzled look on her face. "Ellis, I'm sorry, I don't know why I did that. It's the weirdest thing. I don't know how I got here, I mean in this bed, and I don't know why you're here. I can't explain it but it just doesn't make sense to me. I thought I was...and you were..." She stopped for a second and looked back at him with strong eyes. "Who were you with in San Diego? I mean, were you working with any colleagues on this project? Did you run into anyone there that you know?" It was still a little fuzzy to Tyana, but for some reason, she felt a need to ask him those questions. Ellis worked for a prominent hotel that had several hundred locations around the world. He often went on business trips for sales conferences to oversee grand openings.

"What's gotten into you? Why the questions, or should I say, interrogation? Of course I was working with my colleagues on the project. A few, anyway. That's what I do when opening a new hotel. And, no, I didn't run into anyone else there that I know, other than those on the project. Maybe you should lie down and get some rest. I think you woke up too fast and you were dreaming about something that's still stuck in your mind. Everything's fine, just go to sleep. I

4

know I'm going to hit the sack for a few hours, at least. I need to get into the office no later than noon today." Ellis began to undress and headed to the bathroom to wash up. When he returned, Tyana was sound sleep. He got into bed next to her and put his arms around her. He couldn't help but reflect on the way she had acted when he got home and why she was acting distant, as if he was unfamiliar to her or even estranged. He couldn't make heads or tails out of it. After a few moments of watching her sleep and thinking about her unusual behavior, he dozed off himself.

When Ellis awoke, it was ten-thirty in the morning. He turned over and noticed that Tyana was gone. She had left hours ago for work. He was thinking that he must have been exhausted to not know that she had gotten up and left. He proceeded to get out of bed and make his way to the bathroom. It was certainly going to be a long day for him, having gotten little sleep.

Tyana sat at her desk in her design studio, deep in thought, feeling as if she was having a premonition. It had never happened to her before so she was especially preoccupied with the sensation. She kept asking herself, what was it with Ellis that had her on edge? Just then, her phone rang.

"Tatyana Dominique."

"Tyana, it's me. What are you doing this evening? Do you want to go to a premiere with me? I got free tickets, of course, from one of the other ad agents. Our firm got the lead actor his role in this drama, so we're going to show our support." It was Kellie, her best friend, calling with yet another attempt at getting her away from work to relax and take a break from the rat race.

"That sounds great and I'd love to go, but..." Tyana barely got out the next word when Kellie interrupted.

"But nothing. You always have a 'but'. Work will be there, Tyana. You're the best interior designer in Arizona. You have clients beating down your door if you haven't noticed. You can put a few on hold, you know. You never take any time off to do something fun. Just say you'll go—for once. Please?" Kellie was determined.

"Well, for your information, what I was about to say was, I would love to go; however, I have other plans for this evening. I have dance lessons scheduled with my dance instructor. I went for a couple of lessons already and it's pretty exciting. You should check it out with me. It was more than what I had expected. And Antonio..." Tyana stopped abruptly in mid-sentence as if she had lost her train of thought.

"And Antonio...what?" Kellie asked, trying to prompt her to finish her sentence.

"Kellie, there's something very weird going on and it just hit me again. It feels like déjà vu or something. I just can't quite put my finger on it. I got this strong feeling last night, or rather early this morning, when Ellis came home from San Diego. There was something about him that I was uncomfortable with or anxious about. I didn't understand it or know why the feeling was so strong. I couldn't remember where he had been and for some reason, I felt that there was more to his trip than the usual, but that doesn't make sense.

6

Why this particular trip? And whenever he would come near me to touch me, I would back away by reflex. I don't know why I did that, either. Then, just now, while I was telling you about my dance lessons with Antonio, I had that same feeling again—like there was something familiar about Antonio, something I've already experienced. This is so weird and I don't know why it's happening."

"Girl, you're not making any sense. Maybe you're overworked. That's possible. I think you need to take more time off to relax your mind and do something fun. It's no wonder you're going crazy—just kidding! So, what's up with this dancing stuff? Have you decided to take lessons permanently? What about Ellis—is he joining you? At least it's a step in the right direction, meaning you'll be doing something fun. I love to dance. I just don't think dancing is in Paul's future. I can't seem to get him out of court long enough to do anything with me. He's got more clients so far this year than he had all year last year. But, hey, I'm not complaining. He's thinking about purchasing this boat. Hell, it looks like a yacht to me. I just hope he can find time to get away from the office long enough to take the thing out. But back to you, what about these strange feelings you're having? When did they start?" Kellie knew that Tyana wasn't one to exaggerate.

"I don't know Kel, it's probably nothing. Maybe I'm just tired. I was in a deep sleep when Ellis walked in and that's when it happened for the first time. I've been keeping late hours, working non-stop and juggling projects. I'll dismiss it for now and not give it another thought. It's probably nothing. It sounds pretty silly anyway. I'm

7

sure that there's a perfectly good explanation for it. So, anyway, yes, I've decided to take ballroom dance lessons. I've loved ballroom dancing ever since long ago, when I went to this live ballroom dance competition. I've never really forgotten about it. It stirred something inside me, but I haven't seriously thought about pursing it through the years, with my career and all. But when I went in for my first lesson last week it all came back. I thought about inviting Ellis along, which would make sense, but he's rarely in town and when he is, it would be almost impossible for us to synchronize our schedules. I'll just take a few more lessons, see how I do, then go from there. Chances are, I won't have that much time for anything long-term anyway. Call me tomorrow and tell me how the premiere was. I've got to run—my other line is ringing."

"OK, will do. Have fun tonight!" They ended their conversation and Tyana connected to her other line.

"Tatyana speaking."

"Well, I'm surprised I caught you in your office. Figured you'd be out decorating mansions or something."

"Hey, Trevor! How's it going? Welcome back! How was your honeymoon? How was the trip to Italy? When can we get together so we can get caught up? I want to see all your pictures too—I know Cleo took a bunch. I can't wait to hear about all the gorgeous things she bought and what you saw and did." Tyana was very excited to hear from her good friend, Trevor. They had been extremely close friends for years.

Trevor was a talented and successful architect. He and Tyana had met a few months before she had met Ellis, working on a project together. They had quickly developed a bond and a friendship that had now been cultivated over the years. He always kept a close eye on Tyana and felt especially close to her, almost as if he needed to protect her. He had once been in love with her and had wanted a romantic relationship, but they had decided that their friendship would, by far, be the best thing for them at the time, which turned out to be a good decision. Neither had ever had a closer friendship with a member of the opposite sex. She loved him too, in a special way, and would always have a special place for him in her heart. But Ellis was her true love. There had been no other person that she could imagine being with after she met Ellis.

"The trip was awesome, the weather was perfect, and yes, Cleo did do some damage when it came to souvenir shopping. She got some beautiful things, though, and she's so happy. We actually found some great art pieces that we had shipped home. And the honeymoon itself was spectacular. She's an amazing woman and I'm so lucky to have her as my wife. We had a wonderful time. But I did miss you, Kiddo. What have you been doing since I've been gone? Wait! Let me guess—working, what else? Have you at least taken one day off in the two weeks that we've been gone?" He knew her very well and suspected that she hadn't taken a break, especially if Ellis had been out of town. It usually took him or Kellie to pry her away from her work to do something relaxing.

9

"Well, I certainly missed you too, but it sounds like you were too busy to really miss anyone. It was your honeymoon, for goodness sakes, Trev, I wouldn't expect you to be thinking about anything else." The truth of the matter was, he always thought about her. "I'm glad you're back safe and sound, though. We'll have to get together soon. I'm sorry to have to cut our conversation short, but I have an appointment that I'm going to be late getting to if I don't get out of here very soon. Ellis is home so I'll be tied up tonight, but I'll give you a call tomorrow. Maybe we can catch up then, OK? And thanks for calling. Welcome back!" Tyana and Trevor said their good-byes and hung up.

Tyana's assistant, Melanie, was tidying up in preparation for closing up shop for the day. Melanie didn't put in nearly the hours that Tyana did; however, she worked very hard to keep Tyana's office running as efficiently as possible. She had always felt lucky to have Melanie as the assistant designer. They worked well together and Melanie had a flare for interior design herself, which helped out Tyana tremendously, especially on those rare occasions when she wanted to take some time off to travel with Ellis.

Tyana straightened up only a little, since she was expecting to return to her office after her dance lesson. She still had some things she wanted to finish up before heading home. She promised herself that she wouldn't work late while Ellis was in town. She thought about telling him about her dance lessons before heading to the studio so he would know where she was, but then decided against it. She would rather discuss it with him when she got home. It wasn't a big deal to her and she anticipated it not being a big deal to Ellis, either.

She pulled up to the familiar building and walked toward the entrance. Suddenly she stopped cold in her tracks and quickly turned around, as if she had heard something behind her. She looked around slowly, like she was trying to figure out where she was, but she knew where she was—at the dance studio. Just at that moment, someone exited the dance studio doors, startling Tyana and returning her back to the present. She shook her head and entered the studio.

It was still a lively and magical place, as always. Antonio had shown her around on her first visit and bragged about the fact that it had been recently remodeled. Tyana was still very impressed with the look of the dance studio. It was decorated in a style that she was familiar with, which, remarkably, suited her taste. She couldn't find one thing that she would have done differently, which was strange in itself, she thought. Designers would always find at least one flaw in another designer's work, or see something that they would have designed differently, if not the whole project. She couldn't stop staring at the studio's interior and the detail. It was so alive, fresh, and warm. A person walking through the doors would definitely want to come into the space and be a part of what was happening inside. It was a very comfortable space as well; it had a feeling of energy and excitement. She felt good being there, as if she had been there many times. She felt she was an extension of this place—that somehow she belonged. At that instant, Antonio noticed her standing near the entrance and approached her.

"Tyana! It's so good to see you again. How are you this evening? Can I get you anything?" Antonio was always very courteous and amiable. He was the perfect host to those who entered his "palace", as he often dubbed his studio.

"No thank you. I'm doing well—how about yourself?"

"Just wonderful, thanks for asking. Are you ready for your lesson this evening? I'm very excited about having you as a student. I still can't get over the way you took command of those new steps I showed you the last time—you're a natural. You make my job so easy. I've decided to introduce to you some more new steps. I have the utmost confidence that you'll pick these up with ease as well. Are you sure you haven't done this before? It has taken some students about six months to get where you are walking in the door. I think you're holding out on me—not telling me the whole truth about your background." Antonio truly was amazed at Tyana's dancing skills. She had told him that she had only studied ballet as young girl and into her early teen years, but had given it up once she entered high school and had had no other dance training since. He found that hard to believe after watching her for the first time.

He also found it hard not to notice her beauty and her very sexy body. The day she first walked into his studio he had immediately been attracted to her large dark, alluring eyes; her tall and thin, dancer-like frame; her long, dark, wavy hair; and her warm and bright smile. Antonio had been in the business for almost two decades, and therefore had seen his share of beautiful women. Some were very enticing to him; however, there was something very inviting and warm, yet mysterious about Tyana that not only enticed him, but intrigued him as well. Besides that, he had had a strange feeling that he knew her from somewhere. Since he couldn't place her in any of his past situations, he had dismissed it as probably having seen someone who looked like her. After all, in that business, he'd certainly been almost everywhere and had seen almost everything. He was bound to come across similar people.

"Oh, I think you're being especially nice," Tyana said shyly. Antonio took her hand and led her into one of the several private dance rooms where, as he had promised, he began to teach her the new steps.

They danced several of the new steps with one more to go before they would complete the lesson. The last dance was a rumba. He changed the music to fit the aura of the dance. He refreshed her memory of the basic steps he had shown her the last time she was there. When they had begun to dance, she sensed something very familiar about the music. He was starting to get that familiar feeling again about her. It was a little stronger with him this time, too. He continued to give her instructions while they danced.

Tyana's mind began to wander when Antonio pulled her close to him in a closed stance position. It was at that instant that she had an overwhelming sensation, once again, that she had been in that exact situation before, but that time the sensation included him as well. She almost gasped as the feeling enveloped her for a few seconds. The distraction was so intense it threw her timing off. What she wasn't aware of was that Antonio, simultaneously, felt a similar stirring about her. It was so powerful to him that he lost his count in the middle of the measure. They met each other's eyes and held a steady stare, while the music continue to fill the room and their souls with the soft, dreamy melody.

There was no mention of the little exchange between them; however, they both were having secret thoughts about it in the privacy of their own minds. It was something that neither could consciously ignore.

The lesson continued on smoothly and Tyana was progressing remarkably. Antonio was constantly impressed and excited about being able to teach someone like her, with so much potential. He was actually having fun—it didn't seem like work to teach her. He couldn't help but conjure up ideas about doing special performances, shows, exhibitions, and of course, competitions with her. He was certain that he wanted her as his star student. He was planning to work with her often enough to get her in competition condition. There were several competitions coming up that he definitely had her in mind for. He didn't get the impression that money would be a concern; he needed to make the events appealing and desirable enough for her to want to do them. But there was more to it than just competing or performing—he had a passionate desire to dance with her.

"I'm still amazed by your progress. You have so much talent and skill when it comes to retaining these dance steps. I would like to start working on a few basic routines with you. And, with your permission, I'd like to enter you into a mini competition that'll take place in about three weeks. You'll only be performing with other students at your own level. There's no pressure; it's just a formality to appraise your progress and skills. You'll definitely be ready, so I don't want that to be a concern. You're learning so fast, and dancing appears to be such a natural thing for you. Please think about it. I would be proud to dance with you." Antonio was beaming as he talked about dancing with Tyana. She noticed.

"You say such nice things. I'm just not sure if I can commit to something like that, though. It would depend on my work schedule in the upcoming weeks—how much work I'll have. But I'll certainly consider it. With you as my instructor, I'm sure you can work some magic with me. What kind of dances do you have in mind?" She was actually thrilled at the thought of performing with him. She was getting more excited about her dancing with each lesson. She felt like a kid with a new toy. She, too, beamed as she watched him when he talked more in detail about the mini competition.

Antonio had always been guarded about his private life with both his staff and his clients. He felt that any personal business would only be a distraction from his studio business and purpose. Those who knew Antonio well respected his privacy. He'd been known from time to time to date beautiful women, usually from within the dance business, but never anyone closely associated with his studio. He worked hard at keeping his personal life private and out of the rumor mill. He did that mainly out of respect to his female companions. Antonio was well known in the business and extremely desirable to many women. It often disturbed him, the lengths that some women would go to in order to date or just sleep with him. He wasn't attracted to those women who consistently created situations or attempted to manipulate him in order to get his attention. He found it to be an instant turn-off. It only made them look ridiculous, and he had very little respect for them. He was still surprised by those women who would continue their relentless pursuit of him even after they had learned that he was in a committed relationship. He could only wonder how they would feel if someone did that to their men in an attempt to disrupt their relationships. Like they say, what goes around comes around. He felt sometimes that his good looks were a curse. He received so many offers from women to help him with this thing or that, that it was sometimes hard to know whom he could trust; who had *his* best interest in mind instead of theirs.

For the most part, Antonio didn't have much time for a serious relationship. He was devoted to his business, and his schedule usually left him with little time to date. He would also feel guilty if he couldn't give a relationship the attention it needed. He never wanted to hurt anyone, but sometimes he had to choose his business over everything else. It was usually tough for him when it came to love. He would often bury himself in his work so he wouldn't think about it, but that kind of emptiness still found its way to the surface from time to time. He was also at an age where he was ready to settle down and have some permanence in his life, but it just wasn't easy for him to find someone who could accept his lifestyle and the schedule he maintained.

"Tyana, just leave everything to me. You'll be a star in no time. In fact, you're on your way. You have a lot of talent for this and I want to be able to develop your potential. I think you'll approve of the ideas I have for some upcoming events. Once you become recognized in these events, a whole new world of opportunities will present itself to you and you'll be able to learn more about this world. It's very exciting. Every day that I do this, I discover something new. It's exhilarating and special. You're special." Antonio didn't mean to add that, but it was there before he could think twice. But at the moment he said it, he felt that sensation again, as if he'd said that to her before. The way she was standing and looking at him was very familiar to him. His heart started beating a little faster.

"So, can you come back tomorrow? I'd like to get started right away on preparing you for the mini competition. I could easily add your name to fifteen routines, no sweat." Antonio wanted to ignore the feeling he was having. It was starting to concern him, especially because of his relationship to Tyana. It was never a good idea to get emotionally involved with students. He viewed them strictly as clients, with no personal attachment. It was best to do it that way.

"Fifteen routines sounds aggressive to me. Like I mentioned, it depends on my schedule. Let's talk a little more about that as we get closer to the competition. But tomorrow is fine, although, I won't be available until around eight tomorrow night." Tyana was thinking that that would depend on Ellis' schedule as well. She wanted to spend some time with him while he was home.

Theresa E. Liggins

"Tomorrow night at eight it is. Great, I've got you down. Thanks again for a great lesson and I look forward to seeing you tomorrow." Antonio walked Tyana to the door and hugged her good-bye. He caught a whiff of her fragrance, closed his eyes and slowly breathed in, inhaling it. He had almost lost himself in the moment, but quickly composed himself and pulled back. She sensed something unusual about that hug. She thought it was her imagination or that perhaps she had read too much into it. She said good-bye and left the studio to go home—home to Ellis.

Chapter Two

Tyana drove home thinking about all that had happened to her since early that morning. She felt as if she were possessed or something. Strange things were happening to her and she had no explanation whatsoever for any of them. She thought about returning to the office to finish up her work, but because she was having such a weird day, she decided to make it an early evening and spend some time with Ellis, if he was home. If not, she would just take it easy and maybe watch some TV, which was something she seldom did.

When she arrived home, she noticed that Ellis' car was not in the garage. He wasn't home yet, she thought. It was already seven p.m. and she expected that he would be there by now, but of course, he could have gotten tied up at the office. He did, however, just return from a lengthy business trip. She entered the house and headed toward her office to deposit her things. She sat down in her chair to collect her thoughts.

She sat quietly and reflected on her entire day, beginning with the episode with Ellis. Then her thoughts quickly took her to her ballroom dance lesson with Antonio. She couldn't help but wonder what had happened in there. Did she really feel something familiar and extraordinary with Antonio for that brief moment? She was racking her brain trying to figure out what was going on with her today and why some of the day's events seemed as if they had happened before. Then, she thought that maybe she dreamed those things, but it just seemed too real for a dream.

She agonized over those incidents for nearly an hour, completely losing track of time. She was so deep in thought she almost didn't hear her cell phone ringing.

"Hello?"

"Tyana, it's me. Are you at home or at the office? I tried your number at the office and got no answer." It was Ellis.

"I'm at home, Ellis, where are you? I thought you might be home yourself by now. What time is it anyway?" She hadn't realized the time in a while and noticed that she was sitting in the dark. She turned on the light to look at her watch.

"It's almost nine and I'm still at the office. Something came up and I need to take care of a few things before heading out. I should be there in about an hour or so, OK?" Ellis sounded a little preoccupied to Tyana.

"Ellis, you've been gone for a couple of weeks. I just thought we could spend some time together tonight, catch up and have dinner together. What's so important now?" she asked, feeling a little dejected. She was thinking that she was beginning to lose her edge. She was exhausted from her work and dance lessons, and from trying to uncover her perplexing mystery.

"Tyana, I'm sorry, but something came up regarding some potential clients and I must tend to it immediately. It can't be helped. I'll get there as soon as I can, but don't wait up for me. I'll just grab something from the hotel dining room. Look, I'll get there as soon as

I get free from this situation. I'll see you later." Ellis was a little abrupt and cut their conversation short. She was still holding the phone when he hung up.

"I'm sorry for the interruption, where were we?" Ellis said when he returned to his office.

"No problem. I'm sorry for this unexpected visit, but I felt we needed to meet immediately to discuss these very large potential bookings. I just didn't think it should be left up to the staff in place to handle. These two bookings alone will greatly expand the revenue for the hotel and, if we make the pitch correctly, we could get their renewal business as well. And if all goes well, we're talking quite an enormous bonus for you and your staff. I'd like to help make that happen. I just couldn't waste another day waiting for you to get settled, so I jumped on the first flight out. I know you just returned from that grand opening in San Diego, which, by the way, great job! But there's no time to waste celebrating that when we have to nail these accounts. Now, here's what I propose." Charlotte St. Jean began to spread out her notes and reports she had worked up on the plane. She turned on her laptop and began typing more notes right away.

"Charlotte, you've been so vital to the success of my career, I don't know what I would do without you. You've gone way out of your way on several occasions to see that I've got my "I's" dotted and "T's" crossed. You're certainly an extraordinary businesswoman. How can I ever repay you?"

Ellis and Charlotte had known each other for three years on a professional level, working in the hotel business. Charlotte was a tall, savvy, sexy executive, who worked at the San Diego hotel property. She was Ellis' counterpart, although she had a few years on him as far as experience in sales went. She was thirty-five, single, and very ambitious. Her golden blonde hair and striking model-like features often fooled most of her associates into thinking that she was just another beautiful woman with only her sex appeal to get her by. But her intelligence and credentials quickly dispelled any notion that she was anything but all business. She had moved up quickly within the company, by anyone's standards, based solely on her merits. And in the process, she had gained the respect of everyone she encountered— deservedly so.

It was Charlotte who had helped Ellis get his promotion to regional vice president and was now helping him work on acquiring an additional region. She had secured her position as regional vice president about five years before. She and Ellis met on a project she facilitated. They had several other encounters on projects and soon became friends. Ellis had a strong ambition to move up in the company but initially needed to gain more experience. Once he did acquire the experience, he formed an alliance with Charlotte, recognizing her intelligence and ability to advance so quickly through pure hard work. He would pick her brain and let her know that he respected her leadership and managerial skills. Charlotte was flattered to have a man express an interest in her mind and business sense. At that point, she assisted him whenever she could to help him excel in the business. She was impressed by his background, his education, and his reputation in the business. She knew she wouldn't be wasting her time working with Ellis Montgomery. They purposely kept their meetings and conferences discreet so as not to make waves within the organization and also to disguise the fact that she was giving Ellis exclusive handling and access to some confidential information. In the last three years, Ellis and Charlotte had become devoted working partners. Her short-term goal was to get him transferred to her region, to be able to work more closely and openly with him. She knew that, together, they would make a dynamic team. Ellis shared her objectives.

"Well, let me see…how about, if we pull this off, we celebrate in high fashion and go to the sales convention in Madrid next month? I know it's work, but we can get some leisure time in here and there. Plus, it's a new property and it would be nice to see how it's laid out and who's on the client list. I think the opportunity would provide you with some connections in the international sector. That could definitely come in handy when you come to work in my region. I make it a point to keep close ties with our international departments. And…there will be several exclusive parties to attend, and you can be my escort." Charlotte was always business first. She ran a tight ship and was always thinking one step ahead. She made it a practice to keep her interest and reputation visible among the elite. Her idea of a vacation would be attending a conference in an exotic region. Her lifestyle gave her no opportunity for a traditional relationship. She was never in one location long enough to have long-term relationships. Most of her encounters were casual. For the time being, that was ideal for her. Her career always came first, which, in the past, had caused problems for her romantic partners. She was hardly around—and when she was, she had a propensity to dominate the relationship. She was more into the escort scene, if she needed to attend a formal function. It was easier and, most of the time, turned out to be more advantageous for her in many ways. She got what she wanted and when she no longer required the arrangement, she could move on without incident or discussion.

"Madrid? Next month? That sounds appealing. I'm certainly interested in acquiring international contacts. I'll check my schedule and let you know tomorrow. At least I know I'm not opening any hotels next month, thank goodness. This last one presented so many challenges—I'm glad it's completed."

"Oh, but that's what makes this job so exciting, don't you think? Meeting those challenges head on and pulling off the impossible. That's how you make a name for yourself in this business. I thrive on that kind of excitement. There isn't anything that I would shy away from. But then that's why I'm where I am and others are where they are. Now, how about taking a look at this historical data that I came up with. This should help with the projections you'll need in preparation for your presentation to the client. Once we adjust some of the figures to correspond with your statistics, you should be able to back into your final numbers." Charlotte didn't allow herself to digress too much when she was on a mission. Although this was Ellis' project, she was able to see her gain from the final results;

otherwise, she wouldn't waste her time. "And let me know tomorrow about Madrid. I expect that you'll make any necessary adjustments to your schedule to allow for the time away. Like I said, it'll be well worth your while." She refocused on her laptop.

It was one in the morning before Ellis and Charlotte wrapped up their meeting. Neither had realized the time before then. They organized and put away their files, and he escorted her to her room in the hotel. She had arranged for a presidential suite with all the amenities. She always traveled in style. She felt that life was too short to have regrets or not to live like you want, as long as you could afford it. She could. Since she wasn't usually in one place long, she maintained a modest abode on a beach in southern California. She usually hired someone to stay at her place when she was on extended trips. She had had several different house sitters in the past, but the last few times she'd used the same person, Carlos. Carlos seemed to meet her requirements impeccably and he usually did things the way she wanted—to perfection. Often times his responsibilities would go above and beyond the usual call of duty, which suited him just fine.

"Thanks again Charlotte for meeting with me on this project. I'll work up the numbers in the morning and prepare my final presentation. We can discuss it tomorrow. Have a good evening." Ellis was excited about this endeavor and having, once again, Charlotte's assistance. However, his thoughts weren't far from Tyana, thinking of her reaction to his late-night meeting.

"It's my pleasure. You're brilliant and I like working with brilliant people. It stimulates me. Would you care to come in for a nightcap? It's still early. We can go over the presentation now. My mind's still fresh and I have an angle that you might find interesting—it just might work with this particular group. I understand they're a hard sell." Charlotte was extremely attractive and sexy. It was hard to resist her requests for anything. It was part of her charm and personality. Her sensual aura had a way of pulling in anyone who was weak enough to fall under her spell. Generally, that didn't leave out many. Those around her were usually caught off guard by her confidence and curt nature, which made refusing her difficult.

"As tempting as that sounds, I really should get out of your hair; you've done so much for me already today and I've kept you longer than I should have." Ellis didn't want to bring his personal life into the conversation. A person like Charlotte didn't have much patience for anyone's domestic issues or concerns. After all, he was indebted to her and didn't want to turn her off to voluntarily working with him beyond their usual projects. He knew that she certainly had more important matters to deal with than his. He had always been accommodating to her when they were working together. He knew she expected it and she definitely held the control card and could expose his plan to transfer out.

"Don't be silly, this is exhilarating. I think it's always good practice to capture ideas while they're fresh in your mind. They're in my mind right now. But if you feel you have a handle on your presentation and don't need my two cents, then by all means, don't let me interfere." She knew how to manipulate any situation. It was customary for her to assert herself when necessary. She almost always found it necessary.

"No, I didn't mean…I mean, I would love your input. OK. I'll come in so we can work on the presentation." Ellis looked at his watch again and closed the door behind him. He and Charlotte usually worked together when he was away from home. He was surprised by her impromptu visit to Phoenix and wasn't prepared to handle this situation with Tyana. She had never known the extent of his work relationship with Charlotte. He hadn't shared with Tyana his strategy and alliance with Charlotte. It hadn't been necessary. While Charlotte went into the bedroom to change, Ellis turned off his cell phone. The last thing he wanted was a call from Tyana, to give Charlotte the impression that he had a curfew, or domestic obligations.

Tyana looked at the clock on her nightstand. She was still awake, reading, while she waited up for Ellis. She was shocked to see that it was nearly one-thirty in the morning and she hadn't heard from him since nine. She reached for the phone to dial his office. After four rings, she was connected to his voicemail. She left a brief message inquiring of his whereabouts and hung up. She then dialed his cell phone only to find that it had been turned off. She began to worry and became restless. She talked herself out of panicking, figuring he was probably on his way home. She returned to her book.

Charlotte had changed into something very sexy and casual that accentuated her large breasts and the shapely curves of her body, which were usually disguised by her business attire. She had carefully selected her professional wardrobe to give a hint of her sexuality, but left much to the imagination. She didn't need the clothes to attract anyone; she was quite capable of doing that with her personality and femininity. She and Ellis had seldom worked within the confines of a hotel room. When they got together while he was on the road in her territory, they were usually all business. She was careful not to arouse suspicion on her turf. But this time Charlotte was out of her region and she felt it was late enough that no one would notice.

"OK, that's better," Charlotte said, referring to her attire as she returned to the living room where Ellis was sitting, waiting patiently. "Now, for that nightcap I offered you. What's your pleasure? If I don't have it, we can order it. So speak up." She was already pouring herself a liqueur. She continued to scan the liquor cabinet. "How about scotch on the rocks? That's what you usually order, am I right?"

"You're right. That'll be fine, thanks." Ellis glanced at the clock and saw that it was almost two. He was beginning to get fidgety. She handed him the drink.

"Here, let me turn on the light so we can see what we're doing here." Charlotte reached across Ellis, brushing up against him slightly as she turned on the lamp. Ellis caught a whiff of her fragrance, which sent a tingle down his spine, right to his loins. He felt a stirring in his pants. He had always found her attractive and sexy, but he respected their working relationship and never ventured beyond her appearance as another sexy woman. He was certainly in a position to cross paths with many attractive women. His loyalty to his own relationship had kept him in check. He loved Tyana and respected her. Tyana was just as attractive and beautiful as these other women, so he felt he had a good situation. Plus, she was smart and self-reliant too, which he particularly admired. He had never thought of cheating on Tyana. Ellis immediately tried to turn his thoughts back to his work and away from what Charlotte's fragrance and body were doing to him. He was also getting very tired. He had just returned from a long and exhausting trip, getting in at five a.m., then he put in a full day, which hadn't ended yet. He really wanted to go home and go to bed.

Charlotte began to rattle off her ideas about the presentation. She was wide-awake and full of ideas. Ellis was doing his best to keep up—he was fading fast. Every time he would finish his drink, she was quick to refill the glass. Ellis could barely keep his eyes opened. It was three-thirty.

"Excuse me while I go wash my hands," said Charlotte, letting Ellis know in a polite way that she had to use the restroom. Ellis took another sip of his drink as he continued to yawn. He laid his head back on the sofa while he waited for Charlotte to return.

While Charlotte was in the bathroom, she realized the time and thought she had better let Ellis get home. She needed him fresh for their next meeting. She was due to leave the following morning and wanted to make sure they had made great progress before leaving. When she returned to the living room, she saw Ellis sound asleep with his glass still in his hand. She stared at him for a few moments, admiring his handsome face, his designer suit, looking very sexy as he lay back on her sofa in a model-like pose. She thought of waking him, but he looked so peaceful that she didn't want to disturb him.

She carefully removed the glass from his hand. He must have had at least three doubles, she thought as she smiled at him. She was sure he would be out cold and maybe a little drunk. Even if she were to wake him, she didn't think it was wise for him to drive after having so many drinks. She didn't want to leave him on her sofa though, nor did she want him to sleep in his clothes. She attempted to wake him.

"Ellis, Ellis. We need to get you up and into bed." She tried to shake him awake. He moaned a little, but didn't respond. She tried several more times, but to no avail. Finally she was able to get him to stand up and she helped him walk to her bedroom while she supported him all the way. It took them awhile but they finally reached her bedroom, where he collapsed onto the bed. She untied and removed his tie, then proceeded to unbutton his shirt. She removed it and hung it up in her closet. She took off his shoes and socks, then unbuckled his belt. Once she got his pants unzipped, she struggled a bit, trying to remove them. She never thought twice about undressing him or what his reaction would be about it when he awoke. She was like that. She usually just took charge of situations and didn't concern herself with trivial things. She'd seen her share of naked men, so this one would be no different to her. But as Ellis lay on her bed in only his shorts, Charlotte surprisingly found her body responding to this man. He had the body of a model and was very muscular and fit. She thought that he definitely took care of himself and made it to the gym regularly. She felt her body become warm and fill with desire for this nearly-naked man on her bed. She had always made a conscious effort not to mix business with pleasure. She had never understood the benefit in that. She had had many offers, but never pursued any of them. She didn't want anyone in the business to know her that way or have any gossip on her. She lived by that rule. But at four a.m. in the morning, staring at this sexy heap of flesh on her bed, she suddenly had other thoughts. She was becoming quite aroused.

She decided to ignore her yearning and pulled up the sheets over Ellis' body after she removed her clothes and slipped under the sheets as well. She lay next to Ellis as he slept. Unable to go to sleep next to him, she ran her hands softly over his hairy chest, feeling his prominent pecs. She couldn't stop staring at his sculptured body, wondering what it would be like to feel that against her naked body every night. What would it feel like? Again, her body was reacting with excitement, being so close to this new, uncharted territory. She continued to feel his body with a soft touch until she reached his silk shorts.

She carefully guided her hand through the opening of his shorts and began to fondle him. Her body was definitely heating up now. As she stroked him with long, fluid motions, his body began to respond, ever so slightly. He began to moan, quietly at first. She had to work extra hard to stimulate him given his current state. Her movements accelerated with her fast beating heart. Within moments, Ellis' body began twitching as if it were keeping rhythm with her heartbeats. He was slowly becoming erect from the stimulation by her hand. His moans grew louder. She couldn't stop herself now because his body was being awakened by her touch and she had become more aroused with each stroke. Ellis was now semi-conscious, thinking that he was dreaming this whole situation. After nearly twenty minutes, she noticed that he had a full erection, and without considering the consequences, she climbed on top of him and gently lowered herself onto him until he was inside of her. Her body began to writhe with pleasure with each gyration of her hips. She was experiencing irresistible pleasure as she began to pump faster and harder.

Ellis' eyes opened, but the room was dark and he was unable to make her out. It took him a few seconds to realize what was going on, but he immediately felt sheer pleasure from the woman riding his erection. He began to stroke her buttocks, feeling her soft, smooth skin. He pulled her harder onto himself until he could enter her no further and pumped vigorously. He was still disoriented as he began to moan loudly, then he grabbed Charlotte and turned her over on her back as he skillfully maneuvered himself on top of her. He began thrusting his body into hers with pleasurable force. She felt herself reaching a climax and squeezed herself tightly around him as her body violently began to spasm. Ellis, too, unable to hold back his own sensation, released himself in ecstasy as he shouted: "Oh God, Tyana! I love you, baby!"

Chapter Three

Tyana suddenly awoke, realizing that she had fallen asleep while trying to wait up for Ellis. She looked at Ellis' side of the bed and saw no one there. The sheets had not been disturbed—there was no sign of Ellis being home. Her heart began to pound in her chest. In a panic, she reached for the phone. She began dialing as she glanced at the clock. It was five fifteen in the morning. Where was Ellis?

Ellis' powerful orgasm had left him drained and listless and he slumped down on Charlotte. He lay quiet, still resting inside of her—his body paralyzed from the intense lovemaking episode. He buried his head in the pillow to rest. Moments later, as he lifted his head to kiss the woman beneath him, his eyes began to adjust to the dimly lit room, as daybreak was approaching. He looked up and saw a woman and it wasn't Tyana. He jumped up, startled out of his wits, releasing himself from Charlotte's body.

"What the hell?! Who?! OH MY GOD!! Charlotte?! What the hell is going on here?! What is this?! What are you doing here?! Why are we...?! Shit! How..., when..." Ellis leaped off the bed and began to pace as he was trying to sort out the precarious situation he found himself in. He frantically started looking for his clothes. He still had a semi-erection. He was completely disoriented until he realized he wasn't at home. The curtains were closed and he had no idea that the sunrise was approaching—he had been with Charlotte all night. His mind frantically raced, as he was trying to make sense out of everything, still pacing the room. Then suddenly, his thoughts went to Tyana. He put his hands to his head and closed his eyes. He was starting to feel sick to his stomach. This was unexplainable and his worst nightmare.

"Relax Ellis, it's OK. We had a few drinks; you were in no condition to drive home so you crashed here. I don't know, I guess with our bodies so close to each other, one thing led to another. I asked you if you were sure about making love to me, when you started to come on to me, and you assured me that it was fine—that we were two consenting adults. I mean, the heat was certainly mounting between us. I'm sorry you now feel differently. It wasn't my intention to make you uncomfortable. I should have insisted that we refrain, especially since we're business colleagues. Are you going to be all right? I mean, will you be OK to continue working with me or should we call the whole thing off and I'll no longer concern myself with your project?" Charlotte had a slight smirk on her face when she looked away and got up from the bed to locate her robe. She opened the curtains, exposing the sunrise, then slowly strutted past Ellis, giving him a long look and full view of her naked body in its splendor. She had, once again, successfully accomplished another acquisition.

"I...don't know what to say. I guess I don't remember too much. I must have had too much to drink. I'm sorry for freaking out there." Ellis wasn't clear about Charlotte's explanation, but he wasn't going to question her and appear as if he were successfully seduced against his will. Absolutely not. Furthermore, he wasn't going to let Charlotte walk out of his life now. He was so close to accomplishing his goals and was on his way to making more money than he had ever imagined he could make in this business. Charlotte still had control of his destiny and he wasn't about to let that slip through his fingers— not over some misunderstanding. As he listened to what she said, he was relieved that she didn't think that he had taken advantage of her. What an outcome that could present! She could potentially initiate a sexual harassment charge against him. He knew he had to get himself together and apologize before she got offended. "I hope this doesn't interfere with our working relationship. I certainly respect you, Charlotte. You should know that. I apologize for my inappropriate behavior. We don't need to speak of this incident again. I think you're a beautiful woman...a sexy woman and I should have had better control. Thanks for being OK with this incident." He wasn't sure of what to say, but he had to save the relationship and keep Charlotte on his side. "Please excuse me, I need to get cleaned up and out of here so I can get to work. May I wash up in your bathroom?" He picked up his shorts and proceeded to the bathroom.

"Take your time, Ellis, and hey, don't worry about it. We're OK. Promise. I'm glad you don't want me to stop working with you. I think we have a great future ahead of us as partners. In a few months, we should have you on your way to the top. Oh, and I think you're an amazing lover. The pleasure was all mine." Charlotte winked at him then finally put on her robe.

Tyana wasn't getting anywhere in her attempt to locate Ellis. She was beginning to think that maybe he had been in an accident. She agonized over her missing man with each second that passed. She decided to get up and get dressed in case she needed to leave if a call came in that he was in the hospital. In her haste, she kept bumping into things—she was shaking. Then she finally just sat down on the floor and cried. It was not like him to not call her. Where was he? Was he in trouble? Did he need her? Those were her jumbled thoughts as she wept.

Just then, she heard the door to the garage open. She jumped up and ran to the door. It was Ellis.

"Oh my God, Ellis! Where have you been? I've been sick out of my mind with worry. I've called you everywhere. What happened? Why didn't you call me?" Tyana was hyper but relieved to see him. "Are you all right? I was scared to death!" She ran to him and hugged him. He hugged her back, feeling relieved to be in her arms. His heart started to pound hard against his chest. He held her tightly and closed his eyes.

Ellis had been preparing himself all the way home to deal with her reaction to his all-nighter. He hadn't expected that his guilt would overwhelm him the way that it did at that moment. He had just realized how much he did love her and want her.

"Baby, I'm so sorry. I didn't mean to cause you to worry, believe me. I love you so much. I'm all right. I had to work late and things escalated. We couldn't leave until we were able to come up with some solutions. It was grueling. We were locked up in a conference

36

room. The time just got away from us. None of us realized that it had gotten so late. I'm sorry. It'll never happen again. I promise you that." He continued to hold tightly to her.

"Ellis, you have no idea what it was like not knowing where you were, if you were hurt or in trouble. Please don't put me through that again." She held him tightly too. "Were you drinking?" She smelled the alcohol on him.

"Yes, we all had a few drinks, that's all. Don't worry, baby, I won't put you through that again. I should've been more aware of the time and notified you if I knew I was going to be that late. It won't happen again." Ellis kissed Tyana and she kissed him back. They walked slowly back to the bedroom. She began to undress him. She wanted to be next to him and to feel his warm body next to hers.

"Honey, I should really get ready for work," he said trying to avoid her attempt to get him to make love to her. He was still weak from his recent sexual episode with Charlotte, and he had a bit of a hangover.

"Ellis, please, I've missed you and I've been up practically all night worried. I just need to be next to you. I know you're tired, but I need you, baby. You've been gone for so long on your trip and we haven't been together in a long time." Tyana had removed her robe and was standing before Ellis, very naked. He had never been able to resist her beautiful body. She continued to remove his belt and unbutton his shirt as she pulled him down onto the bed with her. He kissed her as she ran her hands all over his body. His mind was interrupted by thoughts of Charlotte and what he had done. As much as Tyana was enticing him and caressing him, he wasn't able to respond. He was overcome with guilt about his evening of infidelity. He was angry with himself and disgusted by this choice to cheat. He couldn't imagine having gotten himself so intoxicated that he couldn't stay in control. The strangest thing about what he remembered was that he hadn't even thought of making love to Charlotte the whole time they were working in her hotel room. Why did he all of a sudden take her like that? He couldn't reconcile his sketchy memories of the evening.

"Ellis, is everything OK? You don't seem to be in the moment with me," Tyana said, referring to the fact that her attempt to arouse him was futile.

"I'm sorry, I guess I'm just too tired. The whole evening was so draining for me." Ellis removed Tyana off of him and sat up. "You must be exhausted, too. Why don't you lie back and try to get some sleep before you have to go into your office. I'll just go take a shower and change. I need to get to work early. I have so many meetings and a presentation to work on. I don't think I'll be able to make it home for dinner, either. I'm sorry. I promise to get home tonight as early as possible. We can have some uninterrupted time then, OK, baby?" He was trying to deter her from wanting to make love to him right then. He was sure he wouldn't be able to perform mentally or physically. Charlotte had seen to that.

"OK, but you promised and I'll be here when you get home. I love you." She lay back and closed her eyes as she was reminded, by the stirring between her legs, how much she still wanted Ellis.

Tyana had a typical day at work, with the exception of her curiosity about Ellis' all-night meeting. She still couldn't imagine that he had never thought to make a phone call to her to let her know what was going on. Who was he with that no one needed to call anyone to inform them that they would be home late? Certainly, someone had to think about it. Her thoughts continued to churn in her head. She hadn't heard from Ellis at all yet that day. It was approaching four o'clock and she had scheduled a dance lesson with Antonio, which had almost escaped her mind. She had discussed with him the last time she was there the possibility of continuing her dance lessons. She felt such magic when she danced across the ballroom floor. She wanted more of that feeling, at least for the time being. But what she wanted more right now was some quality time with Ellis. She decided her dance lessons could wait another day and called the dance studio to apologetically cancel her lesson for the evening.

Tyana worked until about seven before she wanted to finish up and get home to meet Ellis. She had received a message from him while she was out that he should be home around seven-thirty. She was pleased to hear that. She had really missed him and wanted to spend some uninterrupted time with him. She locked up so she could rush home and take a hot bath to get relaxed and fresh for him. She smiled all the way home, with intermittent thoughts about Antonio and his hug.

"Ellis Montgomery." He was still at work.

"Hi Ellis, this is Charlotte. I'm glad I caught you still at work. I received some information today that will be crucial to your presentation. I just finished a series of meetings with the new steering committee heading up the New York project and I got some interesting information that you can definitely use. Stay put, I'll be right over." Charlotte was calling from her room in the hotel. She always took charge and rarely waited for invitations when she was focused on something—especially if she was going out of her way to help someone else. Everything was orchestrated by her and according to her schedule.

Ellis had just shut down his laptop and was heading out for a quiet, romantic evening with Tyana, in hopes of being redeemed from the night before. He sat frozen in his chair when he heard Charlotte's instructions.

"But Charlotte, I have another appointment which I was on my way out to," said Ellis in an attempt to keep his promise to Tyana. He was still feeling extremely guilty and ashamed and wanted to do nothing but focus on Tyana. He didn't want to give her any reason to suspect anything.

"Ellis, I have to fly out in the morning, are you onboard with this objective or should I find someone who is serious? I don't mean to disrupt your schedule but it's now or never. We're wasting time if we want to do this. I thought you were as ambitious as I am. Was I misinformed?" Charlotte didn't mince words.

"No, Charlotte, I am onboard, I want this acquisition. I'll be here when you get here." Ellis hung up the phone, dropped his briefcase and leaned back in his chair. He was trying to figure out how he was going to break it to Tyana that he wouldn't be home until late…again. He just sat quiet in his chair, thinking. Just then his phone rang.

"Ellis Montgomery."

"Hi honey, I'm glad I caught you. Can you stop on your way home and pick up a bottle of wine? I really feel like red tonight and all we have is white. I guess I haven't paid attention to our inventory. Hey, I just finished a nice luxurious bath with your favorite bath scents. I'm all soft and silky for you. Hurry home." She was no longer concerned about his absence the night before; she was only thinking about having him all to herself tonight.

"Tyana, honey, I don't know how to tell you, but I just received a phone call and an impromptu meeting was just called. I'm sorry, baby, I was just about to leave when the call came in. I don't know how long it'll take but I don't want you wait up." He cringed as he told her.

"Ellis, are you kidding me? What is so damn important that you have to have a meeting at eight o'clock in the evening, after pulling an all-nighter last night?!"

"Tyana, please be understanding. I can't help it. I have to attend. What do you want me to do, tell them I can't attend, even though my career depends on it, because my girlfriend needs me at home?" He hated lying to her.

"Well, I'm sorry, but I haven't seen you for nearly three weeks. What do you want me to say? I miss you, Ellis, and want some time

41

with you. And what do you mean your career depends on this meeting?" She was angry and now confused by his response.

"Baby, just let me make it up to you. When this project is over, we'll go away on a trip, away from phones, faxes, emails, voicemails, everything—just you and me. I have to go now. I'll try to get home as soon as I can. I love you. See you." He hated hanging up and knew she had a valid point. He didn't like what was happening but didn't think he had much choice. He'd gone too far with Charlotte on their venture to make waves now. She could sabotage everything, not to mention she could add insult to injury with a sexual harassment suit. For the first time in his life, Ellis felt he was being manipulated and was no longer in control of his life. All he could think about was getting through this project and out from under Charlotte's reign. He needed his control back. He needed his life with Tyana back, if that was possible.

Tyana slammed down the phone and blew out the candles. She began to sulk over being stood up again until she remembered her dance lesson that she cancelled. She picked up the phone and dialed the dance studio.

"Hi, this is Tyana Dominique, may I speak with Antonio please?" She was hoping that she could still get in for a lesson tonight. She waited for Antonio to come to the phone.

"Hello, this is Antonio," he answered.

"Hi Antonio, this is Tyana. How are you?"

"Hello Tyana, I'm fine. It's good to hear from you. Is everything all right? You cancelled on me tonight."

"Yes, everything's fine. And I'm sorry about the cancellation; that's why I'm calling. My plans have changed and I was wondering if I could still come in for my lesson. I'm very sorry for the late notice and will understand if you're booked." She waited for him to respond.

"Well, sure you can come in—no problem. I'm glad you called, and I'm glad your plans changed. How soon can you get here?" There was a detection of excitement in Antonio's voice.

"Great, thanks. I can be there in about twenty minutes. Thanks again!" She hung up and hurried to change her clothes. She wasn't going to sit at home waiting for Ellis this time. She figured that he would probably get home around the same time she did anyway.

Theresa E. Liggins

Chapter Four

Charlotte barged right into Ellis' office just moments after he had hung up the phone with Tyana. He was hoping that she would not detain him too long. He was certainly interested in what she had to share with him, but after the last meeting, he was a little timid about seeing her again so soon. He still wasn't clear how all that had happened. He just knew he had to be careful not to upset her now that they had become intimate and especially since he apparently had initiated the encounter. It was a whole new ballgame now.

"Hello, Charlotte. Come on in and have a seat. I'm ready to hear what news you have. Can I get you a drink or something from dining?" Ellis was trying to make sure they remained in his office and not in her room. He had been avoiding that area of the hotel all day, hoping not to run into Charlotte or even be reminded of what had taken place just several floors from his office. He was going crazy thinking about what he had done. The worst part was, he just couldn't figure out why or how it happened. His mind was still completely fuzzy on that part. He would be careful next time not to drink so much. He assumed that the combination of an empty stomach and lack of sleep had contributed to his condition. He would know better next time. He would also try and avoid a next time.

"Thanks, Ellis, a drink would be perfect. How about a martini?" He ordered the martini for Charlotte as she settled in and opened her laptop. He noticed that she had already changed into something less

45

business-like and more casual and revealing. She was exposing quite a bit of cleavage and her skirt hugged her hips tightly, leaving no doubt in anyone's mind that she was wearing nothing underneath. He tried not to stare, but the temptation was too great. This was a different side of her that he had not been familiar with in the past, but was quickly becoming too intimately accustomed to for his preference.

Charlotte appeared unfazed by last night's episode, to Ellis' delight. He continued to prepare for his impromptu meeting with her. She got up and closed the door. He looked up over his laptop and started to feel tightness in his throat.

"I just think that these meetings should remain as confidential as possible. We just don't want to jeopardize things at this point, now do we?" She strutted back to her chair across from his desk.

"I agree, although I doubt that anyone's still here at this late hour," he added.

"Ellis, I have brought a lot of notes and I need you to see what's on my laptop. Why don't we move over here to the table so we can spread things out and we both can see these reports together." Charlotte had already begun to move her things to the table and pulled a chair close to her for him. He followed her over. Just then her drink arrived.

"Aren't you having a drink too?" she asked, looking at Ellis while motioning for the dining attendant to wait.

"I'm not that thirsty at the moment. I think I'll pass." He was thinking about last night.

"Don't be silly. You aren't going to make me drink by myself, now, are you? What kind of gentleman are you? Now, what will you have—or do you want me to order for you?"

Ellis looked at the attendant and ordered a club soda.

"He'll have a scotch on the rocks, double. And make it snappy, please, we don't have all evening. And bring me another martini," she snapped at the attendant. The attendant left with the order. "Now, where were we? Oh yes, take a look at these reports. If these don't get your attention, then I don't know what will." She moved her chair in closer to his, leaning against him just enough to rest her right breast against his arm. Her tight blouse was cut so low it barely cleared her nipples. She seemed very comfortable with this style. She crossed her leg to expose her long silky legs through the slit of her skirt that reached her upper thigh. She was only wearing a thong underneath her skirt; there were no panty lines visible. She began to lightly rub her leg against Ellis' leg. He was becoming increasingly uncomfortable. She pretended not to notice.

A few moments later there was a knock at the door. The drinks had arrived. The meeting continued.

Tyana arrived at the dance studio about twenty minutes after hanging up with Antonio. She rushed in and quickly changed her shoes. Antonio greeted her and they proceeded to one of the dance rooms. Their lesson was underway.

They finished the lesson around nine forty-five. The studio was clearing out. Most of the other lessons were completed and the staff

47

was packing up, preparing to leave for the evening. Antonio was always the last to leave and usually the first to arrive each day. He left Tyana for a few minutes to give some instructions to one of his staff. She changed her shoes while he was gone. She was thinking about her lessons and the idea of performing in the mini competition. They had worked on one of the several routines he wanted her to perform. She picked up the dance steps with no problem. He had continued to praise her throughout her lesson. He was growing increasingly excited about his star student. He had ideas and dreams for her. Her thoughts then went to Ellis. She couldn't help but wonder if he was still at his office. She thought about calling him to see if he was there and if he wanted to meet her for dinner somewhere. She figured he would be heading home soon and would be hungry. Everyone left and Antonio returned to Tyana.

"So, how do you feel about these new routines and steps? I think you're doing a superb job and I'm extremely impressed." Antonio felt very proud of Tyana's progress.

"I feel great and I love being here—more than I thought I would. After such long days that I put in, it feels great ending the evening doing something fun and relaxing as this. Of course, you make learning to dance enjoyable and easy. Thank you!" She was just as impressed with him.

"Well, believe me, sometimes, it's not as enjoyable as other times. It's students like you who make my job easy. It's such a pleasure to teach you, Tyana. Thanks for the opportunity." He came in closer to her and embraced her. She wrapped her arms around him in response and hugged him casually at first, then they both tightened their grip. Suddenly, that feeling of connection hit them both like a bolt of lightning. As they held the embrace, their bodies moved in a little closer to one another. Tyana's heart began to pound faster, as did Antonio's. They both thought about the last time they connected like that. He rubbed his hands slowly across her back. She felt a tingle up her spine and shuddered slightly. He felt his body respond to her body being so close to his. He couldn't think straight and felt his insides react with the pleasure of their private moment. He started to perspire slightly. She could sense his body reacting and she found herself getting caught up in the romance that they were generating. He squeezed her gently, feeling total delight in her body being next to his. Their grips became tighter and their breathing heavy. As they reluctantly pulled back, he looked lovingly into her eyes. He was awestruck by her beauty and her mere presence. He didn't know why she was affecting him like this. He could have sworn that she was someone he had been close to before. She gazed back at him; their bodies still in close contact.

"Tyana, I find you attractive and it's not my intention to create an inappropriate situation. You're my student and I respect you. You're paying for dance lessons and my intentions are to teach you to dance. I apologize for my actions just now. This has never happened to me before and I'm not sure what is happening; however, I can't say that I didn't want it." He stepped back from the closeness of her body and took hold of her hands. He paused for a long while, looking down at her hands, then back up at her face. He wasn't sure of what he should say now but knew he was feeling something with her that he shouldn't be and it was making him nervous. He couldn't believe what he was about to say and was desperately wishing he could turn back time and start over.

"Tyana, you're a beautiful woman with a great deal of talent and I'm finding that my concentration when I'm around you is compromised. I should have better control but for some reason I can't seem to muster that control when I'm with you. Therefore, I hope you'll understand when I recommend that you continue your lessons with one of my other instructors. In no way do I want your lessons here to be misconstrued or uncomfortable for either of us. You're so special and talented—I want you to get the most out of your dancing while you're here. It's our goal to provide the best training possible for each student, and I want that for you especially. My actions were inappropriate and I don't want to chance anything like that happening again between us in the studio. It's not fair to you or me." He paused as she spoke.

"Wow, I don't know what to say. I must admit that I felt something as well during our exchange, but I don't think that it was all you, Antonio, so please don't be so hard on yourself. I'm surprised by what happened myself. It's never happened to me before either. It was like there was some irresistible force or something. I'm so embarrassed."

"Don't be, you didn't do anything wrong," he interjected.

She softly touched his arm and continued. "I do enjoy having you as my instructor and I'm sorry, too, that because of what happened, it wouldn't be advisable for us to continue to work together. I wasn't expecting that and I have enormous regret that I can no longer be your student. I respect you, as well as my relationship, and wouldn't want to do anything to jeopardize your position or my relationship. I think you're a great person and dance teacher, Antonio, and I look forward to dancing with you every time I'm here." She paused as she felt a lump develop in her throat.

"I know I look forward to dancing with you, too," he added.

"If you feel that we should be apart from each other, then I have to respect your decision. I'm very sorry. I'll miss you." A single tear fell from Tyana's eye. She was surprised by the feelings she was having.

"I know, me too," said Antonio, looking especially torn by his decision. "I like you a lot and I had wanted nothing more than to dance with you—you Tyana, please know that. I'd like it if you could stay." He was still holding tightly to her hands. "I can arrange for you to work with Lance or John. They're both very experienced and they work with more of our advanced students. You'll fit right in with their style and curriculum. I'm so sorry, Tyana." He was trying very hard not to show any more emotional attachment to her than he already had. "I'll have one of them call you in the morning to work you into their schedule. Tyana, if there's anything you need, please don't hesitate to call me. I really would like for you to remain here and continue with your programs. I am so, so sorry. And thanks so much for being understanding." He walked her to the door, said goodnight, then watched her walk to her car. He returned to his office and sat silently for several hours. He couldn't believe that the best student he'd ever had just slipped through his fingers. He was still baffled as to why it happened. He had been so careful for so many years to not let anything like that happen. Why now? What was it that had caused him to do that? He had no answers. He just sat there feeling great sadness.

Tyana drove away feeling completely bewildered by what had just happened at the dance studio. Her evening had started out on such a high note, dancing with Antonio, making plans and learning new routines for the upcoming mini competition, and ending with her losing her dance partner and instructor, and her plans to perform with him in that competition vanished—all in about three minutes. And what did happen in those three minutes? She still wasn't sure of any of it. Why did she feel something for Antonio like that? She knew she was in love with Ellis and she was perfectly happy with him. Why did she respond to Antonio that way? How did they let that happen—and so suddenly? Perhaps it was for the best that they not be forced together with the dancing if there was going to be a distraction that would cause them any awkwardness. It was already ten-thirty when Tyana found herself driving up to her house. When she entered the garage, she noticed that Ellis' car was missing.

Ellis intermittently glanced at his watch to see the time slipping away. He was exhausted and wanted to go home to sleep in his own bed, next to Tyana. Just then, he realized that she must be at home waiting for him, again. He thought, 'what am I going to tell her?' He needed to end the meeting, but was enthralled with the information Charlotte was sharing with him. He needed that edge desperately. He needed her connections and insight desperately. They continued on.

Tyana called Ellis' office to find out when he would be home. She was tired and wanted to eat something quick and retire to bed. She had had a long and exhausting day. She was still despondent about the situation with Antonio. His office line rang once, but she was immediately connected to his voicemail. She left a brief message. She tried his cell phone, but it, too, connected her to his voicemail. She began to wonder what was going on and why all of a sudden he was making himself inaccessible? This was the second time. Why was it so important for these meetings to be held so late in the evenings? She fixed herself something to eat, then retreated to the bedroom. She was so tired that she just got into bed and watched some TV for awhile, dozing off and on.

"Ellis, I need to take a little break, sweetheart. Please excuse me," said Charlotte as she left his office and headed to the restroom. It was eleven-thirty and Ellis didn't see an end to his meeting with Charlotte. They still had three more reports to dissect. He saw that he had a message on his voicemail and dialed to retrieve it. It was from Tyana. She was looking for him to be home all right. He didn't know if he should call her and explain or just wait until he got home. He decided to call her so she wouldn't worry, but just as he picked up the phone to dial home, Charlotte returned and closed the door behind her. He immediately hung up the phone.

"Is there somewhere you need to be?" she asked when she saw the phone in Ellis' hand.

"No, just checking my messages."

"Good. I think we're making great progress, don't you? I mean, with just a few more meetings to go over some of these projections and iron out any inconsistencies, we should be ready to make the first of the presentations," she said as she sat on the sofa in the corner of Ellis' office. She patted the cushioned beside her, gesturing him to come and sit next to her.

"Aren't you planning on returning next week for subsequent meetings? I didn't think we would be able to conclude everything tonight." He was confused by Charlotte's statement.

"Oh no, dear, I don't want to waste too much time on this by flying back and forth. I changed my flight reservations earlier today to leave in a few more days instead of tomorrow morning. I anticipated that we would need more time. I didn't think you would have a problem with this, and figured you would actually prefer that I stay and see this stage of the project through to completion. I just thought you are as eager as I am to get this presentation ready for the clients. After all, we don't want to drag our heels on this and miss the opportunity to snag these guys. We've got to look like we're serious. Are we in sync on this or am I being presumptuous in my thinking here?" Charlotte was overly aggressive and expected everyone she dealt with to work by the same philosophy. Ellis was definitely aware that he was being backed into a corner with no escape.

"No, no, that's fine Charlotte. I do prefer that," he said as he sat down next to her on the sofa. She had ordered a bottle of wine and some appetizers an hour ago, which they continued to feast on. He was feeling a little woozy from mixing the drinks, but mostly from exhaustion. He knew he had better leave soon while he was sure he could still drive home. Just then, there was a knock on the door. Charlotte got up to answer it. It was room service once again, with a bottle of champagne that she had ordered when she left the room.

"Good, just in time. Put it down over there," she said to the attendant, pointing to the table. "Thanks."

"What's all this, Charlotte?" asked Ellis, astonished by the champagne.

"Oh, don't worry, I picked up the tab on this. I just think that all our hard work called for some celebration—and what better way to celebrate than with Dom?" He didn't quite know what to say or do. She popped the cork and began pouring. They sat back down on the sofa and toasted their partnership.

Three glasses of champagne and one hour later, Ellis wasn't sure he could sustain his composure and was beginning to slur his words. Charlotte, too, had soon felt the effects of the alcohol. She insisted that they wrap up the meeting, and requested that he walk her to her hotel room.

"Charlotte, I need to sit here for a few minutes to get my bearings. I think I had a little too much to drink." He could barely stand and was stalling, not wanting to go anywhere near her room.

"I think you're right, Ellis. Take your time, I don't have far to go. This sofa is awfully comfortable too. Perhaps we can just rest here until we're ready to leave." She wasn't as drunk as he because she had had a full meal before arriving at his office and she had made sure she didn't pour as much wine in her glass or pour it as many times as she had in his. He hadn't watched her closely while she kept refilling his glass throughout the evening. He closed his eyes to rest. Charlotte then removed her blouse to expose her naked, heaving breasts and began to rub herself next to him. He opened one eye to see what was going on and attempted to sit up. She shoved him back into the sofa.

"Charlotte, what are you doing? Your blouse! Why are you naked?" he asked, trying to focus on her.

"Oh, come on now, we both know what we want. You wouldn't be here if you weren't expecting this. I mean, after last night, I get it that you want a little something for me making you work so hard." She was relieved that he hadn't figured out what exactly had happened the night before as she unbuckled his belt and unzipped his pants with one swift motion. He flinched, feeling very uncomfortable and uncertain about what to do next.

Before he could form an idea of how to get out of this situation, Charlotte had her hand inside of his pants and grabbed hold of what she was looking for and removed it to expose him.

"Charlotte, wait. I don't think I can…"

"Don't be silly, just sit back and enjoy the moment. I'm sure you don't get this every day. It's my pleasure." She lowered her mouth onto him, taking him all in at once in order to get him to respond. It wasn't long before she was getting results. She ignored his pleas for her to stop and continued pleasuring him with intensity and skill. She was right, he didn't get that every day, especially not from anyone with as much experience as she had. She was great at what she did and she knew it. He wanted to get up, but was rendered more powerless with each vigorous stroke. Because of all the alcohol he had consumed, it took her a while to bring him to climax. But when she did, he relieved himself with great force, which caused him to let out a resounding cry of excitement. He held onto that feeling of euphoria for nearly a minute. He had never experienced such an overwhelming and paralyzing moment of ecstasy, as far as he could remember. He couldn't stop it. Finally, he was motionless for about five minutes. Meanwhile, Charlotte removed her skirt with one motion and exposed her bareness and removed her thong. She climbed on Ellis' lap, straddling him, and began to kiss him hard on the mouth, sharing the taste and smell of his own body. He soon responded, feeling his heart ache inside as he thought about Tyana. He felt so trapped in this tangled situation that Charlotte had orchestrated. He was so close to the height of his goals and Charlotte still held the vital pieces. He still needed her. He couldn't reject her now and risk everything he'd worked so hard to get. Reluctantly, he kissed her back. She then lay back on the sofa and spread her legs, pulling him toward her, then pushing his face down between her legs. As much as he marveled at her beauty and sensuality, he didn't want her that way. She began to move her hips in anticipation of receiving pleasure from him. He hesitated but then he complied. She instructed him to give her more. He did. He gave her exactly what she wanted until she screamed from the depth of her soul. He left her body still writhing from his performance. She raised up and greeted him with her wet, naked body and enticed him to make love to her again, which he did. She had turned him on to a point of no return. He wasn't sure how it was possible but they both climaxed again after an hour of non-stop hot, animal, fiery sex. It was the most incredible night of passion he had spent with anyone in a very long time. He and Tyana had once shared that kind of passion, but not anymore.

They finally got up from his sofa and gathered their clothes and got dressed. Ellis' body was dripping with perspiration. Charlotte's hair was a tangled mess. They got themselves together in silence and soon left and headed to her hotel room where he left her at the door. She gave him a passionate kiss goodnight and he walked slowly away, feeling weak in the knees and sick in the pit of his stomach.

Chapter Five

The next morning, Tyana awoke and saw Ellis lying next to her. She must have been sleeping hard to not have heard him come in. She had no idea what time he had returned home. She didn't care at this point; she was just glad to see him next to her. She nuzzled up close to him, rubbing her hands and legs on his body. He seemed to be passed out cold. She tried again but got very little reaction from him besides a slight moan. She climbed on top of him and lowered her head toward his chest, kissing him on his chest as she followed her route downward in an attempt to get him to wake up and make love to her. He still wasn't responding. She lowered her focus even further until she took him with her mouth and began to envelop him. He stirred as his senses began to heighten. She continued for several minutes before he opened his eyes suddenly, fearing that Charlotte was upon him again. He jumped up and shouted, "No, I can't!" before he had looked to see that it was Tyana.

"What?" she asked, shocked by his tone.

"Tyana? Is that you, baby? Oh my God, I'm so sorry. What happened?" he asked, not sure where he was or whom he was with.

"Well, who in the hell did you think it was? What's wrong with you, Ellis?"

"I'm sorry, baby. Oh baby I'm so sorry. I didn't mean to shout at you. I guess I was asleep and I don't know...maybe I was dreaming or something." He was trying hard to vindicate himself. He was very embarrassed by his reaction, but had been horrified thinking that it was Charlotte.

"What time did you get home, Ellis? And what are you doing these nights that you can't seem to get home at a decent hour?" She demanded to know what was going on with him.

"I don't know—it was late, I guess. I'm not sure of the time. I didn't want to wake you, honey. I'm sorry about the late nights, but it shouldn't happen too often, it's just this project I'm working on. It's important now that I stay focused and work diligently until I get to a point where I can get a reprieve. It shouldn't be much longer. I promise.

"You've been promising a lot these days—promises that you can't keep. There had better be some reward at the end of this. I have been cutting my days short to be with you while you're home—that's our deal. I already have to put up with you being away so often and I don't complain. You have to do something to give us some quality time. Now, do you have a few moments right now to make love to your neglected girlfriend?" She continued what she had been doing, but he pulled her up and began kissing her. He was hoping that he could get aroused and perform. However, he was getting a bad feeling and couldn't get Charlotte, and what had happened in his office, out of his head. They continued kissing for several minutes, until Tyana's body was twitching with excitement. She was ready for him to take her. It had been nearly a month since she made love to her man. She needed him.

He rolled on top of her and tried to enter her but he couldn't get himself erect. He began to panic, thinking about what he had done with Charlotte, and tried several times again. It wasn't working. Tyana finally realized what was going on and she stopped.

"Ellis, is there a problem? What's the matter, honey?" She noticed that his body was definitely not in the mood.

"Tyana, I guess I'm more tired than I thought. I'm terribly sorry, baby. Can I make it up to you later? I should be rested later tonight. I might have to work late again, but I'll plan to come home early enough to give you a night of ecstasy that you won't forget for a long time. Is that OK?" He was holding his breath, hoping she would go along with his suggestion. He knew that the orgasms that he had had with Charlotte weren't going to allow him to perform again so soon. His body was weary.

She left him to rest some more as she got up to get ready for work. An hour later, she left and he was still asleep. She looked back at him, feeling sorry for his rough schedule. She wanted to do something special for him because he had been working so hard.

Tyana was knee deep in her work when Melanie told her that she had a phone call.

"Tyana speaking," she answered.

"Tyana, this is John from the dance studio. Antonio left me a message to call you and discuss scheduling some progressive lessons with me."

"Oh hi, John. Yes, Antonio mentioned that someone would be calling me. We were discussing the mini competition that I'm scheduled to perform several numbers for and we thought that it would be a good idea for me to get some additional training from other instructors. I want to learn as much as I can in a short period of time." She had to think fast on her feet to explain why she was suddenly switching instructors. She wasn't sure what Antonio might have said to John when he left the message, but she didn't want anyone to suspect that there might have been some sort of problem between Antonio and her.

"That's what we like to hear. It would be my pleasure to train you in preparation for the mini competition. Antonio spoke highly of you and mentioned that you have progressed tremendously in such a short period of time. I recalled seeing you here once or twice. You're quite talented. When can we get started?" John asked with excitement in his voice, happy that he would get to work with the famous Tyana Dominique. Everyone at the studio thought she was exclusive to Antonio. "How about today? Is that possible? I think we shouldn't lose any of the momentum that you and Antonio have created."

"Well, let me see…" She quickly thought about Ellis and their conversation earlier that morning and got the impression that he would tied up again tonight. She would then be available for her dance lesson. "I think I can come in around eight."

"Eight is perfect—I'm available. I'll put you down and see you then. Thanks so much, Tyana, and have a great day." They both hung up.

After Tyana hung up the phone, she just sat staring off into space thinking about Antonio and the last time she had danced with him.

She couldn't imagine dancing with anyone other than him. They were really melding together as dance partners. She was beginning to anticipate his lead and he knew when he could incorporate a new step in the middle of their routine. They genuinely had fun while they danced. She felt a wave of sadness in her heart just thinking about not dancing with him. She didn't understand how that could affect her as much as it did. Her thoughts were becoming too complicated, so she got up and walked to the outer office to talk with Melanie about some current projects. It was a good distraction.

Her meeting with Melanie was eventually interrupted by a call from Kellie. She paused to take her call. "Hello Kel, how's it going? Hey, how was that premiere you attended the other night?"

"It was great. You missed a good performance by this kid. I think he's going to go far in his acting career. He's surprised all of us. So, what's been going on with you?" Kellie was an executive at a very successful advertising agency. She had met Tyana in college while studying communications and theater arts. Tyana had been a theater arts major.

"Did Ellis get back OK and have you two come up for air much? I know how you get when he's away for a long period of time," inquired Kellie, eager to get the goods on her friend.

"Well, not exactly. I haven't been able to spend one frickin' moment with Ellis since he's been back," Tyana said harshly.

"Why? What do you mean? Is everything OK?" Kellie got serious in response to Tyana's tone.

"He's been keeping late nights at the office, Kel. His first night back he didn't come home until five-thirty in the morning and then just turned right around and went back to the office. And last night, the same thing although, I'm not sure what time he came in—I didn't hear him. But I know it was at least three because I was up until about two. He says he's working on some big project or presentation that I haven't heard him speak of at all before now. It sounds like these are spur-of-the-moment meetings, too, because each night he had planned on coming home to be with me but then calls me to tell me he's been detained. I don't understand. He said he might be working again tonight but that he'll try to get away early to spend some time with me," she continued, lowering her voice so Melanie wouldn't overhear. "We haven't made love in almost a month and when I attempted to get close to him this morning, he couldn't...it wouldn't. He's just that tired. I'm trying to be as patient as I can, but it's not easy and I miss him. And I understand that these are important meetings and all, but he's come home smelling like alcohol too, which makes me feel uncomfortable about him driving in that condition. I don't know what to do."

"Wow, that's quite a problem you have there, Tyana. Ellis needs to have a little more consideration for your needs and take a little break for you two to get together. That doesn't sound like him to be that preoccupied. This must be a big project because I don't recall you mentioning him ever being that busy—to keep crazy hours like that. Have you met any of these people he's been meeting with, or talked to any of them? I mean, it all just sounds so peculiar. What's so important that keeps him there that late that you know nothing about?" Kellie was suspicious, which was her nature anyway. She had always been more cautious and suspicious than Tyana. Tyana was a very trusting and somewhat naïve person next to Kellie. Kellie trusted very few. One had to earn her trust.

"I don't know, Kel, he said something about his career depending on this project or something like that. I find that statement weird just from the fact that he's never mentioned it before to me. I got the impression that it was only going to be crazy for a few more days. I'm probably over-reacting. He always knows what he has to do and he's good at what he does, so I should just relax and be patient." Tyana was beginning to calm down some.

"That's your problem, Tyana, you're too patient sometimes. He should be a little more patient and understanding of *you*. You give him so much room and benefit of the doubt all the time. Paul works some crazy hours too when he's working on a big case, but he'll always inform me of what's going on and he calls me if he's going to be too late. That's the least he can do considering the position he puts me in at times. Ellis should do the same for you, Sweetie. You've given him so much of yourself, and I hope I'm not out of line when I say this, but I think you spoil him too much and now he's taking you for granted. He needs to spoil you more. You cater to him when he's home, giving up your schedules and time, but now that he's home, he hasn't spent any time with you. Are you still taking your dance lessons, by the way?" Kellie felt some pity for her friend.

"Kel, I know it seems that way, but I love him and I do what I can to make our relationship easy for both of us. He makes sacrifices as well. He does." Tyana wasn't sure that that was completely true. "Yes, I'm still taking my dance lessons, I guess." Her voice seemed to drop just then.

"What's wrong, Tyana? You suddenly don't sound as excited about your lessons as you have been. Is there something going on? Are you thinking of quitting?" Kellie was very perceptive when it came to Tyana.

"I don't know. I don't think I should talk about it here, maybe later." Tyana was thinking about Melanie just outside her office. "How about we get together soon and we can talk then? I really need to get back to work so I can get home and get ready for my lesson tonight," she said, preparing to hang up.

"Oh, so you are still taking the lessons. Good. OK. Hey, you call me anytime. I love you." They hung up.

Tyana returned to work but couldn't help thinking about everything that Kellie said about Ellis and how she thought he was taking her for granted. Was he? She reflected back on several incidents where his job and schedules had to be considered over hers. She wasn't convinced that he was. She continued to work, refocusing on her job.

Ellis and Charlotte met again, after hours, in Ellis' office. He had come into work early that morning to tidy up his office after the adventurous night he had spent with Charlotte. It left things quite disheveled. It was difficult working across from his sofa all morning, seeing the images in his mind of Charlotte, naked, practically forcing him to make love to her. He couldn't help but think how it was all because of him coming on to her in her hotel room.

He was still reliving that nightmare when Charlotte entered, this time without knocking. He jumped at her presence. He was expecting her, dreading what the evening might have in store for him this time. He was going to make every effort to put a stop to the sex. He couldn't handle it any longer. He knew he needed to be with Tyana and make love to her. Charlotte was making that impossible.

"Good, you're here. I noticed that everyone else has gone home. Where's the loyalty around here? I've got some good stuff for tonight's meeting. I've been in meetings all day and on three conference calls. I tell you, I don't know how some of these idiots have jobs. I recommended one bastard be fired today. He should get his severance in the morning. I don't think he deserves it, but it's policy." Charlotte began to unload her papers from her briefcase, showing no emotions in her last statement. Ellis was shocked by what she had just said. Fired.

They worked well into the evening again. That didn't faze Charlotte at all—it was customary for her to do so. Following protocol, they had several drinks. He wasn't up to drinking at all, but he was playing the part. He figured he had just one more day of this charade and then Charlotte would be on a plane back to California.

"Listen, I think we did all we could here tonight. You seem to have a handle on the presentation and it all seems to be coming together. I'm confident that you'll knock 'em dead. All you have to do is let the presentation speak for itself. You're home free, sweetheart. How about we celebrate this major feat and treat ourselves to a little dip in my hot tub? I've been here for several days now and have yet to use the thing. It looks so inviting. Come on." Charlotte had already packed up her things and was heading out the door. He ran to catch up with her.

"Charlotte, I think I should be heading out. It's been a long week and it's late. You probably have some packing to do anyway."

"Nonsense. I won't hear of it. You've worked your ass off—and a beautiful ass you have, I might add. We owe it to ourselves. We can get a massage first if you like."

"No, no, that's not necessary," he said, realizing that he'd be better off just going along with her on the hot tub deal than to stretch the evening out any further with a massage too. "The hot tub sounds great—for just a little while." He gave in.

When they reached Charlotte's hotel room Ellis looked around to see if anyone was around who would recognize him. The coast was clear. They entered the room where it had all begun. He was getting that sick feeling in the pit of his stomach once again. Charlotte excused herself to change. She left Ellis with instructions to get them drinks from her bar. He poured them both a drink.

"I just remembered that I don't have any trunks here with me. I sent my gym clothes to housekeeping to be washed," he yelled out to Charlotte while she was still in her bedroom. He thought he was in the clear. She emerged wearing nothing.

"Don't be absurd. It's a private hot tub, silly. Who needs to wear anything? I find that clothes can be too restricting. The jets against our naked bodies will feel marvelous. Come on now. Hurry and get out of those clothes. Do you need some help?"

Ellis was perplexed, and found himself staring at Charlotte's unblemished and exquisitely, shapely body. She was truly a sex goddess, he was thinking to himself. Charlotte approached him but he stopped her.

"Here's your drink. I can handle removing my clothes. I just thought...never mind." Ellis quickly complied. In a few moments, he was standing next to her in all his glory as she flagrantly admired his body. She took their drinks and headed to the hot tub.

"Oh, doesn't this feel heavenly?" she said as she lowered herself into the water. He entered right after her.

"Yes, it's great. It's been a few days since I've been to the gym." He didn't know what to say. They continued to sip on their drinks while Charlotte talked a little more about the project.

"What the hell am I doing? We're not here to talk shop, we're here to relax and celebrate." Charlotte moved closer to Ellis' body and ran her hands up his leg, starting at his knee and ending up between his legs. She wasted no time locating her prize. He flinched. "Did I startle you? Why did you jump, Ellis?"

"I...just wasn't expecting it. Uh, what time is your flight tomorrow, Charlotte?" he asked, feeling extremely nervous and full of guilt. He knew Tyana would be home waiting for him.

"Well, I didn't mean to surprise you. I was just helping you get relaxed. You look so tense. I guess we'll have to stay in here until we can work all of that tension out of you." Charlotte closed her eyes and started caressing her breasts. He just watched. He tried to ignore the fact that what she was doing was turning him on. She began to moan softly in response to her touch, as she wrapped her leg around his leg, rubbing her crotch on his leg. She released one hand and grabbed his rear end and pulled him closer to her. She continued to rub herself on his leg. She was quickly becoming aroused, as was he.

He closed his eyes and didn't fight the moment. He knew he wasn't going to win anyway. It wasn't long before he had a full erection and was in need of relief. He was trapped, a prisoner, and Charlotte held the all-important key—the key to the success or demise of his career. When she was good and turned on she quickly straddled his waist but didn't allow him to enter her. He was trying but she kept him just out of her reach. He was getting more aroused by the second. His erection was searching for her opening. She allowed him to reach her crotch but would pull away from him each time he tried to enter her. His body began to shudder intermittently. He was so turned on he was actually starting to feel desperate.

Charlotte saw that he was grimacing and was becoming impatient with her little game, but she didn't care—she was in control. He knew that what he was doing was wrong and couldn't bring himself to openly want her, but he couldn't control what his body was now craving and desperately needed. He admitted to himself that he had fallen under the spell of her body. His body had not known the kind of stimulation that her body had been providing him. His body had become a slave to her loins and he was quickly becoming addicted to her. He needed her to give him the kind of earth-shattering, mind-blowing, release that only she had been able to produce, with ease.

She continued to tease him by allowing him to enter her then quickly pulling him out. That went on for several minutes until he could no longer withstand the pressure. He grabbed her and shoved his erection into her with such force that they almost went under the water. He held her tightly to his body so she couldn't pull away. She struggled but he refused to let her go, almost as if he was possessed. He thrust himself harder and faster, not hearing her cries for him to stop. He didn't stop until he drained himself completely. His body shuddered for several minutes. Charlotte, too, reached the heights of ecstasy but hid that fact from Ellis. His body was still heaving with spasms, still relieving itself so violently that he didn't feel the scratches on his chest made by Charlotte in her attempt to get him to stop.

Theresa E. Liggins

Chapter Six

While Ellis was becoming more tangled up in Charlotte's salacious web, Tyana kept her dance lesson appointment with John. She couldn't help but think about Antonio during her drive to the dance studio. She still couldn't believe all that had taken place and that she was no longer training with Antonio. She arrived right on time and entered the studio with less enthusiasm than before. She stopped and looked around, not certain of who John was. Someone approached her.

"Hi Tyana, I'm John. So glad you could make it in tonight. I have your chart here and Antonio and I have discussed your curriculum to get me up to speed with your progress. I don't want to impede that progress in the slightest, so we can pick right up where you left off. It's not unusual for students to work with several instructors. Actually, that works to their advantage because all the instructors have slightly different styles of teaching. That way you can follow almost any type of lead. Shall we get started?" Tyana kept looking around while John was talking to see if she could spot Antonio, but he was nowhere around. She barely heard a word that John said, but followed him to one of the private dance rooms.

During the first half-hour of her lesson, Tyana strained to focus on her routines. They decided to start from scratch on some of them to incorporate more of John's style than Antonio's. She didn't mind, and in fact preferred that they didn't continue to choreograph what she and Antonio had worked on. Those were their dances, she thought to herself. She found it difficult to stay in the moment with John. By the end of her lesson, she had realized that John was an extremely good dancer and instructor. He was also very attractive as well, but she didn't think he had quite the attributes and whole package that Antonio had. She caught herself comparing them like pieces of fruit, then stopped herself. Was she admitting to herself that she was attracted to Antonio physically? She wasn't sure anymore. All she knew was that she was missing him terribly. It just wasn't the same without him.

At the end of her lesson, she decided to give John the benefit of the doubt and work with him in order to continue her dancing. She loved dancing and didn't want to give it up. Plus, if she were to give it up at this point, she was afraid that people would think it had something to do with Antonio. She and John talked for quite a while after the lesson about her impression of the lesson and of John as her instructor. She told him that everything was fine and that she looked forward to taking lessons from him. She knew in her heart that it wasn't the truth. It was Antonio whom she wanted as her instructor. It was Antonio whom she wanted to dance with and learn new routines with. It was Antonio whom she wanted to be with on the dance floor. They wrapped up their conversation, scheduled more lessons, and then he walked her to the door. She said goodnight to John and left the studio.

It was nine-thirty by now as she sat dazed in her car, still thinking about her lesson, but more about Antonio. She was completely lost in thought and hadn't realized that she was still sitting there when she heard a tap on her car's passenger window. She jumped and turned to see Antonio.

She quickly unlocked the car and opened the door. Antonio leaned in to speak to her. "Hi there. Are you OK? It's ten o'clock and you're sitting out here alone." He was genuinely concerned about her sitting out there in the dark by herself.

"Oh, yes, I'm fine. I guess I should leave. I had some things on my mind and didn't realize the time." Her heart was racing. She felt ridiculous, having Antonio catch her just sitting there with nothing in her hands to make him think that she was busy with something. "Are you leaving for the evening? I just finished my lesson with John," she said, trying to divert the attention away from her sitting in the dark car.

"Ah yes, how did that go? John's one of my top instructors. He does a great job. Did you enjoy the lesson?" Antonio was trying to hide his own feelings about not teaching her.

"The lesson was great. John's a good instructor and I like him a lot. We learned some new steps and worked on a couple of new routines. He thought that it was best that we work on something totally different than what I started with you, in order to incorporate John's style better," she explained.

Antonio found himself staring at her as she spoke. He barely heard what she said about John. He wanted to touch her hands, hold her close to him and dance with her. He had deliberately stayed away from her at the studio while she was there. He wasn't ready to see her dance with someone else when he knew he couldn't. He was upset about not having better control over himself and about exposing his attraction to her. He still wasn't sure why it happened. It was as if he had had an out-of-body experience that night. He was afraid more would come to the surface if they continued dancing together.

"That's a good idea," said Antonio. They both stared long at each other without a word. "Well, I better let you get going, it's late. Drive carefully. I'll see you next time. Bye now." He closed the car door. She started the engine and pulled away. She looked in her rear-view mirror, watching Antonio as he stood on the sidewalk watching her drive away. John stopped and watched them both as he got into his car.

Tyana arrived at an empty house. No Ellis—again. She was losing her patience with his schedule. She checked her cell phone to see if he had called her. He had not. She didn't know what to make of this project that was keeping him working throughout the night and into the morning. It just sounded so out-of-the-blue to her. She didn't think he was being very open about it, either. She had never known him to pull all-nighters before in the many years he'd been with the hotel. She had known about all his projects in the past, even the smaller ones. This was very unusual. She entered the house and tried to busy herself to keep from dwelling on the fact that he was still out. She called his office and got no answer then called his cell—same story. At midnight, she called both numbers again—still no answer.

Tyana put on some jeans and a T-shirt and headed toward the hotel.

76

"Oh, Charlotte, that was amazing," said Ellis as his body finally began to relax. He slowly slid out of her. He opened his eyes and began to feel the stinging sensation on his chest. He looked down and saw that he was bleeding from the scratches made by her nails. "What happened?" He turned to look at Charlotte crying. "What's wrong, Charlotte?"

"Ellis, I don't know what came over you. I begged you to stop and you just continued to ram your penis into me, hurting me. Didn't you hear me plead with you to stop it? I think I'm hurt. You were so big and I didn't..." Charlotte got out of the hot tub, leaving Ellis standing in shock.

"But Charlotte, you wanted it, you were all over me. What do you mean? This was your idea to come in here and...your leg was all over me...what, I don't understand!" She went back into the room. Ellis was frightened and totally shocked by her insinuations and behavior. He couldn't imagine what she was talking about. All the other times, all the flirting, her numerous come-ons. He just stood there in complete disbelief. He got out to tend to his wounds. He found her in the bathroom with blood dripping from between her legs. "Oh my God, Charlotte, what's going on? Where did that come from?"

"Ellis, I would like you to leave now. I don't know what you were thinking or what you're talking about, saying I wanted this! Look at me! I don't know what to think about all this. Are you saying that I asked for this to happen to me? What do you take me for? You forced yourself on me and you wouldn't stop until you finished. You were like a crazed beast. I yelled and yelled but you wouldn't stop, that's when I scratched you but that didn't seem to stop you either. I need to be alone right now to get cleaned up and to see if I require medical attention. I'm very sore and can hardly walk at the moment." She searched for her robe.

"Charlotte, I'm very sorry, I certainly didn't mean to hurt you. I didn't think that you were...I mean, you seemed to be in the moment. I wouldn't do anything that was inappropriate. Can I do something? Are you sure you need to have medical attention? I'm so confused as to what happened. I didn't hear you tell me to stop, I didn't, Charlotte." Ellis was rambling and he felt like he was losing his mind.

"Of course, you didn't. You were too busy getting your rocks off! I'm surprised by what has happened here, Ellis." She continued to stick to her story.

"Please, Charlotte, what do you want me to do? Please don't involve anyone else in this, we can handle it. I'm terrible sorry—it was a misunderstanding. I'm sorry."

"Put your clothes on, Ellis, and please leave me. It's late and I need to catch a plane in the morning. I would like to rest and calm down. This is very traumatic for me. I've never experienced anything like this before and I'm just a little in shock, I guess." She cleaned herself up with a nearby wash cloth.

"I won't leave if you still need me. I want to help."

"I think I would prefer that you do leave—you've done enough, Ellis. I don't want you here right now. I'll call you tomorrow and let you know how I feel, that is if I think I should go to the hospital or something. If I had known you were an aggressive person, I wouldn't have invited you to come to my hotel room. You just go and take care of that presentation. I'm glad you got what you wanted from me, in more ways than one." She shoved Ellis out of her room before he finished dressing. He was standing in the hall with just his pants on. It was one in the morning.

Still dazed and confused, Ellis returned quickly to his office to get himself together. He wasn't sure what the heck had just happened to him. The first thing that came to his mind was him losing his job. What if she filed a rape charge against him, he thought to himself. He just couldn't think straight. He needed to sit down.

When he reached his office, he closed the door behind him and just sat in his chair in the dark with his head slumped over in his hands. He didn't hear Tyana enter.

"Ellis, what the hell are you doing? And why are you half naked?" She started to panic. "What is happening here and you better have a good explanation! It's one in the morning and I find you here, with your clothes off. What the hell are you up to?!" Tyana couldn't even think coherently with the thousands of thoughts that were racing through her head. Ellis was speechless and numb. He just stood there staring at her. She walked over to the table near the window and turned on the lamp. "And your hair is wet! He quickly turned slightly away while he put on his shirt to cover up the scratches made by Charlotte. He turned back around.

"Tyana, I…what are you doing here? Where did you come from; when did you get here?" He was stalling for something logical to say. He was dumbfounded. "I mean, I was just coming back from the workout facility and was closing up to head home."

"What?! What about your meeting? You know I've been home waiting for you and you have time to work out? Ellis, I'm only going to ask you this one more time, what is going on here?" She was beginning to tremble.

"Tyana, the meeting ended a little while ago and I've been so tight from these late meetings that I felt I needed to unwind a little and have a good workout—to feel better. I've been so tense." Ellis was doing the best he could on the spur of the moment.

"Then why do you smell like chlorine?" Tyana wasn't through with her inquisition.

"I took a swim and then soaked in the…hot tub for a few moments. I just left the gym and came in here to get my things. I don't want you to be upset, honey. There's nothing to worry about. I'm finished here, so let's so go, OK? I'm sorry I worried you. These meetings are over for now. We wrapped things up this evening. I'm ready for my presentation and if all goes well, honey, I'll be getting a huge bonus. We can take that trip to Hawaii. Let's start packing!" He did what he could to defuse the potentially volatile situation he saw beginning to brew. He also needed to quickly redirect Tyana's focus from his mounting guilt and lies.

"I don't know, Ellis, I don't understand why you didn't call me, or better yet, come home. You haven't been home yet since you've been back. How can working out at the gym be more of a priority? It just doesn't add up." Her suspicion began to mount as well.

"I know, baby, it seems that way to you, but I wanted to release the tension before coming home to you. You know how working out makes me feel. It gives me more energy too. I didn't think that an hour of a workout would be such a problem. It's been a grueling month for me, baby. I just needed one hour to get revived. Now, let's get out of here and get home. I'm really beat and would love to get some sleep." He was quickly escorting her out of his office. He wanted to get her out of the hotel before Charlotte surfaced. He couldn't handle any more drama.

"Get some sleep, are you kidding? What I've been waiting a month for doesn't include you going home to get some sleep." She stopped him in his tracks and started rubbing her hands on him.

"Tyana, can we please leave?" He was getting nervous and uncomfortable with so many reminders of Charlotte and him in compromising positions.

"No, I've got a better idea. Let's not waste another second. It's late and there's no one around..." She didn't have to finish her sentence for Ellis to know what she was about to suggest. "Come on Ellis, let's do it right here. I've missed you, baby. I need you. I want you now!" She became very amorous and moved in closer to him to hug him. He hugged her back. "Ellis, I love you and I've missed you so much. I hate it when we're apart for so long." She started to remove his clothes.

"I know. I hate it too when we're apart. I'll try to do better and spend more time with you. Can we please go home? I've been in this office all day—all week. I just need a different scenery." He was trying his best to leave the scene of the crime and to get Tyana out of there before he met up with any more surprises.

Tyana had other plans. She wasn't going to chance missing out on another opportunity with Ellis. She closed the door to his office, turned off the light, and undressed herself. He watched, feeling queasy just thinking about having to perform again just after he left himself completely drained with Charlotte. It was too soon for him to be able to get himself up again to make love to her. He knew it all too well. But he also knew that after his last failed performance, he'd better be able to do something. Tyana was standing naked at this point and moved toward the sofa, where she lay down on her back as she motioned Ellis to come to her. He did.

Knowing that he wasn't going to be able to talk himself out of making love to her, he went to her and lay on top of her and began to kiss her. As hard as he tried, he couldn't get himself in the mood to want to have sex, at least not at that moment. He had always wanted her until Charlotte got a hold on him. Now, the only one he was able to respond to was Charlotte. He stalled a little while longer and continued to kiss her, but he was having no reaction to her touch, her body, or her kisses. He was getting nervous. Tyana began to touch him and stroke him but he was limp in her hands. She worked harder at getting a response out of him. Nothing. Ellis was starting to perspire as he, too, attempted to arouse himself.

"Ellis? What's happening? This is the second time this has happened. It's never happened before now and you've worked late numerous times." She was frustrated as well. "Do you want me to try something else? You can never resist that." She was desperate for him to make love to her.

"No, no, that's OK, sweetheart. Just give me a minute." Ellis couldn't imagine how he had gotten himself in this situation—overnight. Why did Charlotte choose to come here? She'd never come here before to meet him. He continued to work diligently on an erection. He closed his eyes as Tyana's hands were on him and he began to imagine that Tyana was Charlotte.

Charlotte was up in her hotel room, getting cleaned up. She poured herself a glass of wine as she ran the water in the shower. She took a sip and smiled as she praised herself for her award-winning performance with Ellis. How duped he was, she thought. It was perfect; he was definitely putty in her hands. She literally had him by the balls. She wasn't about to let him get away from her now. He'll be eating out of her palm. She knew the presentation was all but put to bed and he would be rewarded handsomely for his hard work. He would be taking the credit. She didn't want him to get away from her. Not after discovering how good he was in the sack. She had plans for him. She had to come up with an elaborate scheme to keep him right where she could get at him anytime she wanted after their work together was completed. She knew she had shaken him up pretty good with her threats to seek medical attention because he forced himself on her—and the effects with the blood dripping from between her legs. Her quick thinking to cut her upper thigh slightly with her razor was brilliant, she thought. He didn't suspect a thing.

As she showered under the steamy hot water, she was thinking that she might have gone a little too far and freaked him out too much. She decided she would go and see if he was still in the hotel and talk to him. She would come up with something that would ease his mind about her taking the incident any further. When she got out of the shower, she put on some clothes and headed down to his office. She reached the door but stopped because she heard noises coming from inside. They were moans. The lights were out so she opened the door and peeked into his dark office to see Ellis and Tyana making love on his sofa—the sofa where she had been just the night before. She watched intently, feeling a little offended since he had just had his way with her.

He forced a vision of Charlotte in his mind. He began to moan and move in rhythm to his moans. Tyana worked harder, seeing that he was starting to respond. Ellis began to fondle and kiss her breasts, still keeping his eyes closed. It was working. He managed to get himself aroused as long as he had a mental picture of Charlotte and imagined that she was the one caressing him. It took him a long time and a lot of effort before he was able to climax but he managed to force himself. It wasn't nearly the fireworks that he had exhibited with Charlotte, but he was just relieved that it was over and was able to bring Tyana to her sexual height as well. His job was done but he had realized that he was now under Charlotte's power. Charlotte smirked at their performance. She thought it was pathetic, but was sure they were doing the best they could; after all, he had just been with her. She backed away from the door. He didn't even have the energy to get up, so he just lay there on the sofa while Tyana got dressed. He watched her, thinking how incredible sexy she was, wondering why he wasn't turned on by her just then. He was hoping it was only temporary. They cleaned up and left. Charlotte had been waiting for them to leave, hiding around the corner. She followed them out, keeping a safe distance.

Chapter Seven

The next several days went by without incident. Charlotte was gone, Ellis gave his presentations, and Tyana continued her dance lessons with John, growing more comfortable with him. She seldom saw Antonio at the dance studio, which she just accepted. Only occasionally did she see him instructing another student. She couldn't help but feel heartbroken about Antonio's decision to not teach her any longer. She was unaware that he kept a close watch on her and her progress. He missed her just as much but didn't want to go back on his decision to not teach her—not until he was certain that it could be done without distractions or any interference caused by his emotional attachment.

It had been several weeks when Charlotte phoned Ellis to talk about the new client acquisition. There was no doubt in her mind that Ellis would get the contract. She wanted to congratulate him.

"Hello Ellis," said Charlotte when he answered his line. "How are you? I haven't heard from you in a while."

"Charlotte, hello. It's good to hear from you. Things have been crazy here, as you would imagine, after nailing those accounts. And speaking of that, I want to thank you again for everything you've done. I couldn't have done it without your help. I owe you a lot." He didn't mentioned the incident between them and hoped she wasn't harboring any animosity toward him over it.

"Yes, you do, Ellis. And by the way, I decided not to hold you solely responsible regarding that little incident that transpired on my last night there. I decided to let it go this time. You probably weren't yourself that evening—maybe starved for some gratifying sex and you knew that I would be able to provide what you needed. Some men are often neglected at home and are in need of a woman who knows how to satisfy a man. Perhaps you just became overly stimulated and lost control. I imagine I can have that effect on men sometimes. It's a gift. But I want to warn you that you had better take it easy and play by my rules alone, or else you'll find yourself where you don't want to be. I promise you that." Charlotte was getting her digs in about his sex life. After witnessing his weak performance with Tyana, she was convinced that he didn't have access to a woman who could bring him to the sexual heights that she could. She knew she still had him.

"I understand. It will never happen again. I'm truly sorry for hurting you in any way. It wasn't my intention. You mean a lot to me and I would never do anything to hurt our friendship or working relationship. I hope you forgive me." Ellis was quick to accept responsibility if it meant that his job wasn't in jeopardy. He was grateful.

Charlotte had other plans for him up her sleeve. Once their project was over and she no longer had a legitimate reason to see him, she wanted to make sure she had access to him for personal reasons.

"Good, I'm glad you understand where I'm coming from. Don't worry about your job either, I have only your best interest in mind, sweetheart. As long as you work by my rules, I'll get you to the top." Charlotte was already plotting her next move. "Oh, by the way, I hope you've cleared your schedule for the Madrid trip. We leave in less than four weeks. I'll take care of your flight arrangements and all the accommodations we'll need in Madrid—don't worry about that. You just get yourself prepared. I have several meetings already lined up throughout the conference to get you introduced to the key executives. You better have your shit together before meeting these folks. They don't waste time with anyone who doesn't know what they're talking about. Bottom line. I'll email an agenda to you by end of next week. Look for it and get back to me immediately with any comments." She abruptly ended the conversation after that and hung up.

Ellis wasn't sure if he could actually get away now for that conference in Madrid, but in light of Charlotte's vindication he began to look at his upcoming schedule. Telling Tyana was going to be another hurdle. He was going to Madrid for a week. He had promised Tyana that they would go to Hawaii.

The mini competition was one week away and Tyana and John felt that she was ready. The dances that they had chosen had become easy for her to learn and perfect, as had several routines. She wasn't concerned about her performance. John was a great instructor and easy to work with. He had already discussed several other regional competitions that would give her more of a challenge. She thought about them and decided that she indeed wanted more. She was a natural at dancing and had started focusing more on technique and styling. She and John were having a good time dancing together. Antonio continued to watch from a distance.

Tyana was keeping an aggressive schedule at the studio and becoming addicted to the dancing and the mere relaxation and fun that it provided. She'd met a lot of new people in the process—some who had commissioned her for interior decorating projects as well. This was quickly becoming the most rewarding thing she had done for just herself in a very long time. While Ellis was in town, she would schedule her lessons in the middle of the day, leaving her the evenings to spend with him. When he was out of town, she sometimes danced at the end of the day, which helped her to relax before heading home to an empty house. She had mentioned the dance lessons to Ellis several times; however, he was usually so preoccupied with Charlotte's control over his career and his upcoming trip that he just didn't give her news much consideration. She stopped bringing it up. It certainly didn't interfere with their schedule.

Tyana was also finding that she and Ellis didn't have much of a joint schedule since he returned from San Diego. She tried talking to him about spending more time together, but he would invariably mumble something about his focus on some new project. They were beginning to see less and less of each other because of Charlotte's control over his position and his potential promotion if and when he acquired another region—a position within Charlotte's region. This would mean more money than he had ever anticipated he could make in this business. Charlotte, too, was aware of his salary potential and had set her sights on him. She knew it was only a matter of time before she could get his focus away from that woman she saw him making love to in his office. She thought Tyana was an attractive woman, from what she could tell, but didn't give her much merit when it came down to what she thought Tyana could give Ellis physically. Her plan was to convince him of that.

As expected, Ellis pulled into the garage around midnight. Aside from his job at the hotel and his secret plans to expand his base of operations, orchestrated by Charlotte, he was also avoiding Tyana because of the insurmountable guilt with which he had been plagued. He still found it hard to make love to her, both physically and emotionally. It was hard for him to face her under the circumstances. He found it also hard to perform with her because of what he'd experienced with Charlotte. Charlotte was simply amazing, sexually. He had been so perplexed by this situation because he loved Tyana so much. He couldn't imagine his life without her. Life with her was easy and without drama. Her attention to her career allowed him to concentrate on his. She was beautiful, smart, and sexy. He had it all, or so he'd thought, until he met Charlotte. Charlotte was no Tyana by any stretch of the imagination in terms of morals, but she had a different quality about her that fascinated Ellis. Charlotte didn't let morals dictate her approach to success—they only limited her. Ellis was drawn to her ability to help him make a lot of money and gain a lot of power. He had been financially secure already, before meeting Charlotte, but she had convinced him that he shouldn't settle for just being well off. He quickly bought into her voracious appetite for fame and money.

"Ellis, is that you?" Tyana heard him walking toward the bedroom. He had hoped she would be asleep. He entered the dimly lit bedroom.

"Hi, babe, what are you still doing up?" Ellis avoided eye contact with her.

"I thought I'd wait up for you to talk to you for awhile. We haven't seen too much of each other lately and it would be good to catch up on some things." She was being as understanding and patient with his long hours as she could.

"Well, it's kind of late and I'm beat. Can we do this another time? I really want to get some sleep, honey," he spoke to her as he closed the bathroom door behind him. He took a long shower to be alone with his thoughts.

When he emerged from the bathroom, he found her waiting for him. She was sprawled out naked on the bed. The room was dark with the exception of the candles she had lit all around their bed. Ellis' heart sank. This was what he had been trying to avoid. He slid under the sheets, unable to ignore Tyana's hint for a romantic evening. She initiated contact with him and didn't let up until he complied. Again, it took a lot of concentration from him and imagining that he was with Charlotte instead of Tyana. At that point, his performance took on a more forceful and aggressive style, which caught her by surprise. It was as if he were angry at something. He continued at that pace until he finished.

Tyana was left lying very still, trying to figure out what had just happened. She had felt like she was being attacked as she was thrashed about. She was confused and wondered what had happened to their passion and romance. Their lovemaking had always been that—making love, not whatever that was that Ellis had just done. She watched him for a few moments, thinking that he somehow seemed different to her. Just then he moved in a certain way, and Tyana caught a glimpse of the scratches on his chest, made by Charlotte, that were pretty much healed.

"Ellis, what happened to your chest? When did that happen?" She touched his chest to get a better look.

"What? Oh, that. I don't know, I don't remember." He wasn't prepared with a quick answer for her. He had been able to avoid her for so long so she wouldn't see the scratches that he had forgotten about them.

"What do you mean you don't know? How can you forget something like that? They look as if they were pretty bad at one time. It had to have hurt. What happened?" Tyana was determined to get an explanation for his marred body.

"Oh yeah, I got them at the gym a few weeks ago. One of the protective rubber caps had apparently come off one of the machines and when I was walking by, someone said something to me, I turned around quickly and it scratched my chest." Ellis held his breath after telling that lie. It was the best he could come up with on the fly.

"That's odd. What kind of machine would make a mark like that?" She was still not convinced of his story.

"I don't know, Tyana, just one of the machines. It was a long time ago, I've forgotten all about it. It's not a big deal. Can we drop it?" He was getting edgy. He was again lying to her and he hated it. He had never felt compelled to lie to Tyana before Charlotte had entered his private life. He turned over and pulled the sheets up over him and closed his eyes. She blew out the candles and they went to sleep.

The next morning Tyana began to get herself ready for work as Ellis continued to sleep. She noticed that he was sleeping in late in the mornings, but then keeping later hours in the evenings. She wasn't sure why the change. She continued to dress for work. Just as she was leaving the house, the phone rang. She stopped to answer it before it would wake Ellis.

"Hello."

"Ellis Montgomery please," said the female on the other end.

"I'm sorry, but he can't come to the phone right now, may I ask who's calling? I can take a message for him," she replied, not recognizing the voice as anyone she was familiar with from Ellis' office.

"I'm sorry if I woke you, but if you could let Ellis know that this is a very important call and that he should take it, then I'll let him keep his job," barked Charlotte, not in the mood to deal with the girlfriend. She was aware that he was living with the woman she had seen him with. This could mean that she would have to work a little harder to get him all to herself. She was up to the challenge. Tyana put down the phone and went to wake Ellis.

"Ellis, Ellis!" She shook him awake. "There's a very aggressive woman on the phone for you. Who the hell is she and why is she calling here, threatening to fire you if you don't take her call?" Ellis quickly sat up and reached for the phone. It could only be Charlotte.

"This is Ellis," he answered, sitting straight up in bed. Tyana was still in the room listening to the conversation and waiting for an explanation for the curt voice on the phone. "That's right, but I need to call you back when I get into the office, I don't have that information with me here. I'll be there within the hour." He hung up the phone. He had to put Charlotte off and get off the phone. He couldn't talk to her while Tyana was there. He was shocked that she had called him at his house. He didn't know how she had gotten his number, although he wasn't surprised that she had hunted it down. He was trying to come up with yet another lie for Tyana as he turned around, knowing she would be waiting for an explanation. She stared at him in anticipation for an answer.

"That was someone from the office. There seems to be a problem with one of our clients." He pulled that lame explanation right out of the air. "I need to get into the office right away."

"Who was it, Ellis? That wasn't anyone that I'm familiar with *at the office*," mimicked Tyana in an animated way.

"You don't know her, she's one the VPs. She's not there much. She comes in every so often. Don't worry about it, it's nothing. Now, I better get in the shower and get out of here or they will have my job." He scurried into the bathroom and closed the door. Tyana was left with his explanation. She went on to work.

Tyana couldn't get that woman's voice out of her mind, along with Ellis' reaction and vague explanation of who she was. Why was this obscure, yet obnoxious woman calling Ellis at their home? And why hadn't anyone bothered to identify her? There were so many things that were not adding up as far as Tyana was concerned. She found herself going over the whole scene in her head again and again. With her mind completely boggled and crowded with her thoughts, she slowly approached the stoplight halfway to work, slowing down to stop. She didn't notice that the car behind her wasn't stopping. She was rear-ended as she came to a complete stop. Her seatbelt kept her from lunging forward, but she whacked her head pretty hard on the headrest. She sat still in her car, dazed—not so much from the trauma of the accident, but because she felt that the accident had happened to her before. The feeling was so powerful that it had left her motionless for several minutes.

Chapter Eight

Tyana didn't appear to have any life-threatening injuries, or even serious injuries, for that matter. Witnesses had placed the emergency call and the paramedics were dispatched to the scene. Once the police officer made his report from Tyana's account, as well as witnesses' account of the accident, she was taken to the emergency room of the nearest hospital for observation, to be on the safe side. She didn't feel that she needed to go, but didn't argue against it. She was feeling a little woozy. She had really bumped her head hard.

She was checked over by the attending physician and he reported that she had escaped serious injuries. However, she did have a cervical strain from the whiplash she had endured, as well as a slight concussion. Ellis had been called and he had left his office at once to go to her. He was relieved to find her conscious and alert. He had felt sick to his stomach on the way to the hospital thinking about everything that he'd probably put her through, indirectly and unintentionally, because of his recent situation and how lost he would be without her if something tragic had happened to her. He had driven faster when he thought about all that and reached the hospital within minutes. When they took him to her, he reached out instantly and hugged her firmly.

"Tyana, honey, are you right?" He kissed her with emotions filling up inside, which he hadn't done in a long time. He felt familiar with her once again.

"I'm all right. I'm not hurt badly. I'll just have some soreness tomorrow from the whiplash. They gave me a prescription for that. I also have a terrible headache. They tell me I have a slight concussion. I should be OK in a few days. The car was towed to the dealership. They'll get it transported to the auto body shop they're affiliated with. The other driver just failed to stop behind me and was cited. I think they were OK. Their insurance will take care of the car and any of my medical expenses. I just want to go home."

Ellis took Tyana home as soon as she was cleared to leave. He didn't waste any time, getting her home and comfortable. She was a little surprised by his generous nature all of a sudden, considering his recent distant behavior. Her minor accident that day was probably what he needed to get his priorities straight—at least for now. He got her settled and, once he was sure that she would be fine alone, he went back to the office.

Tyana was ordered to take it easy for the next couple of days to make sure she didn't have any additional complications from the accident. She called Melanie immediately to tell her what had happened. She gave her some instructions and asked for some files to be delivered to her so she could work from home. She called Kellie and Trevor to let them know she would be home for a few days. Kellie was on her way over to see her. Trevor made plans to stop by later that evening after work. Before she lay down to rest, she phoned the dance studio to cancel her lesson that afternoon. Antonio answered the phone.

"Hi Antonio, this is Tyana. How are you?" She wasn't expecting to hear Antonio's voice. It just didn't occur to her that he would be the one to pick up the phone. She was lost for words.

"Hello, Tyana, so good to hear from you. I'm doing well, thank you. How's it going?" Antonio's heart stopped for a second after hearing Tyana's voice. He was happy, to say the least, to hear her voice.

"Well, I'm calling because I need to cancel my lesson with John today. I was in a minor car accident and I'm at home. I'm fine for the most part—just a little shaken up, but I'll be OK. I wanted to let John know that I don't think I'll be in, probably for the remainder of the week. I'll see how things go and how I feel and play it by ear, if that's OK."

Antonio was surprised by Tyana's news and was immediately overwhelmed with concern for her. His tone turned serious. "Tyana, are you sure you're OK? Is there anything I can do for you—do you need anything?" He knew that sounded silly as soon as he had said it. He wasn't responsible for her and he was certain that she had someone who could tend to her, but it was instinctive for him to ask.

"Thanks for your concern, but really, I'm fine. I'm just resting— that's all I need to do right now. It's nothing serious, really. If you could just let John know that I'll call and reschedule my lessons when I know better in a few days how I'll be feeling."

"Sure thing, no problem. It was good to hear from you. Please take care and call anytime if you need anything." He wanted so much to reach out to her, but he knew he couldn't. They hung up.

Tyana sat and held her conversation with Antonio in her head for several minutes. She was experiencing déjà vu again, she felt that she had done this before and that Antonio had been a part of it. It was baffling to her, and also a little annoying. She wanted to know what it meant and why she was having the momentary flashbacks. There had now been too many to be a coincidence. It was starting to rattle her. She was still deep in thought when she was interrupted by a phone call from Ellis.

"Hi babe, how are you feeling? Did I wake you?"

"No, I was just lying here not doing much of anything. Melanie will be by later with some work for me. I don't see why I have to stay confined like this. I feel fine."

"Doctor's orders. Plus, you won't know if you have further injuries for several more hours when your body will begin to tell you where the trauma is. Just relax, Tyana," he ordered her as he was trying to take care of her from a distance. "You're very lucky that you weren't seriously hurt."

"How are things at work? Do you still have your job?" she teasingly asked, thinking about the early morning phone call from the mystery woman.

"What are you talking about?"

"The phone call this morning, Ellis, the woman who threatened your job if you didn't take her call. What was that all about?"

"I told you this morning, it was about a client who needed some special attention. Everything's fine, Tyana, let it go. That reminds me, I'll be going out of town again in about three weeks—another business trip," he informed her, realizing that he couldn't put off telling her about the trip to Spain much longer.

"I see. Where to this time?" she casually asked, expecting that it was another routine trip.

He held his breath. "Madrid, Spain."

"Madrid? When did you find out about this? When are you leaving and how long will you be gone?" She sat upright.

"I found out about it a few weeks ago. It's not a big deal. I leave in three weeks—on a Saturday. I'll be gone for about a week, returning the following Sunday." There—it was out.

"Well, why didn't you say something before now? Who all's going?"

Ellis dreaded this question and having to lie to her again. "No one from this office, just me. I'll be meeting with some colleagues from another region and mostly with our Madrid staff. There's a conference there that I felt I needed to attend to gain some perspective on that region. It's a new property and I need to see how they're operating," he explained while nervously tapping his pen on his desk.

"Why? What does Madrid have to do with you, Ellis?" She wasn't accepting his reasons for going just yet.

"Tyana, it's business. This is what I do."

"Oh yeah, Ellis—since when? When have you been interested in an international region?"

"Since now. I have an aggressive and expansive goal set for me these next few quarters and I'm going to do everything in my power to meet them. You don't quite understand what's going on in the business and I don't have time right now to go into all that with you. I have a lot of work to do before I leave for Spain."

"Well, then I'll go with you. I mean, you promised to take me to Hawaii next month anyway. You got that huge bonus and you promised. You've been away a lot and when you're here, you've been spending about sixteen hours a day at the office. Ellis, you owe me this." Tyana felt that her relationship was being threatened by Ellis' job and she was not going to let that happen.

"No, I'm afraid you can't. Not this time. It's strictly business and I'll be too busy on this trip. It's not a pleasure trip. I'll barely have time to take a leak. I wish you could, but it's not possible. We'll go to Hawaii, I promise—when I get back. Look into some packages and I'll review them with you. Make the necessary arrangements and we're there." Ellis was desperate to get Tyana's thoughts of going to Madrid out of her head. He was trying to remain calm and not give away the fact that he was actually quite anxious. "I really have to go, babe. Call me if you need anything. I love you." Ellis was off the line.

Tyana wasn't sure if she was satisfied with Ellis' answer to her questions and she still didn't know who that woman was on the phone. But since she got a trip to Hawaii out of him, she would cut him some slack, for now.

Melanie arrived with some work for Tyana as requested, and left after Tyana had given her some instructions for the office. Several minutes later, Kellie arrived.

"Hey Mamacita, how are you feeling? I was so shocked when you called and told me about the accident. Are you sure you're not seriously injured anywhere? You were so lucky." Kellie was full of questions and concern for her friend. She gave her a big hug and they both sat down to visit. "Well, if this is what it takes to get some time with you..." Kellie tried to make light of the situation.

"I'm doing fine, considering. It happened so suddenly and I didn't see it coming so I got a pretty good jolt. I'll be fine except for some soreness I'm sure I'll have in the morning. I had to cancel a few of my dance lessons, of course," she said, pouting a little. She swallowed a couple of pain pills.

"So, you're still sticking with it then. You must be really good by now. What's it like? And how's your dance instructor, cool? Hey, weren't you going to tell me something about all that? So, what's up?" Kellie's interest was piqued.

"I dunno Kel, it's weird. Well, I don't have the same instructor who I started out with—Antonio. Something weird happened during one of my lessons with him; he's the owner of the dance studio. It's hard to really explain, but at one point while we were dancing, it seemed as if we had done that before—been together like that. We both stopped in mid dance and just stared at each other with a very magnetic-like stare. It was as if our hearts were speaking to one another and we both understood."

"What? Really? What do you think was going on? What did you do?" asked Kellie with a puzzled look on her face.

103

"I didn't do anything. He didn't do anything. We just finished the lesson and I left. I think he was feeling something odd too because we both just pretended that it didn't happen." She paused for a moment.

"OK, then why isn't he your dance teacher any longer if nothing happened?"

"Well, you see, after another lesson, everyone had left the studio and it was just the two of us. When we finished, I don't remember all the details, but he hugged me just like every other time but this time it was different. He just held me and I held him. Again, it felt very familiar to me, and the way he was acting, it probably felt the same with him—I don't know. Anyway, we just stood there holding tightly to each other. Then we looked into each other's eyes and things just got heated between us. I can't explain why it happened, it just did. Like I said, it was weird. I'm in love with Ellis and have never looked at any man like that, ever, since being with Ellis. It wasn't as if I was thinking about that moment or anticipated it before it happened. It caught me by total surprise, and I think it did him too."

"Yeah, then what happened next? Did you guys kiss or make out?" Kellie could hardly wait to hear what had happened next.

"No Kel, we didn't kiss, but it felt like we were going to, I think. That's when he pulled away and said that he was sorry—he didn't know what had come over him. He had no explanation for it. And he said that he wasn't accustomed to behaving like that with students and didn't want to compromise my lessons or my goals in any way. He was being a perfect gentleman. He then said that the best thing for him to do was to not teach me any longer—that he was afraid that something might happen again. He said he wasn't sorry for feeling what he was feeling but that it wasn't appropriate—that his intentions were to teach me dancing. He wanted to turn me over to John, the instructor that I have now. I respected his position and his decision and said OK. So, I've been working with John ever since. John's nice and a great dancer and instructor, but I miss dancing with Antonio—we really connected and it was fun. I'm not saying it's not fun with John, because it is. It just isn't the same. I try not to think about it when I'm there, but it's hard. I don't even see Antonio around when I'm there. I think he's avoiding me. But when I called to cancel today because of the accident, he answered and like I said, the conversation was pleasant. Even that conversation I had with him seemed like I've had it before with him. Kellie, I don't know if I'm losing my mind or what, but it happens too many times to just ignore it. I don't know what to think."

"Wow, that is bizarre. I don't know what to say about the feelings of déjà vu you keep having, but about the exchanges between you and Antonio—what the heck is that about? Are you attracted to him? Why do you think you are? Is he attractive? How did the conversation with him go today?"

"Yes, he's attractive, but that doesn't mean I'm automatically attracted to him. I don't know what I'm feeling. It's more because he seems familiar to me, like I've known him from somewhere but it doesn't make sense to me. I think about him constantly, which is wrong of me. I'm in love with Ellis. The conversation today was very pleasant. I told him about the accident and he was very concerned."

"Has Ellis been around a lot lately?" Kellie asked.

"Well, not really. He's been gone an awful lot. He was out of town for almost a month. Then when he returned home, he spent several nights, all night, at the office. Now, he's going in a little later in the mornings and coming home after midnight." Tyana hated how that sounded.

"What? Are you kidding? What is keeping him at the office like that? That's not his typical behavior. What the hell is going on at a hotel that is so important and demanding like that? I mean, I know he puts in a lot of hours, just like you, but that schedule doesn't sound right. Is there something new going on with his job that warrants this schedule?" Kellie was getting a bad feeling about this. But she didn't want to alarm Tyana, so she turned her focus back to her and Antonio. "I mean, I'm sure there's a good reason for it. So what about Antonio? Are you going to just continue taking lessons from John or do you think you and Antonio will pick it up again? It sounds like you prefer him anyway. What has Ellis said about you taking these lessons?"

"I don't know, Kel. I'll just continue to take the lessons. I really enjoy them no matter who's teaching me, but I would prefer Antonio. Ellis doesn't even know I'm taking lessons, or if he does, he doesn't seem to care. I tried to tell him several times, but he's always preoccupied and just mumbles something at me. I know he doesn't listen because I'm sure he would have had some opinion on the subject. I'm supposed to dance in my first competition next week, but now that I've been in this accident, I don't know if I'll be able to. I'll find out next week."

"Ellis doesn't know? What's he going to think when you do finally tell him or he finds out?"

"I don't really care at this point—I hardly see him anyway and he hasn't shown much interest in me lately. What can he say? Who knows how long I'll be doing this? When he wants to know what's going on with me, he can take the time to ask. I mean, I have to practically beg for sex these days too. That's not like Ellis. I don't know what is going on with him at work, but it's sure changed him and our relationship."

"Hey Kel, I think the medication is starting to kick in; I'm starting to feel a little drowsy. Maybe we should cut our visit short today. I can call you tomorrow to let you know how I'm feeling. I'll be home for a few days, it seems—maybe," she said as she walked Kellie to the door.

"You just take it easy and take advantage of this and get some rest. I'm sure you need it with your work schedule and these dance lessons. Get better so you can do your competition next week. I want to come and watch!"

Kellie left and Tyana went to bed to sleep off the medication.

Charlotte had called Ellis to give him his itinerary for the Madrid trip. During their conversation, she emailed him a copy.

"So, you'll be flying into San Diego where you'll meet up with me and we'll fly out together to Spain on the following day," said Charlotte as she explained the itinerary to Ellis.

"I better call reservations and get a room at our airport property then for that night," he replied in a matter-of-fact tone.

"Don't be silly, I'll send a car for you when your plane lands and you'll stay with me as my guest. The beach house will be much cozier and it'll give us a chance to strategize our agenda for Madrid. We can't waste time by leaving any gaps in the agenda. We have a lot to accomplish in just a week's time. I'll have the limo pick us up the following morning to take us to the airport. It's all been arranged. You don't have to worry about a thing, just let me do my job, which is to get you what you want. You still want it, right? I mean, if I'm wasting my time here, please let me know now." Charlotte had a way of always implementing her plans.

"Of course I still want it. I just don't want to be an imposition, that's all." Ellis suddenly got an ill feeling of nervousness. It was becoming clear to him what Charlotte was trying to do to him, his career, and his life. He knew he could put an end to it but it probably meant losing his job, his reputation and possibly his relationship with Tyana. He shook those thoughts out of his head.

"Don't be absurd. Listen, I have to run. I'll get back to you in a few days to discuss the conference schedule." She quickly hung up before giving him a chance to say anything further. When she hung up, she sat back in her chair and gloated, but she wouldn't let herself get too carried away just yet. There was still one thing she had to take care of and that was Tyana. She picked up the phone and began to dial.

Chapter Nine

Ellis catered to Tyana as much as he could during her short stay at home following her minor accident, but he still kept long hours at the office, preparing for his Madrid trip. He phoned frequently, checking in on her and to see if she needed anything. Against her doctor's advice, she returned to work after only a few days. She was sore, all right, but she didn't let that keep her from her responsibilities. The few days that she was at home, she felt guilty for not going into the office. She wasn't used to being confined for any length of time. She visited periodically with Kellie and Trevor, but soon became restless and needed to get back to work. Ellis had arranged a rental car for her while her car was being repaired.

Once Tyana got settled back into her design studio, she phoned John at the dance studio to let him know that she felt OK to return. She also felt she would be well enough to participate in the mini competition. It was her first exhibition and she was eager to perform. She had worked too hard and didn't want to forfeit her opportunity over some minor soreness. John was thrilled to hear the good news and encouraged her to cut a few heats if she wasn't up to dancing all of them. She emphatically declined his offer to cut back. She was too excited to even consider it.

When she returned to the dance studio after her brief recovery break, John was there to greet her with open arms. He was surprised to see her back so soon and looking well. They chatted for several minutes to get caught up before heading to work. Just then, Antonio surfaced and approached her.

"Hi, Tyana. It's so good to see you. Welcome back! You're looking well. How are you feeling?" asked Antonio as he hugged her. She hugged him back and felt the familiar arms that had once embraced her passionate soul. She still was confused as to where those feelings were coming from.

"I'm doing well, thanks. I'm just excited to be back in the studio again. I've missed being here." What she wanted to say was that she had missed *him*. John was standing beside them, watching the two with curiosity. Ever since he had witnessed them at her car that one evening, he had had the impression that there was something more to their relationship than just student and instructor. He still wondered why Antonio had just given up teaching her. She was a terrific student and a star in every sense. Any teacher would give his eyeteeth to train her and compete with her, plus she had the financial means to pursue dancing. John didn't understand, but he was willing to keep his eyes peeled for any clues to the mystery. He was convinced that there had to be more to it than what Antonio had explained to him. He watched them closely as they continued talking about the upcoming mini competition.

"Well, I better not hold you up any longer. I'm sure you're eager to get back out on that dance floor. Welcome back again, and I'll see you around." Antonio squeezed Tyana's arm gently, then walked away, looking back only once to see her and John as they walked arm in arm toward the dance floor. There was no doubt that he was pining for her.

Tyana and John danced for about an hour, then sat for a while afterwards to talk about new events that were listed on the schedule. Given Tyana's talent, John wanted her to take advantage of more opportunities to exhibit her dancing. Additional competitions, but local and regional, and a few exhibitions were among the events John spoke with her about. Her face lit up at the prospects that were presented to her. She was growing increasingly comfortable with John as her instructor and the way he had of enticing her with these events. They talked about them for several minutes, making sure that Tyana had enough information to make an informed decision. She said she would think about them and let John know her decision later. John was confident that she was sold on a few, if not all, and took that information back to Antonio after she left.

Antonio was thrilled at the news and wanted to see her compete in more events so she would become known throughout the region. He wanted her to get more competitions under her belt at her level, then advancing her to higher levels would be the next step. From there the decision would be hers; she could go as far as she wanted to go with her dancing. Antonio wanted her to consider teaching. He knew she already had a career that she was very successful with, so he had a lot of work ahead of him to convince her to cross over to the dance business. He had to be very careful of his approach, and the manner in which he would covertly groom her. He outlined an advanced curriculum for her and gave it to John to use. John didn't think twice

113

about the aggressive slant on the dance programs Antonio had profiled for Tyana, considering her talent and pace of learning.

On the night of her first competition, Ellis was tied up with clients and would be working late. Tyana decided not to even mention it to him. He hadn't been interested in what she'd been doing to this point. She wasn't really sure that she wanted anyone to watch her at this stage. She wasn't nervous; she just didn't think it was a big deal. She had talked to Trevor and Kellie earlier about the performance and explained to them that she wasn't expecting them to attend. They both had previous commitments that they would have canceled to be with Tyana. She had insisted that they not change their plans. It would be videotaped anyway and she agreed to share the moment with them that way.

All the students arrived at the dance studio about an hour before the start of the competition in order to set up and change into their costumes. They had a chance to review their heat positions and make any last-minute preparations. The judges were also setting up at their table, making sure that they had all the entries in the proper order and familiarizing themselves with the names of the competitors. Antonio, being the perfect host that he was, was running around making sure that everything was in order and everyone knew exactly where they needed to be and what they needed to do. He also made certain that the students were all very comfortable and well taken care of, and was overseeing the minutest of details. He had staff to take care of those details, but he often liked to see to things personally. That was just the way he preferred it when he hosted any event. Then he finally saw her.

Tyana had surfaced from the women's changing room, looking absolutely stunning. Antonio couldn't take his eyes off of her. She would be performing her smooth dances in the first half so she was wearing a beautiful topaz three-quarter-length gown made simply of multiple layers of sheer fabric, splattered with dark topaz-colored beads. She was lucky enough to find the gown, as well as other appropriate dresses for her Latin dances, at her favorite boutique. This was her first competition and she wasn't sure she wanted to go to a lot of expense for one competition. She still hadn't told John whether she wanted to be entered in the additional competitions or not. When she did decide to make more of a commitment to dancing and enter more competitions, then she would consider acquiring more opulent gowns and costumes. She was too modest to admit that she looked stunning in anything she wore. She turned and saw Antonio staring at her. He went to her.

"You are so beautiful, Tyana. How are you feeling?" he asked in a concerned tone.

"Antonio, hi. I'm feeling great, thanks for asking. I'm a little nervous about my first performance, but excited too. John and I have worked so hard. I hope to do him proud."

"Don't be silly. You'd do anyone proud. I'm very proud of your progress and I'm glad you've decided to stay on here. I'd hate to see your talent go to waste—you have incredible potential, Tyana." He was holding back his enthusiasm about her dancing. He knew in his

115

heart that he would dance with her again. Just thinking about it made his heart race.

"Well, thank you. I better go and find John. I think we're in the first heat." Tyana touched Antonio's arm and slid past him, leaving him with a whiff of her familiar fragrance. There was something very comfortable about her. He felt it again as he watched her walk away from him. He didn't see John standing behind him, in a crowd of instructors and students mingling, watching his body language as he talked with Tyana. It was telling a story. But what was the whole story? John was bound and determined to find out. Antonio took his position, as the competition was about to begin.

The first forty heats were all smooth dances, some solos and a few theater arts. Tyana and John danced gracefully and she did extremely well in all her categories. John was beaming with excitement at being with one of the most talented, not to mention one of the most beautiful, competitors in the place. If there were something going on between Antonio and Tyana, he could certainly understand why. She was fun, bright, talented, and gorgeous. A person could be easily drawn to her congenial personality. John didn't recall her ever mentioning a husband or boyfriend. He wondered, at times, what her private life was about. He knew she owned her own business and was a hard worker, but was that all?

When Tyana and John were on the dance floor among other couples, Antonio found himself watching only her. He was amazed at her footwork, at her level, and her floor presence. She definitely had style and what it took to become a great dancer. He ached inside, having to stand back and watch and not be a part of the ensemble. When he could, John would look back at Antonio watching Tyana—looking completely mesmerized by her. John only smiled. He could see that Antonio was hopelessly in love with her but could only enjoy her from the sidelines. Then John's smile faded. He thought it had to take incredible courage and willpower to do what Antonio was doing—keeping his distance. This had to be eating him up inside. That was probably why he so abruptly turned her over to him, he thought. It had to be. She was a gem. Why wouldn't he keep her for himself? He wondered if Tyana knew. He looked at her and saw the face of a true champion, then smiled as they continued to waltz around the room.

During intermission, the students and instructors were all changing for the second half—the Latin dances. Just like the first half, there were forty heats on the program. Twenty minutes later, the second half was underway. Antonio and his student were one of the first couples out on the floor for heat forty-one. He didn't see Tyana as she emerged from the changing room in a very sexy black number with a prominent slit up one thigh, perfectly chosen to set off her sassy, Latin style. It was an extreme departure from the modest, business-look attire she would wear during the day. It wasn't until she was strutting onto the floor for the next heat with John, as Antonio was exiting, that Antonio saw her. He did a double take.

There weren't very many heats that Antonio was in simultaneously with Tyana and John; therefore, he could stand on the side and just watch her perform. Again, he seemed to stare only at her. John appeared to be dancing his best when dancing with her. She had that effect on him. They complimented each other. Antonio couldn't help but feel envious of John's position as her dance partner. That was supposed to be his position, except he knew he would be her partner again someday.

It was a beautiful event, was the consensus of everyone as it came to a close. Antonio and one of his more advanced students performed a romantic theater arts number to end the program. Tyana watched with her eyes fixed solely on Antonio. She watched him with passion in her heart. He looked especially attractive to her tonight. She yearned to dance with him once again. It was as if their souls were reaching out toward one another. She could feel the tugging at her heart each time it skipped a beat as she watched him. It was difficult to ignore. Suddenly she felt despair and her eyes filled with tears. She was frozen with fear. She hadn't even noticed that the music had stopped and the audience was clapping wildly in appreciation. She just stood there like a spiritless statue. John was standing across the room now watching her watch Antonio. His heart sank as he honed in on her expression and saw a single tear trickle down her face. When she realized her emotions and what was happening, she quickly ran through the crowd, out of sight, and into the restroom. She locked herself in one of the stalls and tore off a piece of toilet paper to wipe her tears. She was starting to realize that there was indeed something more within her regarding her mysterious feelings toward Antonio.

How could it be happening, though? She barely knew him, she thought to herself as she faced the ceiling, her eyes closed. Was that what had been going on with her all this time and why she'd had those peculiar moments with Antonio? And what about Ellis? She knew she was in love with Ellis in spite of his recent preoccupation with his job. There was no room in her life for a romance outside of her relationship with Ellis. Her heart belonged to Ellis and she wasn't about to change that.

Tyana's discovery of her feelings for Antonio had unexpectedly redirected her focus. When she unlocked the bathroom stall door, she locked in her emotions that had surfaced—the emotions that made her long for Antonio. She returned to the changing room to change her clothes to go home. When she got there, she realized that she had been in the restroom longer than she thought. A lot of the students had long since left. There were a few who were still changing, and they praised her on her performance when she entered. She returned the compliments and continued to change.

Upon exiting the changing room, she noticed that the place was nearly empty. She was one of the last to leave. She just wanted to leave quickly, without any delay. She wanted to get home and go to bed. She had had a very long and eventful day. She reached her rental car and began to put her things in the back. As she closed the door and turned to open the driver's side door, she was startled to see Antonio standing before her.

"Oh! You scared me. I didn't see or hear you walk up," she said as she dropped her keys. Antonio bent down to pick them up for her.

"I didn't mean to scare you—didn't you hear me calling you?" he asked, handing the keys back to her.

"No, I guess I didn't hear you. I must be tired after all that dancing. What an evening." She was lost for something to say to him.

"That's what I wanted to talk to you about. I didn't see you afterwards and I wanted to tell you that I thought you did an outstanding job out there—being your first competition. You looked like you were a veteran out there. You were awesome and just looked spectacular." Antonio couldn't say enough about her performance. "You were also very elegant and beautiful tonight. Your costumes were breathtaking. You were the envy of many and the talk of the evening. I watched you as much as I could and was so proud of your performance. I think the judges were impressed, too. You can get your scores the next time you're in the studio. I know John was looking for you a while ago to thank you and tell you that you did an outstanding job, but he couldn't find you—you disappeared on us." He couldn't stop staring at her while he spoke, as if he was absorbing her essence.

"I was changing and got to gabbing with some students. I guess I lost track of time. When you see John, tell him I'm sorry I missed him. Or, I'll call him in the morning." Her mind was jumbled and she felt she was rambling. She started to open her car door.

"Is everything all right? You just performed impeccably and flawlessly, but yet you seem distracted and a little upset or nervous about something. Did something happen in there? Are you all right? Did you do too much tonight—I mean because of your recent accident?" Antonio was keenly watching her body language and

120

wanted to know what was the matter. He also wanted to steal a private moment alone with her. He hadn't had a chance to really talk to her in weeks. He had missed that.

John had been standing in the parking lot, at a distance, talking to some students when he saw Antonio and Tyana talking. He looked on with curious eyes, paying only partial attention to the conversation he was involved in. When the students left, he continued to watch, pretending he was putting something in his trunk.

"Yes, I'm fine. What do you mean? I mean, thank you for your concern, but everything is just fine. I had a wonderful time tonight. I guess I managed to pull off my dances without incident. I owe a lot of the credit to John though—he's a great teacher. I mean, so are you, I didn't mean to imply…"

"Tyana, it's OK. I know what you mean." Antonio could sense that she was distracted by something. He hadn't noticed her appearing that way earlier in the evening, which made him curious about what might have happened since then. "I better let you go, it's late and I shouldn't detain you any longer out here. I just wanted to say congratulations on your first performance. I certainly hope you'll be performing with us in the future. I'd love to see that." He stretched his arms out to her.

"Thanks Antonio. It was a pleasure and I hope to do more competitions. I mean, I plan to." They embraced each other. Tyana closed her eyes and she felt tense as Antonio's arms took hold of her in a loving way. She fought back her desire to just hold on to him.

She needed to get home to Ellis—quickly. "Goodnight. I'll see you soon."

Antonio let her go and she got into her car. John continued to peer at them through his car window. Antonio stood in the place where he had just held Tyana and watched her drive away. He watched her until she was out of sight. John watched Antonio and just shook his head, sensing that Antonio was in too deep with feelings for Tyana, maybe at the point of no return. John drove away. A mysterious car that had been parked down the street also drove away, following Tyana.

Antonio returned to the dance studio to oversee the cleanup. He closed himself up in his office and just sat at his desk in deep contemplation. About an hour later the supervisor of the cleaning crew came knocking on Antonio's door. He jumped at the sound and got up to answer it. He inspected the cleanup and wrote a check for the services. Once everyone had left, he turned out all the lights. Only the spotlight was still shining on the dance floor. As he walked over to turn it out, he stopped in his tracks. He could see, in his mind, a vision of Tyana dancing on the dance floor. She looked so angelic and graceful. There was a soft, glowing aura around her. He just stood and imagined her there. Moments later, he realized what he was doing and turned out the spotlight, locked up the studio, and headed home. He drove all the way in silence.

When Tyana arrived at home, Ellis was there, still up.

"Where the hell have you been?" asked Ellis referring to the time of night. "I tried calling you at your office and your cell phone. What's going on?"

"Excuse me? And when have you been home before three in the morning to be asking me about my hours?" She was instantly defensive. "I've been at the dance studio. I told you about the dance lessons and the competition. You didn't act like you were interested at all in what I was doing."

"Dance lessons? What are you taking dance lessons for? You already know how to dance. And what competition?" Ellis was suddenly alert to Tyana's new hobby and now wanted to know what she'd been spending her time doing away from home. "I wanted to talk to you about my trip to Madrid. I leave in one week." He was instantly no longer interested in her new hobby, but was more worried about how he was going to discuss the trip without giving anything away. He was already feeling extremely guilty for cheating on Tyana and now finding himself wanting what Charlotte could do for him in bed. The reward at the end of it all would be more hefty bonuses and raises.

"A week? That sure came around quickly. We're talking Madrid, Ellis. I don't understand why I can't go with you. So you'll be tied up in conferences all day. We can still have the evenings to ourselves. We haven't been on a vacation together in a long time."

"Tyana, we've already been through this. I can't. Not this time. This is different and I need to stay visible all day, including the evening events to schmooze with the right people. It's mandatory and it's my job. Now, I promised to take you to Hawaii, isn't that enough? It isn't even a good time for me to go away, but I'm willing to make that exception for you. Please don't harass me about this. I need you to just bear with me and tolerate my work and the demands it has on me right now. Now, did you look into a package for Hawaii? When you would like to leave?" He was clearly trying to change the tone of the conversation and forget about his guilty conscience, which was now haunting him.

"No, I haven't had a chance to look into the trip. I've been rather busy myself. I can do it tomorrow. I'll try to find something for three weeks from now. Is that OK?" she asked, taking Ellis' cue to change the conversation. She had to admit Hawaii was a pretty good trade-off for Ellis' absence from their relationship lately. She put her things away and headed for the bathroom to take a quick shower before retiring to bed.

While Ellis lay awake in bed with his thoughts about his conversation with Charlotte earlier that day, Tyana lingered in the shower, alone with her thoughts about her admission of her feelings for Antonio. She could think of little else. Neither Ellis nor Tyana were in the mood to make love to the other that night. They fell asleep embracing only their own thoughts.

Chapter Ten

Charlotte received a full report from her private investigator regarding the company that Tyana was keeping and where she had gone on a regular basis in the last week. Once she saw the pictures of Tyana and Antonio hugging outside the studio that night of the competition, she was convinced that Tyana was a little more than just a client to Antonio. There was something in their eyes as they looked at one another that told her that. That was exactly what she needed to help her get that much closer to getting Ellis for her own personal needs. It was going to be much easier than she had anticipated, she thought as she awaited Ellis' arrival from the airport.

The limo pulled up to her house right on schedule. Ellis got out as she watched him from her window. He was wearing black trousers and a tight-fitting black shirt with a charcoal blazer. She couldn't stop staring at him, thinking how handsome he was, as well as a great lay. Although she had Carlos, who basically took care of all her sexual needs before Ellis, she knew she wanted Ellis more. She also wanted the money that he was about to make because of her. She craved the power of having it all, at any price.

Charlotte greeted Ellis at the door, wearing her favorite thong bikini bathing suit, holding a double scotch in her hand for him. "Come on in. How was your flight?" Charlotte handed Ellis the drink. He put his bags down and took the glass from her.

"It was a good flight. Thanks for the drink and thanks for the ride from the airport." Ellis admired Charlotte in all her glory. He still drooled over her beautiful and curvaceous body. He was quickly becoming aroused right before her, seeing her like that.

"Come on in and put your things down. The pool is nice and heated to the ideal temperature. We can discuss the trip later, after dinner. Here, I'll show you to the bedroom where you can change." She led him toward her bedroom, walking ever so proudly in front of him, giving him a perfect view of her perfect rear end. He noticed nothing else except for the fact that his pants were becoming tighter. She gave him instructions to change into his swimwear and meet her out by the pool.

It took only a few moments for Ellis to change into his swim attire and find Charlotte out at the pool. She was waiting for him in the water. She immediately noticed the bulge in his tight swimwear as he lowered himself into the pool next to her. He was obviously turned on, so she wanted to play coy for awhile. She needed to get him riled first until he couldn't stand it any longer—until he absolutely needed to have her. That's the way she liked it. They continued to swim around and talk as she occasionally rubbed against him. Her bikini top barely covered her prominent breasts, and Ellis' eyes were almost always focused on them. He was indeed becoming hot and bothered. He was also becoming comfortable with their arrangement. He knew what role he had to play in order to achieve his successes. It no longer worried him that much, as he felt that Charlotte wanted—or perhaps needed—him as well. He knew what she could expect to gain with him by her side. They were two very power-hungry individuals on a mission.

After their swim, they decided to take a stroll along the beach before dinner. The sun was just beginning to set and the sky was a multitude of beautiful hues of orange, pink, and purple. They walked toward a dark, secluded cove. Once inside, Charlotte turned toward Ellis and pushed herself up close to him until her breasts were smashed up against his chest. She had a few inches on Tyana, which gave her an advantage. She was closer to Ellis' height, allowing her to be just as aggressive. She grabbed the back of Ellis' head by his hair and pulled him toward her as she opened her mouth and kissed him full on the lips with vigor. She backed him into the side of the cove. He grabbed her hair at the back of her head and returned the kiss with as much intensity, reaching his tongue far into her mouth, exploring every inch. He was getting a hard-on that couldn't be ignored. She was quite excited herself and was feeling the sexual tension mount. He slid his hand down between her legs and began to work his fingers inside her, finding her vulnerable area. She was losing the battle of her will to abstain and hold him off. She began to grind hard to his touch as a fire blazed inside her. She grabbed his erection and stroked him with her skillful hands. They continued to kiss passionately without regard for anything or anyone that might wander nearby. They were hungry for each other and nothing else mattered.

Ellis removed the tiny bikini thong that was standing in the way of his conquest. With one swift motion, he lifted her up as she straddled his waist. A few seconds later he entered her, and they both pumped wildly as they thrashed about in the cove. Their muffled moans could be heard outside the cove as their mouths were still pressed hard together. They continued to provide each other with sexual ecstasy, and as the sun set in the distance, they climaxed in unison. He laid her down on the sand and they continued to kiss each other passionately in the privacy of the dark cove.

Tyana and John continued with the curriculum that Antonio had outlined for John. Tyana was more excited with each lesson about learning new steps and advancing through her programs. She planned to spend more time at the dance studio while Ellis was in Spain. She dreaded going home to an empty house, so instead she booked lessons each evening. She and John also talked of the additional competitions he had mentioned to her a while ago. She thought about them and then thought about Ellis' reaction to her taking dance lessons, then thought about his revised schedule lately, and she decided she wanted to do the competitions. She wanted to do all of them. She truly loved dancing and, after her first performance, she realized that she loved to perform in front of an audience. She and John completed the transaction for her additional lessons and competitions, and she was all set. This was going to be more than just a pastime for her. She felt it was truly the passion that was missing from her life. No one was going to take her dancing from her—not Ellis, and not even her feelings for Antonio.

Tyana had heard very little from Ellis since he had left for Madrid. She had tried to phone him several times, but got no answer in his hotel room. With the time difference, she was certain she could catch him at his room during the mornings there, but that wasn't always the case. He usually phoned her the next day with an excuse for not hearing the phone, but the fact of the matter was he and Charlotte were bound to each other in her room. They had insatiable appetites for one another that couldn't be denied by either of them. When they weren't having raw, animal sex with each other, they were working closely, making several new contacts and attending as many meetings as possible that were on the agenda. They had an aggressive schedule and they intended to keep to it. Ellis was working especially hard, trying to get his name and reputation in with the elite groups. It was working, with Charlotte's help. They were certainly on their way to greater accomplishments—far greater than Charlotte had imagined. There was no stopping them now and certainly no turning back. By the end of the third day, Ellis had even been approached about transferring to the Madrid property. He was astounded and flattered. Charlotte reminded him that he should never turn down an offer from these people. Offers like that were hard to come by. But he needed some time to think about it because he was in the midst of acquiring a position in Charlotte's region that was pretty much all but a done deal. That position would mean a big raise in salary, as would the international position.

Charlotte and Ellis discussed the offer and the opportunities that lay ahead for Ellis. She suggested to him that perhaps he could

129

manage to accept both positions, and maintain them both just until he got things where he wanted them and could give up one. Of course, this would mean he would have to immediately relinquish his present position in Arizona. That was small potatoes compared to the other positions. The more they talked about it, the more it enticed Ellis. He could only think of the benefits of having two very prominent regions—how prosperous he would be—how much power he would have. They celebrated over champagne and hot, steamy sex. Charlotte was especially celebrating the fact that she'd have Ellis in her region, not to mention that she could easily work her way into his commuting schedule to Spain while he maintained a split schedule between the U.S. and abroad. It was all coming together. But she still needed to get Tyana out of his head and out of his life. She couldn't yet presume that Tyana wouldn't be transferring with him. After all, she was just an interior designer, according to the reports from the private investigator. Charlotte still had work to do if she wanted to succeed in getting Tyana out of the picture. She wasn't going to let a lowly interior designer stand in the way of her greatest acquisition.

Tyana was unaware that she had been followed for nearly two weeks now. After the evening of the competition, there wasn't anything noteworthy to report back on her, but the spying continued nonetheless. Charlotte was still curious about the pictures of Tyana with that man, who she later learned was the studio owner. She saw something in their eyes that gave her the impression that she had something to work with. When she didn't get any further reports of them being seen together, she decided to intervene and help the situation along. She needed to work fast because things needed to stay on track with her plans for Ellis. Again, she made several phone calls.

Between Tyana's workload and her dancing, there was little room left in her schedule for anything else, such as her friends, Kellie and Trevor. They each had tried to get in touch with her but she wasn't available. She was focused on becoming the best dancer she could possibly be. And for the first time since establishing her career, she was focused on something other than just her job. This was new for her and she was embracing the change.

After working with Tyana for only a short time, John had some unexpected news to give to Antonio about an opportunity for him to manage his own studio. He had considered it before, but didn't quite have the financial backing at the time. But this offer practically fell in his lap and was one that he couldn't refuse. He would be able to assume the current loan due to the circumstances of the previous owner instead of having to apply for a loan and coming up with a substantial down payment. John hated to have to spring this so suddenly on Antonio and leave all his students, but he didn't think he had a choice. Some of his students could follow him to his new studio once their contracts were up, if they'd like; otherwise, they could all stay with Antonio. Antonio had a state-of-the-art studio and the most advanced staff in the area; few students were willing to give that up. The studio that John would be managing wasn't short of clients, so he wasn't concerned either way. It was a good situation for him and the departure from Antonio's studio would be amicable.

When John met with Tyana to tell her the news, she was happy for John, but was going to miss him as her instructor. She had several thousand dollars already tied up in her contracts with Antonio's studio and commitments for several competitions, and she wouldn't consider breaking her promises to Antonio. In fact, she wasn't sure that she would consider leaving even if that weren't the case. She liked John, of course, but when she was told of John's decision, she didn't consider leaving Antonio for a second. John didn't have much time to wean any of his students because he was expected to take over the new studio immediately. Antonio turned over as many students as he could to other staff members, and took some on himself. He decided, without much deliberation, to take Tyana back as his student. It was risky, but he thought it would be the best solution. He was also still planning to groom her for a teaching position and wanted to make sure that she was getting the proper training that would facilitate his plan. He met with her about the transfer.

"Tyana, thanks for meeting with me on short notice. I know you're aware that John is leaving us for a fantastic opportunity. We're all very excited for him. I know he'll do well. Neither John nor I want you to have any lapse in your training because you're making such great progress, so we've decided that it would be better for you to continue your training with me for now, instead of starting you up with someone new again. And since I've obviously worked with you before, the transition would be seamless. If you have any

132

objections, I would certainly understand, but it would be my pleasure to teach you again." Antonio held his breath, waiting for Tyana to say something—hoping that she wouldn't object to him wanting to teach her again, considering what had happened previously.

Tyana's heart raced. She had wanted nothing more than to dance with Antonio again, but she was still in denial about her feelings for him and didn't want anything to come between her and Ellis. In fact, she was certain that nothing could come between them. However, she had made a commitment to herself and the studio that she would perform in upcoming competitions, which meant she had to keep her aggressive schedule in order to meet her own expectations. She knew without a doubt that she could easily do that with Antonio as her instructor, if she could no longer train with John. John was the second best instructor at the studio, Antonio being the best, of course. She couldn't think of slighting herself at this point. She had to give it a shot. She was pretty certain that she could control her emotions regarding Antonio. After all, she was in love with Ellis. There could be no one else for her, she thought. Or could there?

"Well, I do have a lot of work ahead of me if I want to do well at these competitions. And I would love to have you as my instructor again. OK, let's do it." Tyana would be Antonio's student once again. They were back together. Charlotte's plan had worked.

"That's great! We'll get you ready for the competitions in no time. And Tyana, I want you to know you have nothing to worry about regarding anything happening between us again. You have my word." Antonio almost choked on his words. He knew he was making a promise that he wasn't absolutely certain that he could keep, but he would try. Just being next her to now made him nervous, as he realized how much he had missed her and wanted her. But as her instructor, he owed it to her to remain professional, respect her, and provide the best service to her that he could.

"Thank you, Antonio, but I'm not worried about that." Tyana let him know that she wasn't concerned about anything happening between them outside of the lessons.

They decided not to waste any time and went right to work. With the other students that Antonio had to take on, his schedule was going to be extremely tight for a while until he could get some more instructors freed up to take on additional students. He only had late-night slots available, which left little choice for Tyana, since her own schedule took her into the evening hours as well. It was all set—she would be Antonio's last lesson of each evening.

As promised, they worked very hard and it showed at the end of their lesson. Assessing her skills, Antonio was impressed by how far she'd come since the last time he had danced with her. He'd watched her from a distance, dancing with John, but got a better sense of her dancing now that he was her partner. He thought to himself that it wouldn't be long before she could do all that in her sleep. He kept his focus throughout the lesson and gave her no indication that she had anything to be on guard about.

Charlotte's plan was working well. She had the investigator assign someone to take lessons from Antonio so she could have a spy on the inside. She wanted to know every little detail of what was going on with Tyana and Antonio. And if there was nothing going on, then she wanted that to change. That was her only hope to free Ellis from Tyana so she could have him—and his money—all to herself.

Antonio and Tyana wrapped up their lesson and Tyana proceeded to change her shoes. Antonio discussed starting her on some theater arts routines for the next competition. He suggested that she bring a change of clothes so she could wear something less restricting.

Just then, Antonio received a phone call from someone new who wanted to take dance lessons and requested him by name. Tyana continued to get her things together while he took the call. He was on the phone for several minutes before giving in to the caller's request that only he would give her lessons. She had heard about his great reputation as a dance instructor. She was adamant that she would train with him only, or she wouldn't bother. He really wanted to give her to one of his other teachers since she wasn't an advanced dancer, but he didn't want to turn her away. He figured that he could make the transition later. To make matters worse, she insisted that she could only come late in the evenings. It took some juggling but he was able to once again accommodate her needs. Antonio would typically bend over backwards to please any client. That was his nature.

"Wow...I'm sorry for that interruption. I had a very persistent and determined person on the phone that wanted to take lessons. Her schedule didn't seem very flexible so it took some time to get it all worked out. So, how did you feel the lesson went today?" Antonio and Tyana went over the lesson plan and the end-of-lesson progress report. He made some notes based on their discussion and evaluation, and they prepared to leave. As usual, by eleven p.m., everyone else was long gone. He had made special arrangements in his schedule in order to take Tyana. It was later than he normally worked, but he was flexible.

Tyana arrived home to the empty house and saw that she had received no messages from Ellis all day. That was odd, she thought. She picked up the phone to dial his hotel room in Madrid. She knew it would be very early in the morning there, but she missed him terribly and although he was due to come home in a few days, she still wanted to hear his voice. They had not been intimate in a long time, and she was eager to have his body next to hers. The phone began to ring. It rang several times before it was answered.

"Hello," answered a woman.

"Hello? Is this room 1207?" asked Tyana, thinking she was connected to the wrong room by mistake.

"I'm sorry, whom do you wish to speak with?" asked the stern voice on the other end.

"I thought I was dialing Ellis Montgomery's room—I must have the wrong room," said Tyana.

"Well, he's not here at the moment. You might want to call back later." And with that Charlotte hung up the phone. She took the liberty of answering Ellis' phone while he had an early breakfast meeting to discuss his potential promotion. Charlotte and Ellis had ended up in his room last night to celebrate the pending promotion to the Madrid office. She had expected Tyana to call him at some point and she was right. She had monopolized virtually all of his time, leaving him no time free to make any calls to Tyana. Charlotte then called down to the front desk and asked that no calls be put through to that room for the remainder of the morning—she wanted to get some sleep, since she and Ellis had been up pretty late celebrating. They had also been celebrating the position that he secured in San Diego. The call had come through that evening offering him the position. Charlotte had managed to get him where she wanted him—next to her, both in and out of the office.

Tyana didn't know what to think about the phone call, so she called the hotel again and insisted that they had connected her to the wrong room. They told her that the room was correct, according to their registry, but that there was a "do not disturb" message for that room for the rest of the morning and therefore they couldn't connect her. She reluctantly hung up and began to feel desperate. She tried his cell phone, but only got his voicemail. She left a message for him to phone her immediately.

Ellis returned to his room after his meeting and found Charlotte asleep. He woke her to tell her that they had finalized the plans. He would assume his new responsibilities in two months. Charlotte flung her naked body toward him and kissed him hard on the mouth. He kissed her back and laid her onto the still-moist sheets and removed his clothes. They stayed in bed, entwined for the next couple of hours with no interruptions.

Tyana stayed up half the night with worry, trying to reach Ellis. He wasn't reachable.

Chapter Eleven

Ellis received Tyana's messages and phoned her the first opportunity he got. He found her at her office.

"Tyana speaking," she answered.

"Hi it's me. What's up?"

"What do you mean, what's up? Why wasn't I able to reach you yesterday? And why did you have a *do not disturb* message on your incoming calls?" Tyana was angry to say the least.

"What do you mean? I didn't do that. I didn't get a message from you other than the ones on my cell phone. I didn't have my phone with me during my meetings." Ellis was confused by Tyana's tone.

"Oh really. And were those meetings with the same woman that answered your phone at seven in the morning?! What's going on out there, Ellis? Is this why you were so adamant about me not going with you?!" Tyana was furious.

"What woman? What the hell are you talking about, Tyana?" Ellis was getting a bad feeling about things. He suddenly suspected that Tyana may have had some encounter with Charlotte, then thought it wasn't possible. He dismissed it as just being paranoid.

"What do you mean, what woman? How many do you have with you out there? The woman that answered your phone and said you weren't available to talk to me. That woman! I mean it Ellis, I want to know what you are up to out there. When are you coming home?"

Tyana was trying to conceal her anger from Melanie, who was just outside her office door.

"Tyana, I'm with no woman, I'm working here. Now, I don't know what happened but there was probably some mix-up. I'm sorry that whatever did happen has gotten you so upset. I love you, sweetheart—you know that. Now, about me coming home. I have to extend my trip a little while longer. There have been some new developments and I'm in the middle of possibly getting another region. I need to stay a few days longer to wrap up the terms of my contract and meet with some of the clients whose accounts I'll be handling. I don't have an exact date yet as to when I'll be able to leave, but I should know something hopefully tomorrow. I'm sorry but there's not a whole lot I can do to change that. This is something very important and something that I want very much." Ellis was thinking that Charlotte certainly wouldn't have answered his phone, would she?

"Are you kidding? How much longer, Ellis? We have plans to go to Hawaii in two weeks. And, what new region? Are you transferring? Are *we* transferring? To *where*?"

"Tyana, I don't know how much longer. When I do know, I'll call you and tell you. We'll make it to Hawaii as scheduled." Ellis paused before answering her question about transferring. "The new region is here. They want me to manage the sales staff in Madrid. They're impressed with my work and my reputation and offered me the position and I've accepted it. I'll be commuting to Madrid on a monthly basis, but from San Diego." He held his breath.

"San Diego?" Why from there?" Tyana was becoming more confused and agitated by Ellis' surprises, not to mention that she wasn't finished interrogating him about the woman on his phone.

"Well, you see, I've sort of acquired that region as well."

"You what?! When the hell were you going to tell me all this, Ellis? Were you just going to wait until you started packing? Why San Diego?"

"It came up a while back and I was looking into it. I wasn't sure about that position until just a few days ago, after getting here. I wasn't sure it was going to come through. It was contingent on those meetings I was having when I got back from San Diego that kept me tied up at the office so late at night. It all happened so quickly. I'm sorry I didn't keep you in the loop better, but I didn't have any concrete information and all this had to remain completely confidential—no one in my office knew about it and it had to remain that way until I knew for sure it was a done deal. And now it is. They want me there beginning of next month. I was going to tell you, that's why I called. I just found out. And because of the Madrid offer, we have to move to San Diego. I can't commute to both offices—it wouldn't make sense. I can go ahead to San Diego to start working and you can move out as soon as we're able to sell the house, your business, and get packed up. I wish I could talk to you more about this right now, but I have to go. I'm expected in a conference which is beginning at this very moment."

"But wait, you can't just hang up on me after hitting me with all this information. I have some questions for you, Ellis, and I need some answers now!" Tyana's head was spinning.

"I can't, Tyana, I have to go. We'll talk later. I'll call you, OK? I love you." Ellis disconnected the line. Charlotte overheard the tail end of that conversation.

"There you are! Where the hell have you been? We need to be in this meeting right now! The deal's not completely signed, you know, so now's not the time to start slacking off." When she saw him on his cell phone she suspected that he was talking to Tyana. She wanted to keep him away from her.

"Don't worry, Charlotte, I'm here. Everything's under control. The deal isn't going anywhere. Let's go." Ellis didn't like that fact that he could barely breathe with Charlotte following him around everywhere. He needed to talk to Tyana. The tension was mounting between them because of his distance and he didn't like it. He also didn't like lying to her. He still loved her very much but, hated what he had done to their relationship in order to get what he wanted. And now that he was so close, he wanted to make things right between them again.

Tyana sat for a long time, staring at the phone, hearing the conversation with Ellis in her head. Moving…San Diego…new region…Madrid…It was all too overwhelming for her. She thought first and foremost of her business that she had worked so hard to build, then of her dance lessons—she'd prepaid for a least three

142

months. She thought of the competitions she had signed contracts to do and wanted to do. She thought of Antonio. Almost instantly her eyes began to water when she thought of Antonio. She couldn't leave Antonio. She thought about that throughout the remainder of the day, right up to the time of her next lesson. She grabbed something to eat after leaving work and headed over to the dance studio.

Antonio had just finished his lesson with his newest client, Heather. She had no dance training and he wasn't sure she had a lot of talent, but that was his job—to give her the ability and confidence to dance. He still wasn't sure why she wanted to work only with him. Tyana entered the studio while Antonio was discussing some of the dance programs with Heather. Heather looked at Tyana and immediately determined that Tyana was the same person in the photograph that she had been instructed to watch. She thought that Tyana was even more beautiful in person. Heather was being paid handsomely and had been given explicit instructions to record everything that transpired between Tyana and Antonio. And if there didn't appear to be anything going on between them, then she was to make it happen. She had never made that kind of money before on just one gig, so she wasn't about to blow this opportunity. Heather watched her intently as Tyana went back to the changing room to change her clothes. Antonio continued to talk to her. She pretended to be interested in what he was saying to her in order to rush him through it. It was now time for her to step aside and do her job.

Antonio excused himself and headed to the men's room. When he returned, he saw Heather and Tyana talking together. They saw

Antonio return and broke off their conversation. Tyana was just introducing herself to Heather and welcoming her to the studio, having found out it was Heather's first visit.

"Since I'm new to all this dancing stuff and I don't have a clue, would you mind if I hung out here for just a little while longer and watch some of the other people dance?" asked Heather, wanting to get some information for her employer.

"Sure, be my guest. However, it's late and most everyone is either gone or finishing up. I have one last student here, Tyana. She's a fabulous dancer and has only been taking lessons a short while. I don't think she'll mind if you want to hang around for a little while," said Antonio, looking at Tyana with a smile. Tyana had no objections.

"Great! That would be perfect. I promise I won't be in the way. I'll leave after a little while—it is getting late." Heather positioned herself in a chair in the back of the room where she wouldn't be seen taking notes.

Antonio approached Tyana and took her by the hand to escort her to the main dance floor. They were going to practice their theater arts routines.

Antonio and Tyana were working so hard on learning their new routine that they didn't see Heather leave. She didn't go far. When everyone else in the studio had left, she wanted to return to her car and get set up with her surveillance equipment. Antonio and Tyana were there alone. She wanted to situate herself where she could get some photographs of them through the window, if necessary.

The close body contact between Tyana and Antonio was causing each to become distracted. Their bodies were pressed against each other frequently, Antonio's strong arms were supporting Tyana's body during many of the lifts that were incorporated in the routine. At one point in the routine, Antonio would dip her very low to the floor while closely following her down, keeping his face close to hers. Their eyes were locked onto each other's. Antonio began to breathe heavily as Tyana's heart started beating faster. Through Heather's zoom lens, she was able to see the intensity on their faces as they held that position longer than the routine was designed for. That familiar feeling returned to Tyana, but this time she didn't fight it trying to figure it out—she knew she had felt it before, as if she had been waiting for him her entire life. She didn't care where the feeling originated anymore, or how she knew it to have existed before. She just knew that the phenomenon was stronger than she was and she wanted Antonio. As much as she tried to deny her longing for him, she could no longer. She felt it. Her body began to quiver. Heather's camera captured frame after frame of their stolen moment as their eyes were stuck on each other.

Antonio held her like that for a long time, gazing deep into her soul—and she gazed back at him, matching the intensity as their breathing quickened. He suddenly remembered his promise and slowly returned her to her feet. They continued to dance and didn't speak of the incident.

Once they finished, Antonio locked up as Tyana gathered her things to leave. He walked her out to her car, where they stopped to say goodnight. Antonio looked around the dark parking lot, then back at Tyana. He grabbed her hands and pulled her close to him. He hugged her, and she hugged him back. Her body began to melt in his arms. This time she clung tightly to him, thinking about Ellis' news about Madrid and San Diego, then about the woman who answered his phone. He never did explain that to her satisfaction. She thought about how much she loved Ellis, and how they were drifting apart because of his job. Her thoughts went back to Antonio and how it felt to be dancing with him again. She continued to hug Antonio as her eyes began to water. When he pulled back, he looked her in the eyes and saw the developing tears. He pulled her in toward him again and hugged her tightly as she laid her head against his chest. He stroked her hair. Antonio looked straight ahead, not knowing what was safe to do next. He longed for her like he had not longed for any woman in his life. He had never fallen for anyone so quickly and so hard. Heather continued to click away with her camera, thinking it was great stuff so far. Tyana's tears landed on Antonio's shirt. He looked at her again.

"Tyana, what's the matter?"

"Nothing. I'm sorry for doing this. It's been a long week and I just got some disturbing news and I'm trying to sort out some things. I'll be fine. Thanks for walking me to my car. I better get going." Tyana turned toward her car, releasing the hold Antonio had on her.

"Wait, wait. Are you sure you're OK? Do you want to talk about anything? Did I do anything to make you sad? If so, I'm truly sorry. I…"

"No, no. Antonio, no, you didn't do anything. You've been wonderful. I mean that. It's me. It's my stuff and my situation. It's just all happening so fast." She paused. She could still hear Ellis telling her that they'd be moving to San Diego. "Apparently, I may be moving away in a few months."

He couldn't believe what he had just heard. He was shocked. "What? When? Why?"

"Well, you see, my boyfriend just got a new position and he's being transferred. I just found out before coming here. He's in Spain right now and tells me that he also got a position in Spain. We'll be moving to San Diego for the position there, and then something about commuting to Spain as well to manage an office there. It's crazy and I just found out. I still can't believe this is happening, and so fast." She paused for a few seconds, feeling her body tense up from her frustration. Unsure of how she really felt about Ellis' news, she continued. "I guess I have to go with him, Antonio. He's worked so hard for us and I know he's very excited about all this. It's my place to be with him. I don't want to give up dancing—with you, but I have no choice. I'm going to miss you, all this. For the first time in my life, I've discovered something special—like a dream come true or something. The worse part is, I'm falling in love with…dancing, too. I don't want to leave…it, but I have to. My place is with Ellis." She lowered her head as she turned away from Antonio. She knew she wanted to say she was falling in love with *him* and that she would miss *him*.

Antonio turned her around and hugged her. "I understand, Tyana. I do. I don't want you to leave it either. But hey, let's enjoy it while we can. Let's make the most of the time we have together, OK? Now, why don't you go and get some rest. You said you had a long day, so you're probably exhausted—it's almost midnight now. I'll see you tomorrow night, Tyana. I…look forward to seeing you then." He released her and said goodnight after helping her into her car. After she pulled away, he got in his car and just sat staring blankly ahead. He felt like he had been hit hard in the gut when Tyana told him she was moving with her boyfriend. The first shock had been her telling him she would be moving away. The second shock had come when she announced that she was with someone. He had tried to get away from her before she could see the shock and pain in his face. "She can't leave me," he said to himself. "She just can't." Heather continued to focus her camera on Antonio, taking several shots, as he lowered his head in his hands. After a few moments, he drove home thinking only of her.

When Antonio reached his house, he sat in his car for a few moments, thinking about Tyana and how close he had come several times that evening to losing control with her. He turned the car off and went inside.

Once he got inside the house, he grabbed a beer from the refrigerator and headed to his bedroom to undress and take a long, hot shower. Once he got in the shower, he let the water beat against his muscular body, thinking only of Tyana and his urges for her. Her words about her boyfriend and her plans to move away continued to echo in his head. He still couldn't believe what she had told him. As much as he tried, he couldn't get her out of his head. He stood under the showerhead so the water could fall on his face and drown his troubles. That night, he dreamed only of her. But to him, it was becoming more than just a dream. His heart was longing for Tyana. He desired her and was falling in love with her. He couldn't understand how it could happen so quickly, and with someone he barely knew. But his heart didn't discriminate.

Ellis made plans to stay in Madrid for another week with Charlotte. Since they had worked so hard and he'd managed to secure both positions, she felt they deserved a week's vacation to just play and tour around, expensing it to the company. They were able to justify their extension by saying it was attributable to the new position. The word was out now about Ellis' new job. They still had to be careful about being seen in each other's room because that sort of behavior wasn't tolerated in the business and they'd be risking their jobs. Charlotte did arrange a few meetings here and there during the following week to make their staying on look legit. She was a very smooth operator.

The next few days were tough on Tyana, not hearing too much from Ellis. She needed to talk to him more than ever about all the news he had recently sprung on her. She carried on with her work as best as she could, not knowing what, if anything, to tell her clients. She loved her career and that was all she could think of now. It had taken her many years to establish her reputation and build the kind of client base that she had, and she loved living in the southwest, in

Arizona. They had made Scottsdale their home and she couldn't imagine living anywhere else. She didn't want to move her business and have to start over building a new clientele. She didn't want to have to give up her dancing, her passion. These were things for *her*. They meant a lot to her and she wasn't ready to change all that just yet. She figured the house might take some time to sell, so she could stay put for a little while longer. Perhaps she would feel different about things by then. She continued to work, thinking about Ellis and wondering what he was doing in Madrid. The day flew by as she kept herself busy. It was almost time for her lesson with Antonio.

Heather was having a good time dancing with Antonio, although he wasn't convinced yet that she was very serious about dancing—it was more of a pastime for her. But he didn't care. It seemed to him that she would rather make small talk about his personal life than concentrate on her dancing. He wasn't too comfortable with that.

"So, are you married? I mean, I don't see a ring on your finger or anything. Of course, that doesn't mean much these days."

"No, I'm not married, Heather. Would you like to learn the swing?" Antonio tried to change the subject.

"Oh! I'm sorry, are you gay? That's OK with me too. I have no problems with that lifestyle at all," she continued, trying to get Antonio to open up to her easy questions before she hit him with the more leading questions.

"No, Heather, I'm not gay, either. I'm just a dance teacher trying to teach you the swing." Antonio didn't like to be asked too many personal questions by his clients.

"Well, actually that's great news, because I think you have a secret admirer. I probably shouldn't say anything, but I think that Tyana person that I met last night has a crush on you. Of course, it's easy to see why—you're so good looking and a good dancer. Women go for that, you know."

"Why do you think Tyana has a crush on me?" asked Antonio curiously.

"Oh, I'm sorry, I thought perhaps you already knew that. I mean, from the way she was talking, I thought you were aware of how she feels about you. It's so obvious that she's in love with you—she as much as admitted it last night. I think she's afraid that you don't want her. She said something about having to move away but would stay if only she knew how you really felt about her. She mentioned having a boyfriend, but it didn't sound like that was going well. It sounded to me that she's been thinking about leaving him but feels some sort of obligation to stay. I'm sure if she had a good reason to stay here, she would. I'm almost sure of it. You know, I feel awkward saying all this. I better respect her privacy and not say anything else. I just thought you knew. She spoke of you so personal-like. So, how about that swing dance? It sounds like fun. Let's do it!" Heather had said what she'd planned. The bait was set. She didn't feel the least bit uncomfortable about deceiving Antonio. The money that she would make was worth it. Antonio thought it very strange that Tyana would open up to anyone about something so private—especially to a complete stranger. He got the impression that Tyana was a very private and reserved person about her feelings and her life. Heather

151

did seem to know about her plans to move and about her boyfriend, so he didn't think that Heather could be lying. But was it really true that Tyana was in love with him and that she was looking for a reason to leave her boyfriend? Antonio found he could no longer concentrate completely on his lesson with Heather.

As they finished up, Tyana walked through the door. Antonio was especially happy to see her this time. Heather watched Antonio light up when she entered the studio. She got her things together after scheduling more appointments with Antonio. She left and stationed herself outside with her equipment, waiting in her car. She got comfortable and sat back to watch the evening's festivities.

Chapter Twelve

Antonio felt rather light on his feet, dancing with Tyana after his conversation with Heather. They should get a lot accomplished tonight. They had a competition coming up in a month and she wanted to be ready to perform twenty heats that he scheduled her for. They both felt that she could do it. With the schedule she was keeping at the dance studio, it would be relatively easy for her learn all her routines and dances. Although Antonio was feeling pretty good about things, Tyana was still a little preoccupied because she had been unable to reach Ellis. It had been three days since she'd talk to him. She was getting a bad feeling about the woman that answered his phone, or allegedly answered his phone. Ellis was still trying to convince her that there was some sort of mix-up at the hotel switchboard. She wasn't convinced yet, and now with Ellis' disappearance again, as well as his extended stay in Madrid, she was beginning to have thoughts of suspicion. She wasn't concentrating on her lesson.

Antonio stopped dancing when he noticed Tyana's distraction. "What's happening? Is something wrong? You seemed distracted. Are you feeling OK?" He walked her off the dance floor and offered her a seat nearby. They both sat down as she began to explain herself.

"Everything's fine. I guess I must be thinking about more than just my dances tonight. I don't mean to be difficult. I didn't realize that my concentration was slipping. Do you mind if we stop? I need to go. All of a sudden, I'm not feeling very well." Her mind was on Ellis. She was determined to find out what was going on with him in Madrid and why he hadn't called her in three days.

"No, I don't mind at all. Are you going to be all right? Is there something that I can do for you? Are you thinking about your move?" Antonio wanted to find out what was bothering her so he would know what to say to her to let her know that he could be there for her—probably more so than her boyfriend. He was thinking about what Heather had said earlier.

"I guess I'm thinking about a lot of things, including the move. I'm not sure yet how I feel about this move. The feeling's probably temporary, though. I just need to talk some things over with Ellis." Once Tyana said Ellis' name out loud, her thoughts about him possibly having an affair, which she had tried to suppress, came rushing to the forefront of her mind. It had been a notion that she had been trying to ignore ever since she'd heard the woman's voice on Ellis' hotel room phone in Spain. And now the extended trip he was taking, and not being able to reach him. The signs kept flashing in her mind as if to mock her. She stopped talking as she waited for the enormous lump in her throat to subside. It wasn't budging. Her emotions were building up and her shoulders began to spasm. Antonio lifted her head up so he could see her face. She was crying softly.

"Tyana, honey, what is it?" He pulled her close to his warm body; his first reaction was to hold her like a hurting child. She allowed him to. She needed comforting desperately and Antonio was there and

154

willing. She didn't speak; she just kept crying. He patiently held her until she was ready to respond.

After several minutes of feeling completely protected in Antonio's arms, Tyana made a move to get up. She felt strange being in another man's arms like that, even under the circumstances. She thought that she shouldn't be involving Antonio in her personal problems like she was and that she should leave. She was also getting that strange feeling again that he had been her supporter or her knight in shining armor before. She felt so comfortable with him like that. She was sure these feelings were related to her current fluctuating state of mind. She just needed some rest and most of all she needed to confront Ellis. She got up.

"I really should go." She started getting her things together and began to walk toward the door. Antonio walked in silence right next to her until they reached her car.

"Thanks for being so kind and attentive to me. You certainly don't have to fuss over me, I hope you know that. I just need to go home and get my thoughts together and make some decisions about my life and the impending move. I have to face the fact that it's inevitable and I have to make the best of it. I'll certainly miss you. You've become very special to me. I'm not exactly sure why, but you are. I think you have a good heart and you're a helluva dancer." That made them both smile. They stood silent for a few seconds.

"You're truly special, and I care about you—a great deal." Antonio felt himself getting a little nervous. He wanted to tell her how he really felt about her and he needed to act before it was too late. If she really had feelings for him and she didn't want to leave her home in Scottsdale, he wanted to do everything in his power to help her make the right decision for her, not for Ellis. He was struggling with what to say; it had to be at the right moment. He was about to say something when Tyana interjected.

"Antonio, please be patient with me for a little while. I think it would be best if I take a little break from coming here—just until I can get a few things situated at home. I think my attention is divided right now and that's not fair to you or me when it comes to my lessons. I hope you understand and respect my decision. I don't want to stop dancing because it's the only thing that's keeping me sane at the moment, but I can't seem to concentrate on it right now. I'll be back, I promise. It's just a short break until I can find out how I need to plan my immediate future." She looked away from Antonio as she thought about Ellis once again. "I'll be back in a couple of weeks. I'll be in Hawaii…I mean we'll be in Hawaii next week." She wasn't sure why she added that; perhaps it was to reaffirm her relationship with Ellis—that, if she said it out loud it would remind her and Antonio that it did exist. She was trying very hard to stay focused on Ellis, even though Ellis was making it difficult for her to want to do that. Antonio tried not to show his reaction to her telling him about her trip to Hawaii. His face showed it anyway.

"Its OK, Tyana. I understand. I'm not happy about your staying away from dancing," (*and me*, he wanted to add) "but I do respect your decision to take the time to do what you need to do. But just because you won't be coming in here for a few days doesn't mean you can't call on me at any time. I want you to know that I'm always here if you need me—for anything." Antonio hugged Tyana, then let her go. She got into her car and shut the door. He turned and slowly walked back into the studio to lock up. She drove home feeling torn by her decision to take a break from dancing. She thought it was probably the thing she needed to do right now. She had a lot to do anyway to prepare for the time away from her work, while she and Ellis would be in Hawaii. She couldn't help but notice Antonio's expression when she told him about Hawaii. Her own expression changed as well when she saw his face. She didn't mean to share her personal plans with him but she felt it was important to face reality. She did it as her own reminder. It was for the best.

Ellis and Charlotte continued their vacation in Madrid, living the good life. They did a lot of sightseeing and touring, dined at the best restaurants and celebrated in high fashion. They were virtually inaccessible. Ellis had never been quite as sexually active as he was now. There was no letting up with Charlotte. He had almost forgotten totally about Tyana from time to time, but when he did think of her, he couldn't believe how he had gotten himself in the situation he was in with Charlotte. He was attracted to her, yes, but he wasn't in love with her. He certainly was addicted to what she did for him sexually; there was no denying that. Although he felt guilty about what he was doing, he couldn't seem to stop himself. And just when he thought he could stop, Charlotte was right there, turning up the heat, giving him many reasons to continue to satisfy her ravenous sexual appetite for him. She definitely had a hold on him and his career. He was becoming depressed by his quandary. He was due to return home to Tyana the next day.

While Charlotte and Ellis had been shopping around earlier, Charlotte had found herself admiring an expensive tennis bracelet. After much contemplation and some influence from Charlotte, Ellis had decided to buy it for her—as a thank-you gift for everything she'd done for him, making it possible for him to get the big accounts, then both transfers. He felt that was the least he could do for her. What he didn't realize was that Charlotte had already plotted her thank-you gift, which was lying right next to her, naked.

"It's so breathtaking, Ellis. It's exquisite. Thank you, Darling. You shouldn't have, but I love it and it looks fabulous on my wrist, don't you think?" She was admiring her five-carat diamond bracelet that had cost Ellis a small fortune. She wore nothing but the bracelet as they engaged in another evening of marathon sex. They were completely uninhibited during their sexual episodes. They craved each other like animals in heat. They no longer cared about anything other than what was in store for them once they were in private quarters. They would be leaving the next morning and Ellis would be back home. Charlotte was trying to get her fill of him before they would have to say their good-byes. She was unaware that Ellis would be leaving in a week to take Tyana to Hawaii.

Tyana continued to struggle with the fact that she didn't know what was going on with Ellis in Spain. She kept herself busy with work, clearing her schedule for her vacation to Hawaii. She was able to pick up her car after the damage from the accident had been repaired. She visited several times with Trevor and Kellie, although she decided not to let them in on what had been going on with her and Ellis—or with her and Antonio, for that matter. She cleverly disguised her grief. At that point, she missed Antonio more than Ellis. She thought about Antonio every night before she closed her eyes to sleep and every morning when she awoke. She deliberately chose not to call him, despite his offer; instead, she just suffered alone. She was beginning to find it difficult to want to remain loyal and respectful to her relationship with Ellis because she wasn't sure what kind of relationship she had anymore. Her heart ached all the time over what was happening between Ellis and her, and it ached in a different way for Antonio. Meanwhile, she prepared for Ellis' return home.

Ellis and Charlotte boarded the plane back to the States. It was going to be a long flight, he thought, thinking about returning to Tyana. He didn't know how to face her with such an enormous lie on his conscience. He'd never lied to her before, so he wasn't sure if he could actually pull it off. Too much had happened between Charlotte and him on this trip. She had pressured him into making a physical commitment to her—an arrangement, so to speak. They were now going to be officially physical partners in every sense. When Ellis sobered up from the whirlwind week under Charlotte's spell and was sitting quietly on the plane, he couldn't believe he had entered into such a preposterous agreement and wondered how he had gotten himself into his messy triangle. He'd had too much physical contact with Charlotte already; he was supposed to be Tyana's sexual partner, not Charlotte's. He needed to figure out how he could break it off with Charlotte and not get in any deeper, but was afraid that it was too late. He wanted to stop putting himself in a position where he had to continuously lie to Tyana. He was in very deep and Charlotte wasn't going to allow him to break their agreement. With him moving to southern California soon, she wanted to secure access to him whenever she wanted him. He was unaware that she was also planning to accompany him, whenever she could, when he commuted to Madrid. She had it all planned out. She would soon have access to his bank account, too. The plan would work even better once she got Tyana out of the picture. She was looking forward to her next report from the private investigator to see how things were progressing.

The flight landed in San Diego, where Charlotte and Ellis said their good-byes. She wanted him to stay over with her and fly out the next morning, but he insisted on getting back to Phoenix on the next flight out. As it was, it was going to be very late before he would arrive home. Once Charlotte left the airport, Ellis phoned Tyana to let her know he was on his way. Ellis had only a few days to get his bearings before he was off again, this time to Hawaii with Tyana.

"Tyana speaking." Tyana was still at the office preparing to be away from her clients next week.

"Tyana, it's me. What's going on, babe?" asked Ellis, not sure what to say to her.

"Ellis? Where are you?" Tyana's was less than excited to hear from him. She was dejected and Ellis could tell from her voice.

"I'm in San Diego getting ready to catch a flight home. I should be there shortly. Are you OK? I've missed you."

"I'm fine. Our flight leaves in two days, Ellis. It would have been nice for you to have called a little more often while you were cavorting in Madrid. I needed to let you know that the flight got moved up a few days because of a cancellation. I just hope you'll be ready to go in two days because we *will* be on that plane." She was stern and upset.

"I see. All right Tyana. I'll be there as soon as I can and we can talk about it then. I'll need to check in the office to see what's been going on there and tie up some loose ends. I promised you the trip to Hawaii, so we'll go. Listen, I think they're calling my flight. I better go. I'll see you in a little while." They ended their conversation and Ellis was finally on his way home, an extremely weary, tired, and sexually drained man.

The next few days went by quickly and uneventfully. Ellis did his best to convince Tyana that the decision to stay on in Madrid was job-related and necessary. Tyana did her best to believe him and cleared her head of thoughts about Antonio. She was determined to work at her relationship and enjoy the trip with Ellis. She was hoping that it would help them rekindle their relationship. Ellis managed to get a few days' reprieve from having sex with Tyana. He simply convinced her that he was exhausted from his trip, which wasn't far from the truth, although he was really exhausted from being Charlotte's constant sex slave every night for nearly two weeks.

Tyana knew they would have plenty of intimate time together once they get to Hawaii.

The flight that Tyana booked connected into San Diego before heading to Hawaii. Ellis was very fidgety once they landed at the San Diego airport. They had a few hours delay before leaving for Hawaii. He wasn't comfortable being in that airport with her so soon after landing there with Charlotte. He sat nervously with her while they waited to depart. He wasn't sure why he found himself constantly looking around to see if anyone was watching him with Tyana. How would Charlotte know he would be there? Plus, she hadn't mentioned any plans to fly out on that day. He dismissed the paranoid thoughts and excused himself to go to the restroom, leaving Tyana sitting in the gate area to wait. She decided to look around in the gift shops while she waited for him.

"Oh, excuse me, I'm sorry. I didn't mean to bump into you like that."

"Oh, pardon. I wasn't looking where I was going myself," said Tyana back to the stranger. Tyana couldn't help but notice how striking the tall woman was, with her long blonde hair pulled tightly back in a ponytail. She was wearing sunglasses, which didn't detract from her beauty, but gave her more of a mysterious aura. She was dressed in expensive, yet causal attire. Tyana noticed her designer taste.

"All this traveling just makes a person disoriented sometimes. I cannot believe I'm back here in this airport again. You know, you look familiar—pardon my asking, but were you just on a flight here the other day from Europe?"

Tyana looked at the woman strangely when she asked her that. "No, it wasn't me," she responded.

"I'm sorry, I just got back from Madrid, and I could have sworn that you were on that flight. You just look so familiar for some reason. Have you ever been to Madrid?" asked Charlotte.

Tyana's heart stopped. She looked around to see if she could see Ellis. She looked back again at the woman, trying to see through her dark shades. "No, never been to Madrid. You must be mistaking me for someone else," answered Tyana, feeling an ache in the pit of her stomach. Just then, Charlotte cut her off.

"I'm sorry to have bothered you, I must get going, they're calling my flight." With that, Charlotte rushed off. Once she got around the corner, she looked back at Tyana to see her still standing where she had left her, staring off into space and looking a bit frazzled.

Charlotte had received word from her private investigator that Tyana and Ellis were preparing for a trip to Hawaii and was able to obtain the flight information. Charlotte wanted to see Tyana in the light of day and see how hard, if at all, she would have to work to get Ellis freed from her. After seeing her, she realized her work was definitely cut out for her. Charlotte wasn't the jealous type, she didn't have to be; however, she was surprised by Tyana's beauty and style. She could understand Ellis' attraction to her. It was an impromptu decision to make contact with Tyana. She wanted to rattle her a bit. She also wanted to make sure she gave Tyana something to think about during their vacation in Hawaii. Charlotte was very perturbed at Ellis for taking Tyana to Hawaii just days after being in Madrid with her, especially in light of their new arrangement. She knew she could upset things for him at work over this, but that could possibly backfire for her too, so she thought this tactic would be more subtle and effective.

Tyana was still standing in a daze when Ellis found her. "Tyana, I've been looking all over for you. What are you doing just standing here?" asked Ellis, wondering what was the matter with her and why she looked so strange.

"I…I don't know what I came in here for. There was this woman who bumped into me and then she started talking to me. She said I looked familiar or something and that she thought I was in Madrid because she was just there—something like that. Ellis?" Tyana was beginning to get a sick feeling. "Do you know this person? I mean, you were just there, I mean on the flight; she said she was on a flight from Madrid a few days ago—sounds like the same flight you were on. She was very tall, blonde and very beautiful—rather sexy and mysterious looking. Was it maybe someone you worked with?" Ellis' heart began to race as he quickly scanned the area. He, too, was beginning to feel ill. "Ellis? What's going on?"

"You're just imagining things. I don't know of any woman like that who was on the plane. Do you know how many passengers were on that flight? It was a 747, for goodness sakes, Tyana. It was just a coincidence. Now, let's go sit down; I'm sure they're about to board soon."

Ellis kept looking around as they walked back to the gate area. He would be absolutely furious with Charlotte if she decided to pull something and stalk Tyana like that. He also knew his relationship and his career would be in jeopardy if it got out—what he was doing with Charlotte. He was extremely nervous and his mind was going a million miles a minute thinking of the consequences of his decision to become sexually involved with Charlotte. And to think that he purchased that expensive jewelry for her and made that ridiculous arrangement to be her sexual partner. If it *was* Charlotte there spying on him, how did she know about the trip? Tyana had made all the arrangements and he hadn't said anything to anyone in his office about where exactly he was going. He was beginning to drive himself mad, thinking that Charlotte might know what he did with Tyana and worse, who Tyana was. And if that was Charlotte who was following him at the airport, then what was she planning to do next? He shuddered to think.

Charlotte watched them from a distance until they boarded the plane. Within moments they were gone.

The plane landed safely on the island of Maui, and Ellis and Tyana began their vacation in paradise. Tyana had spent the majority of the flight thinking about that beautiful woman in the airport and how it seemed too much of a coincidence. Ellis thought about Tyana's description of the strange woman in the airport and how closely that description matched Charlotte's. He couldn't think of much else. Suddenly, Tyana had a frightening thought when she remembered the woman's voice. She could swear that it sounded

165

somewhat like the woman on Ellis' phone in Madrid. Then she figured that her paranoia was getting the best of her. She really couldn't prove that it was the same voice. She was consumed with her gut feeling about this whole situation. She was hoping her gut was wrong this time as she stared suspiciously at Ellis on their way to the hotel.

They reached the hotel, got to their room, unpacked, and for a moment just stared out at the beautiful Pacific Ocean from their hotel room balcony. The view was absolutely breathtaking. They soaked it all up in silence for a long while, until, without a single word spoken between them, Ellis scooped Tyana up with his strong arms and carried her to the bed. He laid her down gently while looking deep into her eyes. He saw her faded spirit, and knew he was to blame for that. He knew it was up to him to change that. With the breeze pouring into their room from the open balcony door, he began to undress himself and her at the same time. She didn't object, and even found her body yearning for the man that her heart had been disconnected from for so many weeks. He, too, was longing for her familiar body and touch. He hadn't realized how much he had missed her until that moment as he looked at her with hungry eyes. She lay naked next to him as her body began to melt inside in anticipation of what was coming. He pulled her close to him and began kissing her on her lips, gingerly at first. She returned the kisses as she put her hand to his face with a soft touch. He was now kissing her with greater passion. They explored one another like they hadn't in a long time. All thoughts of Charlotte left both their heads as he entered her waiting body.   Within moments their bodies were writhing with unleashed excitement they had not known in a long time. Minute by minute, Ellis was reminded of the subtle way Tyana's body behaved in getting his body to respond to hers. It was exhilarating, once again. They held onto each other tightly as they continued to please each other. They continued like that for a long time until neither could withstand the pressure building up inside. They had missed that special feeling that they had experienced with each other. Then without warning, they relieved themselves simultaneously, with sheer ecstasy from the tremendous power of their passion. Their bodies were glistening with perspiration as they quieted themselves, still shuddering from the momentum. The room was quiet for a long time with only the sound of the ocean in the distance. They fell asleep as Ellis held her tightly in his arms. For the first time in a long while, he was completely relaxed and at peace.

Chapter Thirteen

Ellis and Tyana managed to salvage the romance in their relationship during their vacation in Hawaii. Tyana forced the images of that woman at the airport and the images of Antonio from her mind for most of the vacation. Ellis, however, was still carrying the burden of guilt of his affair with him everywhere he went. He was having a good time on the outside, but inside, he was a mess with intermittent visions of Charlotte's beautiful nude body entering his mind. Those images were tormenting him and causing him tremendous ambivalence about his decision to partner with Charlotte—and now about his relationship with Tyana. Tyana was indeed beautiful, sexy, and smart and he loved her, but would he have the long-term satisfaction with her than he could possibly have with Charlotte? He didn't currently love Charlotte, but was enamored with her powerful influence, her successes, and especially what she did for him in the bedroom. He told himself every day that he didn't love Charlotte because he was in love with Tyana. But now he wasn't sure if he could sustain his love for Tyana, given everything he'd experienced with Charlotte. He was acclimating quickly to Charlotte's opulent lifestyle and her influential connections in the business and other outside elite contacts, not to mention her sexual authority. He had definitely fallen victim to her control, unsuspecting that she had intentionally set him up.

For the remainder of their time in Hawaii, Ellis was especially accommodating and attentive to Tyana. He knew he had put her through a lot while he was secretly occupied with Charlotte, and he was thinking about the possible demise of their relationship because of his affair—an affair that he wasn't sure he wanted to end anymore. His time with Tyana had given him a new perspective on his life and on what was becoming more important to him—Charlotte.

Tyana was blissfully unaware of Ellis' thoughts about possibly moving on. But she was having a great time, thinking that they were renewing their love for one another. She was also having more thoughts about the woman in the gift shop at the airport. She just couldn't keep her out of her mind. She was just so eye-catching and exceptionally beautiful, Tyana was dumbfounded that Ellis wouldn't have noticed her on his flight or either before or after he boarded. It would be virtually impossible to not notice her in even the largest of crowds. Her face, her nails, her hair, her clothes, her shoes, her jewelry...Her jewelry! Tyana had just recalled seeing a very expensive-looking and attractive tennis bracelet on her wrist. She remembered how it caught her eye when she raised her hand to her head to swipe back her perfectly-styled hair. That's when Tyana had noticed her manicured nails and then the bracelet. The bracelet was blinding and very extravagant, she had thought. She was sure that even if anyone was so blind as to not have noticed her, they couldn't have missed the bracelet. As she lay on the beach next to Ellis, she couldn't stop thinking about the mysterious woman and the bracelet.

"Ellis, remember the woman I told you about who bumped into me at the airport and said she was on the Madrid flight?" Ellis' body tightened up. He had been hoping that that subject was dead forever. He nodded as Tyana continued.

"Well, I just remembered that I saw this huge, extravagant diamond bracelet on her wrist when she was talking to me. It was as if she wanted me to see it. She kept waving her right hand around, as if on purpose. I didn't think to mention it at first; I guess I was wrapped up in the fact that she was on your flight. I know you said you don't remember her, but that bracelet...how could you not remember seeing something like that?" Tyana was becoming obsessed with this person and with her feelings that Ellis should have noticed her. She realized as she said it that it was possible that he hadn't noticed anyone's jewelry on the flight. She then thought it was ridiculous to think that he would notice a piece of jewelry without noticing the woman, but, she felt so sure that the woman she bumped into at the airport was someone he knew. Maybe it was the subtle reaction she detected in him when she would mention this woman. She wanted to continue her interrogation.

Ellis started sweating when Tyana told him of the bracelet. It couldn't have been the same bracelet he had bought for Charlotte, could it? It couldn't have been Charlotte at the airport talking to Tyana, could it? Ellis took a long drink of his Mai Tai, almost choking on it. Tyana's full account of the woman at the airport, down to her bracelet, was an exact description of Charlotte. He didn't understand. Why was Charlotte there, and was it really a coincidence

171

that she just happened to bump into Tyana? Ellis dwelled on these thoughts long and hard, trying to figure out Charlotte's motive for spying on him and confronting Tyana. He was beginning to get nervous, wondering once again what she was doing and what she was capable of doing next. He knew that she was capable of just about anything. What Charlotte wanted, Charlotte got. He started to get angry at the fact that Charlotte could be snooping around in his personal life with Tyana. Somehow he needed to find out if that had in fact been Charlotte, although he was ninety percent sure now that it had. No matter what they decided to do together, he didn't want her harassing Tyana for a second. Tyana didn't deserve that; she didn't deserve any of this.

"Ellis? Did you hear me?" asked Tyana as she noticed Ellis staring off into space.

"Yes, Tyana, I heard you. No, I didn't notice anyone with jewelry. I told you I don't know the woman or her bracelet. Why do you insist on talking about this? It was just a coincidence, nothing more. Do you think I know every tall blonde that was on that flight?" Ellis was becoming short-tempered in response to Tyana's interrogation. He got up and took a stroll down the beach. Tyana watched him with curiosity. She didn't understand why he was being so touchy about that subject, but she decided to back off.

At the end of their week's vacation in Hawaii, they weren't as close and in love with each other as they had been at the beginning of the week. They both had become preoccupied with their own private thoughts: Tyana with Ellis' reaction when she mentioned the blonde in the airport, and Ellis with the possibility of Charlotte following him, and with his wanting to be with her more than he wanted to be with Tyana. He was shocked by this feeling. Tyana had meant everything to him for so many years. They had been in love and had had so much respect for one another, until Charlotte decided to help him with his career. But he still felt responsible for Tyana.

They returned home and resumed their familiar schedules. Tyana played catch-up with her clients and projects; Ellis had a monumental workload waiting for him. He also had to begin preparing for his transfer to San Diego. He had to report to work there in three short weeks. He and Tyana met with a real estate agent about putting their house on the market. Things were moving forward toward the move to San Diego. Tyana was still not happy about leaving her clients, her friends, her home, Antonio. She had forced herself to not think about Antonio all week, but because things between Ellis and her were not quite exactly where she had anticipated they would be, thoughts of Antonio were creeping back into her mind. She was eager to get back to her dancing, but she wasn't sure she could find time to do it. She had the competitions coming up and needed to prepare for them. She decided that she had to make time for dancing, and therefore would call Antonio soon.

In Tyana's absence, Antonio had kept himself busy with all the students that he had to take on because of John's abrupt departure. He was hoping to hire another advanced instructor soon to ease his load. Coincidentally, Heather had taken a few days off as well, during the same time Tyana had been gone. She had given Antonio some excuse about needing to take care of a sick relative. Actually, she planned to resume her schedule once she was assured of Tyana's return. Meanwhile, the private investigator that Charlotte had hired was back on Tyana's trail, now that she was back from Hawaii.

It was late in the evening but Tyana decided to call Antonio anyway. She didn't want to wait any longer. He answered the phone.

"Hi Antonio, this is Tyana. How are you?" Tyana found herself feeling a little nervous when she heard his voice.

"Hi, I'm fine. How are you? How was your trip?" He didn't really want to know, but thought it was polite to ask.

"I'm good. Just a little busy since being gone, but everything's fine. The trip was good. Of course, Hawaii was beautiful and the weather, perfect. I'm calling to see when you can fit me in your schedule. The competitions are coming up fast and I need to get busy dancing if I want to do well." Antonio's face lit up when he heard that she wanted to come back. He was hoping she wouldn't disappear for good. He had thought about her every day while she had been gone.

"Great! I'm glad to hear that. You can start back any time— tonight?" Antonio didn't want to waste another day missing her.

"I guess tonight works for me. Are you sure it isn't too late? It's already eight-thirty. Can we still keep the same schedule? I have a busy workload here and I can't afford to get away in the middle of my day." She was looking forward to seeing him as well.

"No, it's not too late, come on by. The same schedule is fine. I'll look forward to seeing you in a little while." They said their good-byes and hung up. It was several minutes before he remembered what he had been doing before she called.

Ellis got a surprise call from Charlotte on his first day back in the office.

"Well, I see you managed to find your way back to work. I understand you took a little vacation last week. My, my, don't we have a lot of free time on our hands these days. I would think that with the new accounts, and your transfers to San Diego and Madrid, you would be up to your eyeballs in work." Charlotte didn't mince words too often.

"Hello Charlotte. Yes, I took a few days off. It was personal and something that was previously scheduled. Our layover in Madrid, however, wasn't scheduled, which was what really set me back here. Now, what can I do for you?" Ellis was in no mood to justify his personal life to Charlotte. He was making that point. He felt that he had given her and done for her everything that she'd wanted, but he had to draw the line where Tyana was concerned. He couldn't help still wondering if she had actually been following him. He wasn't going to bring it up unless Charlotte forced him to. He would be working with her in San Diego and needed to keep peace between them. He didn't want to get things riled up now.

"I see. Well, I called to find out where things stand on your transfer here. We have a lot to do and I wanted to start scheduling some meetings and conference calls that you would need to attend. Do you think you can accommodate me on that?" Charlotte was

175

prepared to keep her control over Ellis, and until she was able to get Tyana out of Ellis' life, she was prepared to make his life uncomfortable for as long as it took. "Oh, by the way, Kyle Stockton and I had a meeting to discuss the new business in this region. We determined that you need to be here by end of next week, instead of in three weeks, if we're going to stay on target for our fourth-quarter goals. The paperwork has already been submitted for your transfer. Kyle has been in touch with your superiors there to confirm the dates. You should be hearing something very soon. Just thought you should know in case you feel a need to take any more 'previously scheduled' time away to shirk your responsibilities." Charlotte hadn't planned on pushing for the revised schedule for Ellis' transfer, but she felt she needed to turn up the heat a bit and disrupt his personal life. Perhaps that little change in plans would at least separate Ellis and Tyana for the time being until she could separate them permanently.

"What?! Why wasn't this discussed with me first? This is bullshit! I can't possibly turn over my entire workload in one week. We still have to hire someone to take my place here. There's too much going on in this office to just leave next week. The original schedule was tight enough as it was. This is preposterous!" Ellis was furious and slammed down a file he was holding onto his desk. Charlotte could hear his anger.

"Well, Ellis, the decision was made last week, while you were spending your leisure time away doing God knows what. Are you sure you have the ambition for this region, and Madrid? That's quite a responsibility and I'm not sure you have the drive to handle it. One can't be lethargic in these regions." Charlotte was ruthless with her disparaging comments about Ellis' work ethic. She was really just venting her disapproval over his trip to Hawaii with Tyana.

"Look! Do not question me about my work ethic. You know how capable I am, so don't start with me, Charlotte! I've done nothing but bend over backwards to do exactly what was required of me and more to get everything that I deserve! Now, I suggest you watch yourself when dealing with me. Questioning my ability to do my job and how I do it isn't something I take lightly!"

She interrupted him. "Just a damn minute! Now, like I said, if you were here you would be more prepared—period! But since you weren't you don't talk to me about what I question. I helped you get these transfers and you just remember that. And if you think you can continue to tell me where my boundaries are with you, think again, Mr. Montgomery. If you don't want our little adventures to get out before you even get transferred and to find yourself with a lot more time for your leisure vacations, then I would strongly suggest that you carefully consider the next words out of your mouth to me! It's your call. I'll expect to see your transfer documents on my desk in two days. And if you still want to work here and keep *everything* discreet, I'll see you in this office next week." She hung up on him.

Ellis immediately left his office to find out what was going on with his transfer. He didn't want anymore surprises or threats from Charlotte. He was getting a bad feeling about her and what her motives were where he was concerned. He also had to figure out a way to tell Tyana that he was leaving without her next week. As he walked down the hall, he couldn't understand why Charlotte was being so contemptuous about his vacation. He didn't understand why she felt she could now control his personal life; after all, their personal arrangement to become sexual partners had been made with the understanding that it would remain purely an arrangement of convenience, with no strings attached. They agreed to respect each other's private lives and business. In fact, it was Charlotte who had been adamant that things between them remain casual and easy, that they didn't owe anyone any explanations in the event the arrangement was no longer suitable for either one. Ellis was baffled by her tone regarding his vacation. She couldn't have known where he was or who he was with, he thought, unless it really was her at the airport. But why was she there if she hadn't been out of town or away from the office? And how could she have known he would be there, was the question?

Tyana walked into the dance studio feeling a little anxious about seeing Antonio. She was eager to dance again, but she needed to keep her feelings in check where Antonio was concerned. She owed it to Ellis. She was determined to stay true to their relationship and give it the attention it needed to help make it work. That was the least she felt she should do. She knew Ellis had been distracted and under a lot of pressure lately, but that was no reason to abandon the relationship.

It was late and everyone was gone, except for Antonio. He saw her come in and greeted her right away. The private investigator was right outside. Soon Heather would be called back to watch Tyana from within the studio.

"It's so good to see you again." Antonio hugged Tyana. They embraced as if they hadn't seen each other in weeks. Tyana couldn't control the way her body reacted to him when he touched her. "Shall we?" Antonio escorted her to the dance floor. He didn't want to wait another second.

They worked very hard on the routines they'd selected for the competitions, which were starting in only a few weeks. The first one was being held in Colorado and the second one was going to be in Florida in five months, with several exhibitions in-between.

After the lesson, they chatted briefly about the competition events and what was to be expected. Tyana was getting very excited about it until she thought about Ellis' job transfer. Her smile quickly faded and her shoulders slumped.

"What's the matter, Tyana?" asked Antonio, noticing her change in demeanor.

"I'll be able to go to Colorado, but I'm not too sure about Florida. We might be moved by then. Everything is still up in the air over that situation. We've talked to a realtor and have put the house on the market." As soon as the words came out of Tyana's mouth, Antonio understood. He didn't want to hear her talk about leaving him. He had to do something if what Heather said about Tyana's feelings was true. He couldn't let her get away so easily. He was hoping that her feelings for him hadn't changed since going on that trip to Hawaii with her boyfriend. How could he know for sure?

"I see. Well, let's just focus on one competition for now and not think about the one in Florida just yet. We'll cross that bridge when we come to it. I don't want you to be distracted from the work you have to do now in order to do well in Colorado." They packed up to leave. As usual, they walked out together after Antonio locked up his studio. When they reached Tyana's car, they stopped. Antonio faced her.

"Tyana, I want you to know that I'm willing to do anything to make your time here pleasurable and meaningful. I'm very fond of you and I enjoy being with you. I wish there was something I could do to get you to stay." Tyana interrupted him.

"I feel the same about you, Antonio, and you have always made me feel comfortable and special here—I enjoy being here, with you. But I have to go where I'm expected to be. I'm afraid I don't have a choice with this." Tyana began to get choked up. She knew in her heart that she was lying to herself. She didn't want to go any more than Antonio wanted her to go. She turned away from Antonio to get into her car. "I have to go." She fumbled with the car door, and dropped her dance shoes.

"Tyana." Antonio grabbed her and turned her around sharply. He held onto her with both hands on her arms. He looked into her eyes with the same pain that he saw in hers. "Please, don't go if you don't want to go. I don't know what I can safely say to you right now but I don't get the impression that you really want to go. I don't think you want to go. Just tell me what I can do to help you realize that." She was surprised by his intensity with her, both physical and emotional. She didn't want to expose her true feelings to him. She was still trying to convince herself that she needed to be with Ellis.

"Antonio, I'm sorry. There's nothing anyone can do at this point. It's been settled that I have to go. I'll be here at long as I can until the house sells, but after that, I must go. Please understand that. I better go now. I'll see you tomorrow night." She released herself from his grip and got into her car. She drove away quickly, leaving Antonio standing and watching her. She drove for about a block and then pulled over and sobbed. She didn't want to leave Antonio; it was quite evident to her now. Her soul was crying out to him. She wanted to go back there and throw herself in his arms where she once felt so safe and secure. She didn't feel that with Ellis lately, he'd been so distracted and distant. She cried, for her heart was now opening up and letting Antonio in. She cried because she had to leave him and do the right thing by her relationship with Ellis. She still loved Ellis but she was falling in love with Antonio. She still didn't understand why or how it had happened but she knew in her heart that Antonio was the one she really wanted and needed.

The private investigator caught the whole conversation between Tyana and Antonio on film. He followed her and captured her crying in her car just a block away. He could tell that these were two people desperately in love with one another, struggling against the powerful forces of their love that was determined to unite them. He shook his head in pity as he continued to follow her home where Ellis was waiting.

Ellis had gotten all the answers to his questions regarding his transfer. It was true, the San Diego office had requested an earlier start date for him and after much resistance they were granted their request. There wasn't anything he could do about it. It was settled. He would be reporting to work in Charlotte's office in one week. Because of the size and profitability of that region, he would be working directly with Charlotte initially in order to obtain some influential clients that they had targeted.   Together, with their experience and reputation, they were expected to achieve these objectives without any trouble. The stakes were definitely raised for Ellis and he had better be ready to win at all costs. It would benefit him to stick close to Charlotte all the way until he could make a name for himself in that region. Right now, he had very little control where his job was concerned, and he was frustrated. He heard Tyana come in. He waited for her in the bedroom.

"You've put in a long day today." Ellis was trying to make conversation, noticing the late time that Tyana was getting home.

"Yes, it was a long day, but I was at my dance lesson after I finished up work. I'm just getting home from there. How long have you been home?" She was trying to pull herself together from crying all the way home.

"I've been home a short while myself. What's wrong with you? Your eyes are all red and you don't look happy. Did something happen?" Ellis noticed that she looked sad.

"No, I'm fine. I'm just tired, that's all." She went into the bathroom to check her face.

"What's up with these dance lessons you say you're taking? Are you still doing that? Why?" Ellis was suddenly curious about her new hobby.

"Ellis, I told you I was taking the lessons. Don't sound so surprised. I like to dance and I'm enjoying them. I've mentioned it to you several times, but you didn't seem even remotely interested in it so I haven't talked to you about it in a while. And I plan to dance in competitions if I can, and I want to learn as much as I can. It's fun for me and helps me relax," she explained to him from the bathroom. He ignored her explanation and focused on what he wanted to discuss.

"Tyana, I need to talk to you about the transfer." She emerged from the bathroom to listen. "There's been a change in plans. It seems my transfer was moved up by several weeks. They need me there next week—permanently. I just got word today that I'm officially transferred as of next week and there isn't anything that I can do to postpone it—I've tried." Ellis looked directly at Tyana while he spoke. She stood still in her tracks and didn't move. She stared blankly back at Ellis in disbelief. She didn't know what to think next.

"Why did this happen? What are we going to do? I mean, this obviously means you're leaving next week without me because there isn't enough time for me to get everything together to go with you: my job, my clients, Melanie, the house, packing the house. I can't believe this. We didn't have that much time before but this is ridiculous. They just expect that I be left here alone to deal with everything myself?" Tyana began to pace the floor; her mind was going a million miles a minute. She was clearly upset.

"I know. It's not what I want either but I have no choice in the matter. I won't be able to get my office properly prepared for my departure. I have staff to hire and loose ends to tie up. It's absurd and I can't do anything to challenge the decision. They've heard my concerns but that didn't change the plan. Apparently the workload in San Diego warrants it and I'm expected to jump right in and meet my goals. The bigger problem is that I have to acclimate myself quickly and start producing while also preparing for the transfer to Madrid. I'm sorry that I didn't have better news for you. I'll need you to handle things with the house while I'm gone. I just don't see how I can stay on top of that when I have to be flying back to Madrid in a few weeks to finalized that transfer."

"Just a minute, Ellis. How can you just come in here and dump this news on me like nothing, then start giving me instructions on what to do because you won't be here to take care of it yourself? You know, you've dumped a lot of changes on me in just a short period of time and I'm trying to adjust the best I can, but you need to give me a break and understand how all this is affecting me. Maybe for once realize the changes and sacrifices that I have to make to accommodate your life!" Tyana was overwhelmed by everything Ellis was throwing at her, not to mention her constant thoughts of the woman in the airport, the voice on Ellis' hotel phone in Madrid, and Antonio. She was struggling with her emotions regarding Antonio and Ellis. She couldn't believe that there was someone else in her heart other than Ellis, and she was trying to be loyal to her commitment to Ellis and forego her feelings for Antonio. All that she was coping with emotionally was enough to drive her insane.

"Tyana, this promotion benefits the both of us in case you've overlooked that detail. I've worked my ass off to get where I've finally gotten and I'm sorry if all this is a big inconvenience to you but whether you like it or not, this is reality and we have to deal with it, and I have to leave next week. Now are you going to get yourself together and help get this place sold so we can get settled in San Diego? Do you think you can pull yourself away from your precious interior design work and your self-gratifying dance lessons to do that?" Ellis stormed off into the bathroom and slammed the door behind him. Tyana left the room and headed toward her home office where, once inside, she closed the door. She sat at her desk in the dark as the moonlight from the full moon shined through the window onto her face. She turned around in her chair to face the window and stared out into the vast world. Tears began to stream down her face as she thought about Antonio, knowing that if she wanted to make her relationship with Ellis work, she would have to get a grip on her roller-coaster emotions regarding Antonio and say good-bye to him—once and for all.

Chapter Fourteen

The next week Ellis worked feverishly to get his affairs in order to be able to report to his new office in San Diego, where Charlotte would be waiting and that much closer to getting him all to herself. Tyana worked hard at her own projects in anticipation of selling her business. They put the house on the market and she was preparing it for showings in hopes of it selling soon. She helped Ellis get packed in order to move as many personal items as he could to his temporary home at the hotel. Tyana would travel to San Diego on the weekends in order to look for a house. In spite of being extremely busy with all that, she still managed to continue her dance lessons. She was more determined than ever to not miss a single evening. She wanted to be with Antonio as much as she could before having to leave him. If she had to leave him then that was compromise. Her competition in Colorado was fast approaching and she was worried she wouldn't be ready in time.

Tyana and Antonio worked harder with each lesson to get her ready for the competition. She never brought up the exchange between them, or his words to her. She pretended it didn't happen. She didn't have the strength to get into their feelings for each other, especially when she was trying to deny hers. It took everything she had for her to just concentrate on her dancing. She was exhausted most nights before even reaching the dance studio from all the work she had to do to coordinate the impending move. Ellis had been gone a week already and, although there was still tension between them because of the challenges they both endured, Tyana still missed him. She would work continuously throughout the day to get everything prepared for the move while performing her own job, then attend her dance lessons late in the evenings. She maintained a non-stop pace like that for weeks, which thoroughly drained her of all her energy. She could barely get up each morning just to do it all over again. Not only was she was beginning to feel tired all the time, but it was becoming a struggle to get through the days without feeling as if she was going to collapse. But she couldn't slow down if she was planning to do all the things she needed to do.

Ellis and Charlotte were together again. Ellis assumed his new position and hit the ground running. He and Charlotte were setting an incredible pace for themselves, trying to quickly get Ellis acclimated and introduced to all the key people and staff. They kept very late and long hours, daily. Charlotte had invited Ellis to stay at her house on the beach his first night in town and several nights after that. He instinctively accepted her invitations. It wasn't long before he began to yearn for the magic of her body to transform him once again and reunite him with her fiery passion. He was truly craving her as she craved him. It wasn't that he was feeling any less guilty for what he was doing to Tyana and their relationship, it was that he was becoming accustomed to Charlotte and his arrangement, as if it were part of the new responsibilities of his new position. He was certain that she was behind the fiasco that forced him to go to San Diego earlier than planned. She had enough clout to be able to manipulate most situations within her jurisdiction. But if all she wanted was his body to keep her contented, then he was willing to oblige. He felt he was getting something out of it as well.

They were ravenous for each other and would stay up half the nights satisfying their voracious sexual appetites. Ellis wasn't in his hotel room much those nights, and so he didn't know that Tyana had been trying to reach him. Because they both had busy schedules, the late evenings were the only times they could really connect by phone on a personal level, and even that was hit-or-miss due to Ellis' sleeping arrangements. The only time she seemed to be able to reach him was during working hours, and even that was for only about five minutes at a time. Charlotte managed to stick close to Ellis as she continued to show him the ropes.

Tyana hadn't been feeling well lately and, with Ellis' disappearing acts again throughout the nights, she was beginning to worry, too. She had dealt with being disconnected from him in Spain and now in San Diego. She lay awake late in the evenings trying to piece together what she couldn't help imagining about Ellis' new work schedules and habits. And she still couldn't dismiss the woman at the airport and the voice in Madrid. A woman, perhaps this woman, was whom he was with when she had been unable to reach him. Was it a coincidence that she ran into a woman in San Diego who had been in Madrid at the same time that Ellis was? And now that he was in San Diego, he was unavailable to her as well. Something just didn't feel right. She worried herself sick that evening to the point where she had to rush to the bathroom to vomit. She lay on the bathroom floor and cried, not knowing what to think or do next. She had a million decisions to make about the house and Ellis' mail and she couldn't reach him.

Tyana now had to concentrate harder on the competition that was coming up that weekend. She had to finalize her costumes, get her hair and nails done, do some last minute shopping for accessories, pack for the weekend, and increase her dance lesson schedule for some last-minute refining. The arrangements were made and all the participating students were given their itineraries. To her surprise, Heather was assigned as her roommate. Tyana hadn't expected Heather to participate because she hadn't been taking lessons that long. She liked her for the most part, but found her a little too inquisitive for her taste. Tyana left for Colorado without getting to talk to Ellis first. She had to leave him a message to let him know where she would be. It hurt her to know that he was now inaccessible to her most of the time. She could hardly concentrate on anything but his whereabouts.

Heather spent a lot of time with Antonio throughout the weekend in Colorado, being extra friendly and pretending that she needed special attention with her dancing. Tyana watched from the sidelines, wondering what Heather was doing and thinking that she was obviously flirting with him. Tyana felt sick to her stomach, as Heather insisted on hanging all over Antonio. Tyana and Antonio danced well, but he could tell she was bothered and distracted about something. He couldn't get her to open up to him no matter how hard he tried. Each evening she retreated to her hotel room to be alone instead of attending the various parties given in the students' honor. Antonio often looked for her, but was never successful in locating her. Heather made sure she wasn't far from Antonio's side. Tyana couldn't bear to watch Heather force herself on him so she made herself scarce.

"What are you doing cooped up in here? Why aren't you downstairs at the party with everyone else? We're all having a blast. I just wanted to freshen up a bit before heading out. A bunch of us are going to a Salsa club not far from here. You should go. I want to look my best because Antonio's going too. Isn't he hot? I can't believe we danced so well today. It's hard not to with him as your lead." Heather was talking a mile a minute. Tyana could only sit and watch her as she darted in and out of the bathroom. When Heather mentioned Antonio going to the club, Tyana tightened up. She wanted to be the one on Antonio's arm tonight. She didn't want Heather preying in on him like a vulture. Heather was beginning to irritate her.

"I'm not feeling too well. I think I'll just stay in tonight. Thanks for the invitation, though. You go and have a great time. You can tell me all about it in the morning." Tyana excused herself and went into the bathroom and closed the door behind her.

Heather's instructions from her employer were to act interested in Antonio and see what kind of reaction she would get out of Tyana. If Tyana appeared bothered by it, she was to turn up the heat and talk only about Antonio in Tyana's presence. If there were something between them, this would be the indicator. And if Tyana felt

191

threatened by Heather where Antonio was concerned, this could motivate Tyana to expose her feelings to Antonio or make advances toward him. Tyana found herself feeling sick again. She was certainly stressed from her thoughts of Ellis and now of Heather and Antonio, plus she felt exhausted from her unrelenting schedule. When Heather returned to the room nearly three hours later, she heard Tyana in the bathroom, being violently ill. She called out to her, but Tyana was too sick to answer and too weak to get up. She remained sick like that for another half-hour before she was able to go back to bed. Heather was still up when Tyana returned to bed.

"Are you OK? You didn't sound too good in there. Are you ill with something?" Heather looked at her with concerned eyes.

"I'm all right, thanks. I don't know, maybe it was something I ate. I'm just exhausted right now and want to get some sleep. My first heat is at eleven tomorrow. Luckily, I don't have that many dances tomorrow and I can finish up early." Tyana crawled under the sheets and pulled up the covers as she lay back to close her eyes. She was moving very slowly so as not to upset her stomach again. She looked extremely pale and Heather was becoming worried. She didn't know if she should call someone. She watched Tyana for a long while, until she fell asleep. Heather got up and made some notes, but couldn't help feeling pity for her. Tyana didn't know that her life was being scrutinized and a plot had been orchestrated to break up her relationship with Ellis. Heather also had worked at this game long enough to know better than to become emotionally attached to the subjects. She needed to do her job and get paid. She put her pad away and went to bed.

The rest of the weekend was difficult for Tyana. She still wasn't feeling well, but did the best she could on the dance floor. Antonio watched her with care, sensing that something was wrong; she didn't look well to him either. He tried to ask her about it several times, but she put him off, saying that she was just a little tired. He didn't push the issue. She kept mostly to herself, thinking that she had no right to be jealous of Heather's friendship with Antonio. She had Ellis and her own relationship to think of; she wasn't in a position to feel resentment toward anyone who would be interested in Antonio. But even still, it was hard to watch Heather with him. She busied herself until they had to leave. Even on the plane, Heather managed to get a seat next to Antonio and appeared to flirt with him throughout the entire flight. Tyana sat several rows back and across the aisle with other students. She found herself watching them continuously except when she closed her eyes because she was feeling queasy. She noticed that Heather was a beautiful and spunky young woman with a lively personality. Tyana was certain that Heather had no trouble getting any man she wanted. She couldn't wait to get off the plane and to be back home where she could hide behind her work.

Ellis agreed to spend the weekend with Charlotte once he learned that Tyana was going to be out of town and wouldn't be able to fly to San Diego to look for a house. They stayed at Charlotte's beach house, where they spent most of their time either on the beach soaking up the sun or in her bed engaging in naughty, physical sex. They never got dressed the entire weekend. Ellis was beginning to think that he was spending too much time with Charlotte, knowing that Tyana would be joining him at some point and he wouldn't be able to maintain his secret life with Charlotte, at least not to the degree that he had been. He had to inform Charlotte of that fact as well. He had never expected their arrangement to become so exclusive and monopolizing. He had figured it to be more sporadic and casual. In the last several months, he had spent far more time with Charlotte than he had with Tyana, whom he lived with. Now he was working with Charlotte and making love to her practically every day. When Ellis hadn't been able to get to her beach house, they would meet very discreetly in his hotel room during lunch hours when fewer people were around, and where they were able to get their sexual fix. They didn't use Ellis' hotel room too often because of the risk. They would both be immediately terminated if they were discovered, and they were aware of that.

Once Tyana was back home, she continued right where she left off, dealing with the house and the realtor. There had been several showings of her house while she had been in Colorado. The realtor informed her that she was sure to get an offer from one of the couples very shortly. They were impressed with the house and it was perfect for them. Tyana hadn't factored in selling the house so quickly once they put it on the market. It was a beautiful house, and of course she had decorated it herself, which gave it a lot of warmth and character. Both the interior and exterior were the envy of the neighborhood.

A few weeks had passed and, true to her word, the realtor phoned Tyana to tell her of the offer made—for asking price at that. This meant Tyana had to decide now what to do with her own business and how to get a house in San Diego quickly. With her work schedule at her design studio, she wasn't able to go to San Diego the past weekend either to see Ellis or to look for a house. She was planning to do that next weekend. She and Ellis spoke at least once a day for a few moments in order to make decisions and arrangements concerning the house and other financial concerns. Since they were living apart, temporarily, Ellis had opened bank accounts in his name only in San Diego. Charlotte saw some bank information lying on his desk and took the liberty of leafing through them, noticing that his new San Diego accounts had only his name on them. She wasn't sure if this was the norm for him, but it was nonetheless a good sign from her perspective.

Tyana was still struggling with exhaustion and nausea. She had to cancel her dance lessons on several occasions because she wasn't up to going. She would instead go home from work and crash until the next morning. She was convinced that her physical state was due to the overwhelming pressure and stress of Ellis being away and being inaccessible at times. Then there was her workload and the idea of having to sell her business, her ambiguous feelings toward Antonio, her dance schedule, and periodic thoughts about the woman in the San Diego airport. She desperately needed to rest and slow her mind down. She hadn't been able to eat much in the last few weeks and she was still getting sick throughout the day. Sleeping was also becoming a problem. It was all making her miserable. She talked about some of it with Kellie, who tried to persuade her to see her doctor or take a vacation. The latter was not an option. She didn't really have time in her schedule to go to the doctor, but finally agreed to do it under protest. Kellie was picking her up at home that morning to make sure she went.

"Maybe she can prescribe some sleeping pills or something to help you relax. You can't keep going like this. You look bad, Kiddo, I'm sorry to say. You just look so tired and pale. Why haven't you called me sooner to tell me what's been going on with you?" asked Kellie as she drove Tyana to her doctor.

"Kellie, I'm fine, I just need to get to San Diego and get settled, that's all. And you certainly didn't have to drive me to the doctor. I'm capable of driving myself, you know. I know I haven't been an especially reliable friend lately, but with everything going on, there really hasn't been that much time in my day to do everything that needed to be done. But that's no excuse for not calling or seeing you. I'm going to really miss you when I leave. We should be spending more time together instead of me having to spend all my time dealing with the house stuff and my own business, especially now. I'm going crazy out of my head thinking about having to sell my business. I've talked to Melanie and she's going to take over for awhile until I find the time to do the legal stuff. I just don't want to leave my clients in a lurch in the middle of their projects. I'll stay here as long as I can to see most of them through to completion, but I can't stay forever, although I wish I could." Tyana was starting to feel ill again just thinking about her business and her life being uprooted so suddenly. Just then, Kellie noticed the sudden change in Tyana's demeanor and coloring.

"Hey, do you want me to pull over? You don't look so good. We should be there in about two minutes. Can you hang on?" Kellie was starting to think that Tyana's condition was more serious than she had thought. She began to drive faster.

"No, no, keep going. I'm OK. It's just a wave that I get when I think about everything at once. I'm overwhelmed and the worst part is Ellis isn't here to assist with these things, especially the house. We got an offer and the couple wants to move in less than a month. I have to pack everything and store it, I guess. We have no home in San Diego or here. I haven't had time to get there and I can't seem to get Ellis to take some time off to look himself. He said he's too busy with everything there and he has to get ready to fly to Madrid week after next for two weeks. Can you believe this life we have now? It's insane and that's where I think I'm headed—to insanity." Tyana finished her sentence just as Kellie pulled into the parking lot. She parked in the first spot she saw and they got out.

Kellie sat out in the waiting area for Tyana, thinking about everything that Tyana was dealing with right now and how unfair it was that Ellis wasn't helping her. Kellie got the impression from listening to Tyana that Ellis wasn't very responsive or available to her since relocating to San Diego. She thought that was odd, considering how close they had been for so long. They had been inseparable for the most part, and completely considerate of each other. She did know that Ellis' work schedule had gotten crazier and that he wasn't home much, but she hadn't realized that he was more or less becoming estranged from Tyana lately.

After her exam, Tyana patiently waited for the doctor to return with a diagnosis and probably some instructions to slow down and get more rest. She couldn't stop herself from thinking about Heather and watching her trying to get her claws into Antonio while they were in Colorado. She had to admit that she couldn't take seeing or hearing about it much longer. She knew her feelings for Antonio were growing stronger and she had to do something to let him know before it was too late. She thought it would be insane to confront him with her feelings, putting him in that position, but that was the only way she would stay in Scottsdale and she really wanted to stay. She knew that he wanted her too, but she'd put him off so many times. Perhaps he was growing impatient with her and was having more fun with Heather. The longer she thought about it, the more she realized that she was in love with Antonio and wanted to stay with him. This was all so hard on her because she respected and cared for Ellis and they had been through so much together. She didn't feel right walking out on him now, with everything that was going on. It would be a difficult decision, at best; to give him up for another man just based on her feelings. She felt loyal to Ellis, but she was convinced now that her heart was truly with Antonio, and when she had thoughts of him, those thoughts were of forever. She finally decided that she would tell Antonio very soon and then let Ellis know—that would be the hard part. When she thought about telling Antonio that she was in love with him, her face lit up. She knew it was the right thing for her now. Suddenly, she couldn't wait to get out of the doctor's office to go to Antonio. She just hoped that there was still time to do it—that Antonio still wanted her.

Just then the doctor entered the room with her test results.

After several more minutes, Tyana got dressed and returned to the waiting area where Kellie was sitting. She motioned to Kellie that she was ready to leave. She was rather quiet as they walked out together and only looked straight ahead. Kellie said something to Tyana as they exited the building but Tyana didn't respond, instead continuing to look straight ahead. Once they got in the car, Kellie looked directly into Tyana's eyes and demanded a report of what her doctor had said to her. Kellie was getting worried from the look on Tyana's face. She didn't know what to think.

"Tyana, what is it? You're scaring me, so please say something," demanded Kellie, still holding the keys in her hand.

"Oh my God," repeated Tyana to herself several times, then began to cry. She looked out the side window, looking away from Kellie and began to cry harder.

"What, Tyana? What is it? Look at me!" Kellie pulled her distraught friend around to face her.

Theresa E. Liggins

Chapter Fifteen

Ellis and Charlotte met at Charlotte's house for a late night dinner one evening. He was planning to tell her about Tyana coming to San Diego next weekend and how they had to reduce the amount of personal time they spent together so as to not arouse Tyana's suspicion. He also wanted to let her know that he would be off limits to her for awhile once Tyana arrived permanently, until they got settled and she was back to work. Seeing each other outside of work would be too risky otherwise.

"When do you leave for Madrid, Ellis?" asked Charlotte as she rubbed her body against him. She then began to unzip his pants right there in the middle of the kitchen while they were preparing their meal.

"Can't we eat first? I'm starved. I leave next week." He was becoming distracted by Charlotte's maneuvers.

"Well, I just thought we can start with dessert while we wait for the steaks to broil." She slipped her hands into his pants and found his rising erection. She carefully removed his stiff penis and began to smother it with her mouth, not giving him a chance to refuse her invitation for dessert. He backed into the counter and lost all concentration on what they had been doing. She worked skillfully for several minutes, with rigorous precision, until she rendered him powerless, exhausting him. He moaned loudly as he reached his climax, grabbing hold of her hair, holding her on him. She kept her momentum going until he could no longer withstand the intense sensation she was creating. Any attempts he made to get her to surrender her control were futile. He finally managed to push her off of him and he swiftly picked her up and laid her on the table, ripping off her delicate, lacy underwear. It was his turn for dessert. His body was still quivering from her performance, which intensified his desire to bestow the same effect on her. She wasn't prepared for what he was able to do to her within a matter of minutes. Her moans matched his in volume. He knew she was having a tremendous orgasm but continued his pace until she, too, pleaded for him to release her. Her pleas went ignored. He couldn't stop. He didn't want to stop. She responded with several more orgasms until her entire body shuddered uncontrollably. He finally decided that she had had enough and he pulled away from her. She just lay on her kitchen table motionless as Ellis got up. It was several moments before she was able to move.

Kellie drove Tyana to her house and sat with her while Tyana lay quietly on her bed. Kellie stroked her hair and just let her be as she softly cried. Kellie didn't know why she was taking the news of her pregnancy so hard. She thought she might be happy about something like that. After all, it was Ellis' baby and that could only enhance their relationship.

Tyana's mind was racing out of control. She couldn't maintain a single thought for more than several seconds. She and Ellis hadn't exactly had the ideal relationship lately. Then there was the move away from her home, not to mention her recent decision to pursue a relationship with Antonio. That was obviously not going to happen now, in light of her condition. When she tried to put things into perspective, thoughts of Antonio continued to enter her mind. She wanted to continue her dancing, but in a few months she might have to give that up too. More importantly, she didn't feel this was the best time for this to happen to them because of Ellis' new positions. He would have to be away a lot, commuting to Madrid every other month. The timing was off. And speaking of timing, she couldn't figure out how she had gotten pregnant, since she had been so careful all the years she and Ellis had been together. The last time they had even made love was when they were in Hawaii. It had to have been that first night they were there. She was caught off guard when Ellis had come on to her and she didn't realize until now that she must have forgotten to use her diaphram. She had never even thought about it. That had happened before, but this time she obviously hadn't been aware of the timing with her cycle. How irresponsible, she thought.

"Sweetie, why are you crying? Aren't you happy about the baby?" asked Kellie, confused by Tyana's emotions.

"I don't know, Kellie. I guess I'm still in shock over the news. It never occurred to me that this is the reason for me feeling so lousy lately. I knew I was tired and run down, but never this. I've been so busy. I guess I hadn't noticed that I was late. I can't believe I could have been that preoccupied. It's the timing, too. Ellis is in San Diego and I'm here with all the responsibilities of everything and now this burden. It's too much. I don't think this is a good time to add a pregnancy in the midst of all this chaos." She paused as she sat up. She decided that she needed to speak candidly with Kellie at this point.

"Kellie, there's more. I didn't say anything at first because perhaps I was in denial myself or thought I was over-reacting, but my relationship with Ellis is strained. We haven't been intimate since Hawaii—and with him gone now, he's not as accessible to me as he should be, considering everything that's going on. I call him late in the evenings and I get no answer. The only time I can really reach him is when he's at work. He's been acting weird since his workload increased; then there's the trip to Madrid. When I asked if I could accompany him, he was emphatic about me not going; said he would be too busy." She paused again as she wiped the tears from her eyes. She continued with more confessions. "Then there was this very attractive woman who bumped into me at the airport in San Diego when we were connecting to Hawaii. She just happened to mention that she was on the flight a few days before from Madrid—the same flight Ellis was on. There was something about her and the way she spoke to me. I confronted Ellis with it but he claimed he never saw anyone who fit her description. But what has me quite concerned is when I called him in Madrid at his hotel room, a woman answered his phone. Again, he excused it as being some mix-up at the hotel—said that there was no one else in his room the entire time. But when I asked for him, the woman just said he wasn't there. She didn't say I had the wrong room. And now each time I try to reach him late at night in San Diego, I get no answer. It just all seems too suspicious to me. I don't know what to think. So, you see I'm not exactly thrilled about my news given the circumstances." Tyana cried harder just imagining that Ellis was having an affair and possibly lying to her. She also thought of Antonio and how she can't pursue him now.

Kellie was speechless after hearing Tyana's account of Ellis' behavior. She didn't know how she had been able to keep all that bottled up inside. She didn't understand why she hadn't confronted Ellis yet with these suspicions. Everything she said sounded as if she at least had a legitimate gripe about his disappearance and neglect. Now she understood why Tyana was so upset about the pregnancy. Tears began to form in her eyes too. She knew she had to be a comfort to Tyana now and help her through her situation. But she also thought that Tyana should tell Ellis about the baby.

"No, I'm not telling him—at least not now. I need to get myself together and figure out the best solution for me, and what it is I need to do in order to get some balance back in my life. That's the most important thing for me, and my baby. So please don't say anything to anyone about this. I don't want anyone else to know until Ellis knows. I don't want him to find out any other way," begged Tyana.

"OK. You have my word. But you have to promise me that you'll take care of yourself in the interim. You're exhausted, Tyana. You can't continue at this pace. Please be careful now and give yourself the rest and care that you and the baby need. And if you need anything or need help, please call me. I'll be here in a flash. I'll help you with the house or anything that you need; just say the word."

Kellie kissed her on her forehead and left her to rest. Her doctor had ordered her to bed for the rest of the day.

Tyana slept until eight o'clock that evening. When she realized the time, she remembered that she hadn't canceled her dance lesson with Antonio and she was scheduled to be there at ten. She picked up the phone to call, but changed her mind. She didn't want to miss her lesson. It was the only thing that gave her pleasure these days. It would only be for an hour, then she would go back home and back to bed. She didn't see the harm in that. Plus, she had several local dancing engagements with Antonio coming up, not to mention the big competition scheduled in about four months in Florida. She still wanted to do those. She suddenly thought of her pregnancy and wondered how that would affect her doing the competition in Florida. Perhaps she wouldn't be showing yet for the Florida competition, she thought, therefore she wouldn't need to cancel it. So, she had a lot to prepare for, especially if she moved to San Diego before the Florida trip. She would want to get as far as she could with dancing in case she had to leave town before the competition but then meet Antonio in Florida. She put the phone back down, got out of bed, and started to get dressed for her lesson.

"Oh, Ellis," murmured Charlotte as she slowly came to life on her kitchen table. With every movement, her legs would convulse violently from her recent explosion. "I can't move. What did you do to me? Why didn't you stop?" She hadn't realized before the immense power he had over her in that way. She slowly sat up knowing that she had become completely vulnerable to him just then. This didn't happen with other men. She had never let it happen—to let them see her weak under their sexual powers. How did she let Ellis get to her like that? She struggled to get up. Ellis, too, felt weak but yet refreshed, knowing he got the best of that round. He turned off the broiler, then picked her up and carried her to her bed. The steaks would have to wait. He began to remove her blouse to expose her succulent breasts. When it came to Charlotte, he had developed an endless desire to be physical with her and couldn't get enough. That had never happened to him with any other woman, at least not quite to the level that he and Charlotte were at. She just lay there while he began to kiss her breasts. She was still light-headed and defenseless against his will to have her as much as he wanted that evening. He kissed her neck, her ears, her belly, but especially her breasts where he stayed for a long time, thinking in the back of his mind how he wouldn't be able to have her anytime he wanted in the near future. He didn't know how, but he was getting excited once again. Charlotte could only lay listless while he shoved his awaiting erection into her and took her again. He carried on with her for nearly forty-five minutes when the unthinkable began to happen to her. She couldn't stop it. This time she screamed fiercely when her body erupted. She was in pain from the sheer force of her climax. "No, no! Please stop, I can't!" she shouted. That only excited him, and he gave in to the intensity when he felt her insides pulsating. They both fell silent, spent. It was several hours before they got around to eating their dinner that night.

Tyana showed up at the dance studio on time. She witnessed Heather and Antonio still dancing on the floor. Heather, too, had entered the competitions that Tyana had entered and insisted that she get some extra training with Antonio so she could compete in Tyana's categories. She told Antonio that she was using Tyana as her inspiration. As they walked off the floor, Heather held onto Antonio's arm, occasionally rubbing her breasts against it. Tyana watched but pretended not to notice. She was beginning to feel sick again. Tyana went to the changing room to put on her dance shoes. Heather entered the room a few minutes later.

"Hi Tyana! How are you feeling now? Better? You certainly looked ill in Colorado. I hope you're doing better. I didn't think you'd be able to continue your lessons for a while, you were so sick. Did you have the flu or something?" asked Heather, not giving Tyana a chance to answer. "I had the flu once and boy was I sick. That was a sight. Hey, do you mind if I switch lessons with you? I want to be Antonio's last lesson of the evenings from now on." She leaned into Tyana's ear. "I want to spend some time with him after our lessons and just talk. I think he's such a hottie and he's not married, so I wanted to see if I can get something going with him, you know, just for fun. We had so much fun in Colorado and I think I was picking up on some vibes from him that he might be interested too. I'm sure he doesn't want to flaunt that kind of thing in front of anyone here, so if I were his last student, then he would be open to respond. This is just between you and me, OK? I trust you, Tyana. You just seem to have that honest face, I guess. I wasn't going to say anything to you, but Antonio mentioned once that you were seeing someone so I knew you weren't taking that last slot for your own personal reasons." Heather winked at Tyana. Tyana was feeling disgusted at the thought of Heather and Antonio being together. She was wondering if Antonio had come on to Heather in Colorado. Tyana had noticed that he certainly hadn't been talking to her much or displaying any emotions with her since Colorado, as he had before the trip and before she told him that she was moving to San Diego. All of a sudden, she felt a wave of nausea consuming her and she quickly ran to the bathroom. Heather made some notes on her pad and left.

Tyana was in the bathroom for quite a while. Antonio came back to look for her. He waited for her to come out. She finally surfaced after about ten minutes.

"Is everything all right, Tyana? You don't look so well," said Antonio, noticing her watery eyes and flushed appearance.

"I'm fine. I'm ready for my lesson." They walked to the dance floor.

Tyana was performing a little sluggishly throughout her entire lesson. Antonio wanted to talk to her but was trying to respect her wishes and not pry. It was tearing him up inside to watch her as she struggled to concentrate. At times she looked as if she was on the verge of collapse. He made her stop to take a break. He got her some water.

"I think we should call it a night. You don't look too well. Let's continue tomorrow if you're up to it." He helped her up so she could change her shoes. When she returned, she met him at the scheduling desk.

"Tyana, I need to ask you a favor. Can I switch your lessons with Heather? She has some conflict with her current schedule and can't make it here until after nine. I know we needed to accommodate your schedule as well, but this would just be for about a week or so, until she can make other arrangements. If you can't, I'll understand. We can work something else out." He didn't want to change her lessons but Heather seemed so convincing to him when she fed him a lie about having other obligations that were too important to reschedule. She wanted to get Tyana worried about the possibility of something going on between her and Antonio. She was following orders by setting the bait for Tyana, letting her think that it was Antonio's idea to want to reschedule them—that there was a possibility that he was interested in *her*. Tyana didn't know what to say. Now, she was pregnant with Ellis' baby and Antonio would soon find out and would want nothing to do with her, especially after she pretty much rejected his personal feelings toward her. She just wanted to get through her lessons and her competition in Florida and walk out of his life. She had no right to fall for him now. She had no business to have any feelings for him—especially now. She needed to let him go from her heart. Her voice trembled when she spoke to him regarding his request to change her schedule.

"Uh, sure. That's fine. If I can't make it some days, I'll just call you and let you know. Heather's coming along great with her lessons, I see." She was holding back her hurt feelings.

"Yes, she is. She wants to get more time in the studio. She has her sights set on getting more out of her lessons than just sticking to her current program and asked if I could help her progress to the next level. I was happy to hear that, especially from her. She wasn't giving me the impression that she wanted more in the beginning but I think that's changing now—she's really opening up and I really want to support her. She's showing me that she has a lot of potential to grasp and accept what I have to offer her." Antonio didn't realize what his words sounded like in Tyana's head, not knowing about the conversation Heather had just had with her. Tyana felt her emotions slip out of her restraint. She got up and, in her haste, walked out. Antonio looked confused and went after her.

"Tyana, wait!" He caught up with her in the parking lot. "Where are you going? We didn't change your lesson time." Just then he saw that she was crying. She knew she was dealing with a lot of emotional issues, but the pregnancy hormones were adding to her emotional instability. "What is it? Come here." He pulled her into his chest. He couldn't help it. He had wanted to hold her for such a long time that seeing her like that forced him to let his guard down.

"Antonio, I really need to go. I'm very tired. I didn't realize how tired I was. I just had too much on my mind, with the house selling so quickly and all. I guess I should tell you that I don't imagine I will be able to continue taking lessons after the Florida competition. I'll be moving to San Diego soon." Antonio didn't want to hear those words from her. He didn't want to lose her. He wasn't convinced yet by her reaction that she really wanted to go. She didn't want to hear his response, so she tried to pull away from his grip but he wouldn't let her go. Even if she wasn't to move to San Diego, she knew she had to walk out of Antonio's life.

"Tyana, please. Just talk to me. You're leaving soon? When?" Antonio hadn't really prepared himself for her to actually leave. He had been in denial, thinking that she would change her mind. He had hoped that he could change her mind, but there were limitations on what he could and could not say to her, especially when it dealt with matters of the heart. Right now his heart was aching for her. He was still holding tightly to her. Heather was nearby with her equipment taking it all in.

"Ellis is already in San Diego and the house just sold last week. I have less than a month to pack our things and turn the house over. I still have my business to decide what to do with. My assistant designer will continue to work on and keep things going if I have to leave before I sell it. It all depends on how fast I find a house in San Diego and when we can close on it. I'll leave at that point. I figured I would stay on here and continue with my lessons and prepare for the Florida competition. It might take us a while to find a house and close, so that should take me up to at least the competition. That's what's going on…to say the least." She wasn't exactly telling him the whole story. The fact that she thought Ellis was having an affair, and that she was now pregnant with his baby, not to mention falling in love with Antonio—that was the whole, convoluted story. She began to tremble in his arms.

"I don't know what to say, except that I'll miss you when you leave. I wish you weren't going. I haven't danced with anyone like you in a very long time and I'll miss that. I know I've told you before that I think you're special, but I want you to know that you're special to *me*." Antonio didn't know what else to say at that particular moment. He sensed that she was pretty much going to go through with her plans; therefore, he didn't want to make her remaining days with him uncomfortable. But there was so much more he wanted to tell her and needed to tell her. He just needed a little more of a sign from her that it was OK to open up.

Tyana was on the verge of saying more, of letting him know that she didn't want to go and that he meant something very special to her, but now with the news of the baby she dared not put that burden on him. She held back her true feelings.

"Thanks, you're special to me too, but I must do what I feel is in my heart to be the right thing and that is to move on. I'll truly miss dancing with you, too. You've given me the greatest gift that I'll always cherish throughout my life. I won't forget that. But you have Heather now; she's become special to you now, I guess." It just slipped out. She turned away as she found it difficult to face him. "I think she'll be good for you and you should pursue her if that's what you really want to do." She pulled away from him and started to unlock her car.

"Wait, what are you talking about? What about Heather? She's not special to me in the sense that you are. Why did you say that?" He was confused by her comment.

"She said that you and she…I really shouldn't get involved with your personal business. I shouldn't have said anything. What you and Heather do together is your business. I have no right to say anything." She turned away again.

"Tyana, tell me. What are you talking about? Heather is a student, nothing more. That's it. She's a great girl, but I'm her instructor and nothing else to her. Where would you get a crazy idea that I would want to pursue her in a personal way?" He was astounded that she would think such a thing. He was desperate now to get her to understand his intentions.

"She told me that you were interested in her and that if she switched slots with me then you two would have some privacy to pursue something personal or intimate after her lessons, that you would have more freedom to make advances toward her—something to that effect. Then you also asked me to switch slots with her; you said that you wanted to help her get more from her lessons; that you have a lot to offer her, etc., etc." Tyana could barely continue.

"Oh my God, Tyana, you misunderstood. She must have misconstrued my intentions. I have not and never will make any advances toward her. I have no personal intentions with her, nor am I interested in her that way. I can't believe she said that to you. Is that what she said was her only reason for wanting to switch lesson times with you? She told me that she had an important obligation that she was committed to and needed the later time. Please believe me when I say I wasn't part of any plot to replace you with her. I don't work that way. I'm not in the habit of dating my students or sleeping with them. What I feel for you is totally and completely a first for me, as far as someone that I'm instructing goes, and it's an isolated situation. I've struggled for a long time with trying to ignore the feelings and put them out of my head. But I couldn't, Tyana, no matter how hard I tried. I still have no plans to make our relationship uncomfortable while you're training with me. I promise you that. I respect you and my business too much to do anything unethical. But I can no longer deny my feelings to myself or to you. You see I don't want you to leave because of how I feel about you. I love being with you, I love dancing with you; you make my day brighter when I see your face. I never expected this to happen, but I'm not sorry either. I may have said way too much, but I needed you to know." Tyana became emotional and relieved, hearing those words from Antonio. She had waited so long to hear them but now the timing was all wrong for her. She couldn't believe the timing of everything. He pulled her close to him and hugged her tightly. She let him, and wrapped her arms around him as well. She cried softly. He kissed her forehead and closed his eyes. There was no turning back for him at this point. She held him tighter as if afraid to let him go. They embraced each other for several minutes without a word. She needed the embrace.

Antonio pulled away slightly to look into Tyana's eyes. He could still see so much pain in them. He kissed her wet eyes—each of them. As he started to lean in toward her to kiss her on the lips, she pulled back.

"I can't Antonio. I just can't—not now. I'm so sorry. I can't explain it and I'm sorry but I don't want to hurt you. I care about you too much to do that. I have to go now. I'm really sorry—really sorry." Tyana wiped the tears from her eyes and got into her car. She turned to look at Antonio who could do nothing but stare at her. He looked as if she had just opened his chest and ripped his heart right out. She drove home. Heather caught the entire moment between them.

Tyana called the studio the next morning and cancelled all her lessons. She could no longer bear to face the man she desired, knowing how she had hurt him. She wanted him to forget about her while she prepared to move to San Diego to be with Ellis and tell him about their baby. No matter what, she had a responsibility to her baby and felt she wasn't in a position to pull Antonio into her complicated life now.

Antonio spent the next few days feeling very despondent over his situation with Tyana and the fact that she cancelled her lessons. Coincidentally, Heather cancelled her lessons as well after she learned of Tyana's dismissal. She told Antonio that she had to leave town for awhile. He didn't care. He cared only about Tyana, and now she was gone.

Ellis had put off telling Charlotte that Tyana was due in for the weekend. Her plane was expected to land in one hour, so he had to tell her now.

"What do you mean, we won't be spending the weekend together? What's more important?" asked Charlotte while she closed the door to his office. She approached him with a sexy strut and sat on his desk facing him while he was sitting in his chair.

"Well, Tyana is coming in this weekend so we can look for a house and I need to be with her. As a matter of fact, she'll be here in an hour. You know my situation and our agreement is flexible because of that reason. I don't have a choice right now. And I also need to you be aware that when she moves here, I'll be less available to be with you. I'm sure you understood that. I'll do what I can so we can be together but my first priority and responsibility is to Tyana." By this time, Charlotte had lowered herself just beneath Ellis' desk. She was rubbing him through his zipped pants and then rapidly unzipped his pants.

"Charlotte! Not here! Are you crazy? Someone can come in here. Stop it!" He tried to back away, but his chair backed into the wall behind him. He struggled with her to get his pants zipped back up but she already had him out of his pants and began to devour him. He sat there nervously, torn between the risk of getting caught and the sensation of her mouth and hands working fast to satisfy him. She was determined to send him off to Tyana, thinking only of her. She didn't like hearing that Tyana was coming into town or that she had to play second string to her. She wanted to keep him reminded of her and give him something to think about while he was with Tyana. Charlotte would be patient. She was getting the reports on Tyana and Antonio and figured it was only a matter of time before she would have Ellis to herself. She'd do what she could, of course, to speed up the process.

Within minutes, Ellis' body stiffened as he relieved himself, leaving him calm and spent, although not relaxed, given their location. Charlotte quickly got up, smoothed out her clothes, and reapplied her lipstick. "Have fun," she said as she left his office. Ellis left for the airport thinking about Charlotte and wondered if she would really give him space to be with Tyana.

Chapter Sixteen

When Tyana saw Ellis in the airport terminal waiting for her, she felt indifferent. She wasn't as excited to see him, given his absence, as she normally would have been. He was still as attractive to her as always and he was looking especially sexy and fresh, she thought as she walked toward him. She couldn't help but wonder what happened to them. They had been the perfect couple for so many years, the epitome of happiness and trust. They were always together and full of life, eager to share experiences. They used to spend a lot of time with each other. What happened? As she got closer, her thoughts returned to the ones she had been having recently about his fidelity to her. There was no doubt in her mind that anyone would be attracted to him, but was he really attracted to someone else—more than he was to her? Had he become involved with someone else, and if so, to what extent? He just looked different to her now in some peculiar way. His actions, too, were becoming unusual. She had always been very keenly aware of the details regarding Ellis, so these little variations in his behavior stood out. And how would he feel about the baby? They'd never talked about having a family; they had been too occupied with their careers to even notice that they weren't married yet or having any conversations about their future plans. It just never came up. If he were having an affair, what would this mean to her and their baby?

Ellis embraced Tyana and kissed her. They retrieved her bags and headed back to his hotel while they discussed his new position.

"This is a beautiful hotel. A lot grander than I had imagined it to be—very nice." She held onto his hand as they made their way through the hotel lobby to the elevators. Charlotte was watching from the upper level lounge with a view to the atrium.

"Yes, it is a beautiful property; large, too. I have a nice view of the ocean from my office. The rooms are quite nice." He was trying to make small talk. They reached his floor within moments. Once they were inside his room, he locked the door behind him and turned to Tyana. "You look amazing, it's good to see you again. I've missed you." He kissed her hard on the mouth, catching her off guard. She returned the kiss, matching his passion. He really had missed her because he'd rarely thought of her since being with Charlotte. She looked different to him for some reason. He couldn't put his finger on what it was, but he knew he was still very much attracted to her. She looked around the room to see how much space he had and to see if there were any signs of someone else being there. Everything checked out. It was a beautiful, spacious luxury suite with all the amenities. Tyana was impressed with his setup.

"Are you hungry? Would you like to go and get something to eat?" asked Ellis, not quite sure what to do next. Charlotte had made it nearly impossible for him to want to make love to Tyana. His body was still recovering from her visit to his office a short while ago. But he couldn't stop staring at Tyana and thinking how attracted he still was to her.

"I'm not starving right now, but maybe in a little while. How about you, are you hungry?" Tyana sat down on his bed. He sat next to her and could smell her familiar fragrance. He had missed that smell that drove him wild with lust for her at one time. "I think I would rather rest a little bit right now, if you don't mind. Can we eat in about an hour?" She began to take off her shoes while she looked for something comfortable from her bags to slip into. Ellis watched her intently. He had almost forgotten how beautiful and sexy she was.

When she lay back on the bed, Ellis went to her and began to kiss her. She wasn't expecting him to be so attentive to her, so she reacted with a surprised gesture. He ignored it and continued to kiss her. He may not have been quite able to have intercourse with her, but he wanted to satisfy her. It had been a long time since they had been together and he suddenly had an urge to express his feelings for her. He had so much ambivalence about his feelings toward both women. His feelings for each were special, though different. He methodically removed her clothes and began to pleasure her. She lay back, looking up at the ceiling, fighting back the emotions that were starting to overwhelm her. She couldn't help herself, but thought of Antonio. She held back her emotions as her body tensed up and she began to moan with pleasure. She had also missed being with Ellis like that.

Antonio managed to get through his days in the dance studio without Tyana there because he had no choice, but his spirit was certainly empty and many were starting to notice a change in him. He just didn't have that bounce in his step lately.

Ellis left Tyana to rest and returned to his office to prepare for his trip to Madrid that coming Monday. He was scheduled to be in Madrid for two weeks this time, but after that, he would stay one month in San Diego, then one month in Spain. That was the deal. When he finished for the day, he would be with Tyana for the entire weekend. He would go with her to the airport on Monday morning to catch his flight to Madrid and she would catch her flight back to Arizona. Charlotte was none too pleased that she couldn't spend the weekend with him before he left for Madrid.

They looked at seven houses over weekend. They were exhausted and all the houses were beginning to look alike. Amazingly they were getting along great during their visit. She still hadn't completely decided when she wanted to tell him about the baby though. Several times she had bouts of nausea and had to explain it away as something she had eaten. Ellis didn't suspect anything, although he questioned her lethargic disposition all weekend. He had never known her to be as tired and sluggish as he saw her then. She had no trouble convincing him that it was due to the packing, her job, her dance schedule, all the things that typically would make her tired anyway. She was distracted most of the time, thinking about the baby that was growing inside of her and what that meant to her now and would mean in her future. She often wondered if she even had a future with Ellis; would her baby have a loving parental unit or single parents?

Those thoughts depressed her. That wasn't what she had ever imagined would happen to her. She wanted to talk to her mother, but she still didn't want to tell anyone else until Ellis himself knew. And she often thought of Antonio and how she'd left things with him. He had revealed his feelings for her and she knew that had to be a difficult and risky thing for him to do; he must have cared for her very much to do it. She hated the fact that she had to reject him when she, too, had strong feelings for him and wanted him to know. She desperately wanted him to know.

"Tyana? Where are you? You've been doing that a lot lately. What are you thinking about?" They were riding back up in the elevator to their suite. It was the end of an exhausting weekend and they had to pack to catch their flights in the morning.

"Oh, I guess I had houses on the brain. We saw so many, I was trying to remember one from the other to make sure I didn't overlook any outstanding detail about them before eliminating any of them. What were you saying?" She managed to sell that lie to him.

"I was asking, were you able to talk to Kellie's husband, Paul, about drawing up the legal papers for selling your business?" He held the elevator doors open for her as they exited.

"Oh, no, I haven't had a chance to. I haven't completely decided what I want to do about it yet," she replied as she walked off the elevator.

"What do you mean, you don't know what you want to do about it?" He was wondering if she was changing her mind about moving with him. He had planned on her coming but was still torn about his

223

relationship with Charlotte and what he really wanted to do about his relationship with Tyana. "When did you have second thoughts?" They had reached their suite.

"It's not that. I just haven't had a lot of time to really think anything entirely through. I'll still be there for another month or two so I'll know by then what I want to do." She was on the verge of collapse from fatigue.

Tyana agreed to be more proactive in preparing for her relocation to San Diego. They shared an intimate evening before having to be separated again for weeks. Ellis thought about her all night and how special their lovemaking was. He knew he wasn't being fair to her by cheating and having a secret love affair with Charlotte, and he felt that he was still in love with Tyana and her passion. But he didn't miss her anymore because he had Charlotte who took care of him when he wasn't with her. He was more confused now than ever about what he wanted.

They left bright and early the next morning to catch their flights. They said their good-byes in the airport and headed toward their respective gates. Tyana had just sat down in the gate area to wait to board the plane when she remembered that she needed some job information from Ellis so she could update his insurance policy. She quickly headed toward his gate. His flight was due to leave after hers, so she knew she could still catch him there.

"What are you doing here?" asked Ellis, surprised and nervous to see Charlotte standing in front of him.

"Well, you didn't think I was going to let you out of my sight for two weeks, did you? Plus, Stockton wanted me to be the liaison during this transition period since I've had the most experience with this region since inception. There are some highly sensitive deals going on at the moment and we just want to make sure everything remains on schedule." Charlotte sat down next to Ellis and leaned in close to him. "I missed you last night. Hey, how about some coffee? Let's go over to the coffee shop for awhile and get out of this stuffy area." They left the gate area together.

Tyana walked briskly to get to Ellis' gate, but found no trace of him there. She looked all around but didn't see him anywhere. She waited as long as she could before she needed to head back to her own gate. As she walked back, something caught her eye in the coffee shop she was passing. She did a double take and turned to see a very attractive, smartly-dressed blonde. It couldn't be, she thought to herself. She stopped and stared and suddenly realized that the woman in the coffee shop was the same woman that had bumped into her before at that very same airport! She had features and an essence about her that made everyone stop and take notice. What a coincidence, Tyana thought, to see her here again. Then suddenly Tyana's heart began to pound hard and erratically. She became weak in the knees and almost lost her balance. She quickly got out of the way of the flow of traffic and leaned up against a wall for support. She couldn't believe her eyes when she saw Ellis sitting with the woman. She stood paralyzed for a few moments just trying to comprehend what she was seeing. They looked quite comfortable with each other as they drank their coffees. Then Ellis reached into his briefcase and pulled out a file that they both became engrossed with. Why were they together? Did he know her? Why did Ellis say he didn't know of any such woman when she described her to him? Was she someone he worked with? Are they traveling to Madrid together? Was she the same woman that answered his phone in Madrid the last time he was there? She watched Charlotte move in closer to Ellis, practically sitting on his lap, and he didn't flinch. Then she saw her put her hand on Ellis' thigh and begin to rub it up and down, intimately, for a long time. Tyana's breathing became shallow and she started to perspire. She felt light-headed and her stomach began to turn inside out, so she ran to the nearest restroom where she was violently ill. When she came out, they were gone and her flight number was being called for final boarding. She didn't know what to do. If she were to go back to his gate, she would miss her flight and she had to go to work. She stood in the middle of the floor and began to cry as she desperately tried to conceal her emotions. She headed back toward her gate and boarded the plane home. As she sat silently in her seat, she felt as if she were in shock, immobilized by what she had just seen in the airport. She had trouble breathing and her heart was ripping apart inside. Was this why they were becoming disconnected from one another? How long have they been lovers, she asked herself, giving in to the fact that they were obviously close. Why did he have to cheat on her instead of just coming to her and telling her? She was feeling so deceived by him, which was what hurt the most. How could he sleep with her and me at the same time, she asked herself over and over. She was beginning to imagine the whole scenario. That woman was so beautiful and they looked striking together. If they were lovers, then she had been with him in Madrid and she was going back to Madrid with him. Did she live in San Diego? Is that why he wanted the transfer there? Tyana wondered what he was planning to do when she moved there to live with him. Was he just planning on living a double life? And was it really a coincidence that she had bumped into her at the airport the last time, now that she thought about it? What were this woman's motives? Tyana's mind was racing with so many ideas about what was happening to Ellis, to her, to them, and now to her baby. The biggest question was what would he do once he knew about the baby? Should she just not tell him now? She didn't know the answer to that one. She first wanted to find out what his plans were with the blonde. The plane was already landing in Phoenix. She was home.

Charlotte and Ellis boarded their flight to Madrid. He was surprised by Charlotte's impromptu decision to join him in Madrid, but inside, he had to admit he was pleased to see her. He had really grown fond of her and attached to her physically. She always made him feel empowered when she was with him. She was the most desired woman in almost all their regions and he was proud to have her, especially in light of her reputation for never fraternizing with her colleagues. And the fact that she was one of the most powerful and influential women in their regions also gave him an ego boost. But deep down, his heart was used to Tyana.

227

They spent their first night in Madrid in Charlotte's hotel room. Ellis had called Tyana earlier to let her know he had arrived, but got her voice mail so he left the message. When Tyana eventually got the message, all she could think about was the fact that he was there with *her*. She knew it would be very early in the morning in Spain but she called him anyway. At four in the morning, Ellis didn't answer his hotel phone. Tyana knew what that probably meant and instantly felt sick. She left a message for him to call her with his work information for the insurance company then she just hung up. Her voice was low and a little raspy from being slightly dehydrated. She had been crying and occasionally throwing up. Her body was becoming more and more stressed by all the changes. She put the phone down and clutched her abdomen and wept for her baby.

The next few weeks were hard on Tyana, knowing that Ellis was in Madrid with the beautiful woman and, most likely, spending his nights with her. She was losing weight and felt exhausted all the time. Melanie had noticed the change in her but figured she had a lot on her plate with the impending move and her business and it was all taking a toll on her. She helped her out as much as she could.

Tyana continued to agonize over when to tell Ellis about his baby. She finally had to talk to someone to help her make that decision. She gave in and called Trevor. The one person she knew would be absolutely straight with her was Trevor. He agreed to meet her at her house that evening.

"Hi Trevor, come on in. How's Cleo and married life?" she asked him as she closed the door behind him.

"Everything's just wonderful, Tyana, but what about you? You didn't sound like yourself over the phone and I detected that this wasn't just one of our casual social visits. What's up? Are you losing weight? You aren't looking your optimum, I'm sorry to say." Trevor had made a total assessment of her when she answered the door. She was looking pale and very sad.

"Come on in and have a seat, Trev. I do need to talk to you about something serious. I hate to dump my issues on you, but I really need your help with something." Tyana moved rather slowly back to her bedroom. "I hope you don't mind visiting with me back here. You're right, I'm not feeling too well and I really need to lie down while we visit."

"OK, what's the matter? Are you all right?" He was becoming more concerned about her health.

"No, I'm not exactly all right. That's what I want to talk to you about. Here, sit." Tyana crawled into bed and invited Trevor to sit on the bed next to her. He stared at her with complete interest.

"Trevor, this is hard enough to talk about, so please just let me finish before you interject. And the fact that I'm not feeling too well at the moment makes it that much harder to sit here and talk about it."

"You've got it. I'm all ears."

"I have just about enough evidence to know that Ellis is having an affair; he's seeing someone in the San Diego office at the hotel." Trevor's eye widened and he started to get up in anger. "Trevor, please, just sit and hear the whole story." He sat back down as Tyana continued.

"Like I said, I have about all the evidence I need at this point to at least accuse him of being involved with someone else." She went on to tell him about the incident in Madrid on Ellis' first trip when she had called his hotel room, then about the numerous times he hadn't answered his phone late at night in the hotel. And how he had insisted that she not go on that trip with him. Then the trip had been extended at the last moment and he had been unreachable. She told him about the woman bumping into her at the San Diego airport on their way to Hawaii. She told him about them being distant, both emotionally and geographically, and about Ellis' changed behavior. She told him about the most recent event when she had seen them together in the San Diego airport just before he'd left for Madrid. And again, not being able to reach him in the late hours of the night in his hotel room. She had just then remembered that prior to all that, when he was home after returning from San Diego, he had pulled a couple of all-nighters, saying he was tied up in meetings. She had forgotten about that. She now wondered if that woman had been here. Had he been with her here those nights? And she recalled now, that when he would eventually come home, he wasn't interested in making love to her.

"Damn!" Tyana got up and ran to the bathroom and threw up again. She was crying and vomiting. Her throat was raw.

"Tyana, can I get you something, do you need anything?" asked Trevor through the closed door.

"No," she said through her tears. "Give me a minute." After a few moments, she washed up and returned to bed, where Trevor had waited patiently for her.

"You look awful, Sweetie. Are you sick like this because of what you think Ellis is doing?" Trevor was stunned by all the information Tyana was giving him. His heart ached for her. He handed her a tissue.

"Sorry about that. It's been happening lately from time to time. I'll be all right though. I hope. I do think Ellis is having an affair, though. The signs are all there. The thing that hurts me the most is that he's sleeping with me, too, and lying to me. That hurts me so much. I don't know what's worse: to be confronted and told about it or finding out this way. Either way sucks, but I just don't like being lied to. And who knows how long this has been going on? My guess is at least since he began going to San Diego. That's been a while now."

"Tyana, I'm blown away by all this. Who would have suspected? Not me. Why do think he did this—I mean to you? You're absolutely beautiful and you're an amazing woman; you're smart, sexy, funny, sweet, kind, caring, I could go on and on. Any man would give his right arm to have someone half as good as you...Can I ask you something?" He looked puzzled.

"Sure, I guess."

"With everything you're telling me about Ellis and this woman, I would have expected you to be more devastated and angry and pissed off, but you seem reasonably OK with this knowledge, or suspicion. Or are you in some sort of shock?" He was usually direct like that.

"Trevor, I have something else to tell you. I haven't told a soul and I trust you to not say anything—not even to Cleo, please. It's serious and I'm confused." She paused and took a deep breath as she wiped her eyes some more. "I am upset about Ellis and what he's doing. He's lying to me and he's never lied to me before. I'm not devastated that he's fallen for someone else, but fucking her before telling me, yes! You see, I've fallen for someone too. It wasn't planned or expected, it just happened. And the difference between Ellis and me is I've been denying those feelings because I respected our relationship and Ellis. I've been agonizing over what to do about Ellis. I've always been loyal to him and our relationship, putting them first. I've basically put any notion of having feelings for anyone else out of my head. Everything's been about him and I denied following my heart and here he's been fucking some blonde in San Diego! He just doesn't care about anyone but himself. And now he's in Madrid and he's with her again. He doesn't even think about what all this could do to our relationship, what this could do to..." Tyana began to cry openly and Trevor reached for her and comforted her. She cried that way for about five minutes.

"Who's the man, Tyana? He must be someone very special; it isn't like you to fall for just anyone. And I know how much you love Ellis. You're right, this is serious. What do you want to do now? How can I help you?" He looked at Tyana with sadness in his face.

"I'm not going to do anything about it. I just can't. Not now, maybe not ever."

"Why not? If Ellis is having an affair, you two don't seem to have much of a relationship right now unless you tell him you know and he decides to end it and you can forgive him and get past it. Do you think that is really what's going to happen? Are you planning to confront him about this? I think you should know what's going on for sure. You need to know so you can move on with your life. How does this other man feel about you? I mean, does he know about how you feel?" Trevor waited for Tyana to answer.

"I don't want to pursue the man, Trevor. I can't pursue him. Yes, he has feelings for me, but I haven't exactly allowed myself to tell him how I really feel about him. He knows about Ellis and knows that I'll be moving to San Diego to be with him soon. It's not important anymore because I *have* to go to San Diego."

"But you're not still planning on moving there now, are you? I don't think that's wise or good for you under the circumstances." She wasn't making much sense to him.

"Yes. I mean, I don't know. It's no longer important what I need or what's good for me. It's not about me anymore. I have to do the right thing." Tyana's pain was deepening. She shut her eyes and began to tremble as she tried to hold back the tears. She was beginning to feel sick again. She excused herself to the bathroom once more.

Trevor was getting more worried about her. It was several minutes before she emerged, looking even more pale and weak.

"Is this what Ellis' affair is doing to you? You need to see a doctor. This isn't good, Tyana." He was desperate to help his friend. She looked at him with watery, bloodshot eyes and took his hand.

"Trevor, I'm pregnant. It's Ellis' baby."

Chapter Seventeen

Ellis and Charlotte managed to breeze through the daily meetings for Ellis' transition to his new office, and indulged in whirlwind sex in the evenings. He was glad she was with him on this trip, as he had become accustomed to his evenings being filled with raw passion that only she had been able to give him. There was nothing gentle or serene about their lovemaking. He was making love to her with his body only, not his heart. He wanted it wild and fierce with her. All his adult life, he had only been in loving and meaningful relationships that involved matters of the heart. Not here; not with Charlotte. He had an arrangement with her that didn't include love. He had never known this kind of loveless attraction. It was exhilarating, unpredictable, uninhibited, and tempestuous. He was addicted to it and didn't want to give it up.

Ellis was aware that he couldn't continue at this level with Charlotte once Tyana moved to San Diego. He needed to figure out how to coordinate his time with Charlotte. She was still essential to the success of his career. Until he had made a complete transition and was established in both locations, he still needed her influence. And right now he just plain needed her. He had developed a perpetual craving for her.

Trevor's reaction to Tyana's news was that of utter shock. She cried in his arms for a long time. He phoned his wife to let her know that he would be a little later getting home than he had planned. He couldn't leave Tyana now. She was in a lot of emotional pain. They talked some more and Trevor helped her to get something to eat. She was weak and on the brink of dehydration. Now he understood her need to move to San Diego with Ellis. Now he understood the pain of Ellis' affair, even though she had feelings for another man. And now he understood her not wanting to pursue those feelings with the other man. His final conclusion, with all the facts, was that she must tell Ellis. He was adamant about that.

"Tyana, I think you should tell him right away. I certainly think he's scum for cheating on you and not having the decency to tell you, but he's the father of your baby and he has a right to know. I know you two still love each other despite your drifting hearts, so you must tell him this. It could change how he feels about what he's doing. You shouldn't have to carry the entire burden yourself; he's a part of this creation and should know—the sooner the better, Tyana. I think you'll benefit from having him know as well. You've gone this far alone. It's time you get some help now. He has a responsibility and you must make him aware of that responsibility. Don't do this to yourself. How far along are you anyway? When did you find out?" Trevor held her hands.

"I'm just about six weeks. It must have happened while we were in Hawaii. Before that, I was always careful and he was gone so much, we hardly had an intimate moment together. And now, it's making sense." Tyana was digressing a bit as she was thinking back on when she got pregnant. "Now I know why we weren't intimate much when he got back from San Diego. He was working late hours and when he would come home to me, I tried to make love to him, but he wouldn't or couldn't, and now I know that it's because he'd been with her, obviously." She started crying again.

"Now Tyana, don't do this to yourself. You don't know that for sure. In fact, you don't have concrete evidence of any of it. I think you should tell Ellis about the baby, and then confront him about the woman. See what he says. Let him tell you whether or not he's cheating. Then you'll have the facts and can make sound decisions based on that. And maybe you can pursue your love interest." He was trying to reason with her.

"I can't possibly pursue someone else now. I'm pregnant, Trevor. Who would want me like this? He cannot know. I won't do it to him." She got quiet.

"Tyana? Who's the man you're in love with?" asked Trevor.

"Why do you think I'm in love with him?" She looked sharply at him.

"Because I know you. You wouldn't put yourself through this kind of anguish over anybody who didn't mean something special to you. And I know how much you love Ellis. No ordinary person could ever divert your attention and your heart away from Ellis—nobody. So, who is this lucky man?" He smiled at her. She knew he was right.

"His name is Antonio Lorenzo. He's my dance instructor from the dance studio. I still don't know why or how it happened, Trev. I can't explain it. I was there and when we saw each other, it was like I felt something wonderful when I was with him, as if I'd known him before. He was so familiar to me. And when we danced, it was as if we'd danced before. It was so eerie to me and I got that feeling several times while I was with him. I've seen him stare at me in an odd way on several occasions as if he was sensing the same thing. I know it all sounds ridiculous but it's true. I tried to ignore the feelings and him, but they got stronger each time I saw him. It was virtually impossible to ignore. We never spoke a word about it, but yet it felt like our hearts were speaking to one another whenever we were together. And dancing with him felt so magical. Our bodies fit perfectly; it was so harmonious. I never wanted it to stop but I knew I had made a commitment to Ellis and I love him. And, when I found out that we were moving to San Diego, I knew my place was with Ellis, that I had an obligation to him, and I tried very hard to stop my feelings for Antonio. I just couldn't. But after all the things that were happening with Ellis and when he was becoming so distant from me and our relationship, I decided that I would pursue Antonio and tell him how I felt about him—that I'm in love with him. But just when I decided to tell him, I found out about the baby. I couldn't go through with it then. So I told Antonio I was going to San Diego with Ellis. That's when he tried to open up to me to let me know how he felt about me—that maybe by telling me, I would stay—I dunno. But I didn't tell him about the baby and nothing he said could make me open up to him at that point. I didn't think it would be fair to him to involve him in my life now with Ellis' baby growing inside of me. At that point, I wanted to go to San Diego anyway—whether Ellis and I stay together or not. If I stayed here, it would be hard to be near Antonio. And if I do decide to tell Ellis about the baby, he would want to be near his child. I know that whatever happens between Ellis and me, Ellis wouldn't turn his back on his child. Things are just so complicated now." She took a deep breath as she lay back on her pillow.

"I think you should tell Ellis, and very soon. Please. As far as Antonio goes, I think you have very deep feelings for this man, and I'm sure he feels the same for you. You owe it to yourself to be happy. Give this Antonio guy the right to decide what he wants. You don't know that he wouldn't still want you even though you're pregnant. If he really loves you, it wouldn't matter. Don't just shut him out without explaining your reasons. But I'll leave that one up to you to think on. You know him better than I do, so I can't really say what to do there. Having a baby is a serious, life-changing event. So, when are you going to tell Ellis?" he asked again leaning in to hug her. She hugged him back.

"All right, all right, I'll tell him. I'll tell him when he gets back from Madrid. I would rather tell him something like this in person, so I'll go to San Diego next weekend." After awhile, Tyana drifted off to sleep and Trevor left.

Ellis and Charlotte returned from Madrid, tanned and refreshed. They came back to a mountain of work and spent the next week working even more closely, collaborating on several projects. Some of their colleagues were beginning to suspect that something was going on between them because they had been together almost constantly since Ellis' arrival, but any rumors were quickly dispelled because of Charlotte's reputation of not fraternizing with her business associates. And because Ellis wasn't in love with Charlotte, he didn't have an enamored air about him when he was with her. He was strictly business when he was on the job. His job was the most important thing to him. Running a very close second was Tyana.

Tyana had left several messages for Ellis since his return to San Diego but he had been too busy to call her back. Charlotte saw to that. She knew that Tyana would be moving to San Diego soon if she didn't do something to change that. Charlotte had also learned from her sources that Tyana was no longer taking dance lessons. No one was able to determine why she had quit, so Charlotte felt she then had to take matters into her own hands. When Tyana and Ellis finally spoke, she told him that she would be coming out for the weekend to continue their search for a home. She told him she would leave a message with her flight information once she made her reservations.

Tyana worked frantically to get things in order so she could take the weekend off and fly to San Diego. She had a lot of catching up to do from being incapacitated by her morning sickness, which usually affected her most of the day. She still hadn't told anyone else about her pregnancy. She wanted to tell Ellis next. She realized that she had an obligation to tell him.

She left a message with Ellis' assistant about her flight information. She thought about calling until she connected with him to make sure he got the message, but his assistant told her that Ellis would be tied up most of the day in meetings but he would definitely get her message. She had then gotten too busy herself and didn't get a chance to call him again. Part of her was apprehensive about talking to him, since she had seen him with that woman in the airport. She still got sick to her stomach at the thought of him sleeping with someone else. She would wait to see him in San Diego before speaking with him. She didn't want him to detect any pain in her voice.

She had left the message for Ellis that her flight would get in at three in the afternoon on Friday. The message was placed on Ellis' desk right on top of everything so he would see it. Ellis had several morning meetings that day and hadn't seen the message yet. He knew that Tyana was arriving on Friday, but was waiting to hear back from her regarding the time. Charlotte entered Ellis' office, before he returned, to leave a report that he would need for one of his meetings. She also wanted to leave her panties in his desk drawer, just as a reminder of last night's lustful episode. She enjoyed leaving her "calling card", so to speak, as a reminder of her.

When she laid the report on top of his desk, she couldn't help but notice the message with Tyana's name on it. She picked it up and read it. Three this afternoon, she thought. That would give her no time with Ellis that day. He would be tied up with the girlfriend until Monday and she would be put back on the shelf. Without another thought, she took a pen and changed the three to an eight. She smiled and placed the note back on the desk and left, keeping her panties with her.

Trevor insisted on taking Tyana to the airport. He wanted to see her off and wish her luck. She had called Kellie before she left to tell her about her plans to tell Ellis about the baby and confront him about the woman. Kellie wished her luck and was planning to see her immediately when she returned.

Ellis finally returned to his office and saw Tyana's message with her flight information. Eight o'clock would give him plenty of time to finish up there and even change before meeting her plane. He was planning to take her out to a nice restaurant after picking her up. He immediately left his office again to meet with some of his staff to give them instructions for Monday. He left his cell phone on his desk; he would get it before leaving for the airport.

On his way back to his office, he was headed off by Charlotte. It was already four-thirty, so she was certain that Tyana would be calling him from the airport looking for him. She enticed him to come to her office where she could have some privacy with him. She removed her panties and played with them under his nose. She knew she would be able to tempt him before he would be off for the weekend. With much convincing and coaxing, she managed to entice him back to his room. They were very careful not to be spotted on guest floors together. He figured he had a few hours yet before he would have to pick up Tyana.

Tyana's flight was uneventful although a little late because they were late taking off. She arrived in San Diego before she had realized the time. She exited the plane and headed toward baggage claim, looking for Ellis on her way down the escalator. She figured he probably got detained at work or in traffic. She would get her luggage and wait for him curbside. She checked her cell phone for a message. There was no message. She waited and waited. She phoned him several times but got his voicemail. She left a message at his office and room and on his cell phone that she was at the airport waiting for him. His assistant had left early that day so anyone calling Ellis would be at the mercy of his voicemail.

Charlotte noticed the message light on his room phone and, when Ellis was in the bathroom, she picked up the phone and retrieved his message. It was from Tyana. She hung up before Ellis returned. She started to get undressed when he suggested that they not make love on the bed, but on the sofa instead. She began to undress him and insisted on going down on him. She knew he would want to do the same for her. That was more personal and she wanted them to have a very personal encounter. She needed his thoughts to be only of her. It wasn't long before Ellis was enjoying Charlotte's performance as he lay back and closed his eyes. She massaged and stroked him hard and fast. He tried to hold out as long as he could before climaxing, but he gave in. She had worked her magic on him once again and he was relishing the moment. He pulled her up close to him and kissed her hard, turning her over to make love to her. He glanced at the clock. It was five-thirty; he still had plenty of time to enjoy himself with her and give her some of the same pleasure she had given him.

Tyana had finally decided to catch a cab and go on to the hotel. She continued trying to reach Ellis to let him know, but he wasn't in his office and his cell phone was still on his desk. Twenty minutes later, the cab had deposited her at the hotel entrance. It was five-thirty. She was hungry and exhausted. She had been feeling particularly strange all day, but figured it was just her nerves. She was indeed nervous about seeing Ellis.

Ellis parted Charlotte's legs and began to kiss her hungrily. He was definitely hot for her and didn't want to waste any time, knowing he had to pick Tyana up soon. Charlotte's moans only made him want her more; he could no longer think of anything or anyone else. He was in the moment with Charlotte and they both were enjoying the rush the excitement provided.

Tyana had gone to Ellis' office first to see if she could find him. She entered his office but he wasn't in there. So she had proceeded to his hotel suite. She still had her keycard so she thought she would just put her bags down and relax until he surfaced. She had left a message for him at the front desk that she was in the hotel. He would find her, if she didn't find him first. She reached the suite and inserted the keycard in the door.

Charlotte was trying very hard to slow Ellis' pace with her, but he was too much in the moment and ignored her request to slow down. Her heart was beginning to beat faster and she felt herself nearing a climax. She couldn't hold it back any longer and began to spasm violently, moaning loudly now. He continued on, driving her completely wild and out of control with pleasure. She continued to scream with affirmation, insisting that he keep doing what he was doing. He complied. Tyana could only stare at them in utter shock and disbelief. She was horrified as she watched Ellis performing oral sex with the same blonde woman from the airport, whose long legs were tightly wrapped around his body as she continued to moan, squirm, and exclaim in ecstasy. "Take me!"

Tyana opened her mouth to scream in terror but nothing came out. Ellis and Charlotte were still involved. Tears began to flow down her face and she turned instantly pale, shaking all over uncontrollably. She backed away toward the door, unable to take her eyes off of them. She turned sharply to run out and fell over her bags that she didn't remember dropping on the floor. The commotion got Ellis and Charlotte's attention. Ellis quickly raised up and turned toward the door in a panic to see what was going on. His first thought was that it was housekeeping.

"Oh shit! Tyana! Oh shit!" Ellis quickly jumped up and grabbed for his shorts, wiping his face. He was mortified to see her there. Charlotte sat up and smiled wryly. Tyana struggled to get up. Once she reached her feet she ran out of the room. She didn't know where to go, being disoriented in the hotel, but she just had to keep running to escape the nightmare. Ellis grabbed his pants and struggled to put them on. "Get out of here," he said to Charlotte as he left the room to run after Tyana.

Tyana reached the elevators and pushed the down button but she could hear Ellis fast approaching her. She saw the door to the stairs and ran toward it. She pushed opened the door and began to run down the stairs. She didn't know where she would go but all she knew was she had to get out of there, away from him. She kept running with the images of Ellis' head between another woman's legs. She cried harder and ran faster, becoming blinded by her tears. Her body was trembling as she ran down the stairs, skipping a few at a time. She heard footsteps behind her, and when she looked back to see Ellis gaining on her, she lost her footing and fell down six steps to the landing. The chase was over. Ellis reached her and carefully picked her up into his shaky arms. He called out to her but she didn't answer. She was out cold. He shouted for someone to get help.

Chapter Eighteen

Tyana had regained consciousness in the emergency room of the nearest hospital but had to be sedated because of the pain. Ellis was sitting next to her with his head bowed in his hands. He had been pacing nervously, waiting to hear the details of her injuries. He had been unable to talk to her for a couple of hours while they examined her. He had been filled with enormous guilt from the second he saw her in the hotel room. He just sat next to her and watched her through the tears in his eyes. She lay quietly with monitors hooked up to her. The attending physician entered the room and addressed Ellis, since he had brought her in and was her emergency contact.

"Ms. Dominique has suffered a slight concussion, which we are monitoring. All her vitals seem to be OK; however, we are giving her fluids intravenously because she showed signs of being dehydrated. Her other test results have come back OK, meaning she isn't in any immediate danger and has no other serious injuries, other than a sprained wrist. We'll be moving her to a private room because of the miscarriage. She'll have to stay here so we can monitor her for forty-eight hours." The physician looked at Ellis with concern. He had suddenly become weak in the knees and turned pale. The doctor had to help him sit down. "Mr. Montgomery, are you all right? Do you need to lie down?" Ellis was in shock.

"She was pregnant?" he asked in a crackled voice. He was given an affirmative nod. He began to cry as he looked over at her. She looked so tiny and frail. He got up and went to her side. He slowly bent down to kiss her gently on her forehead and whispered to her. "I'm so sorry, Tyana. I love you, baby. I'm so sorry." He couldn't tear himself away from her.

"Mr. Montgomery. Are you going to be all right? We need to move her to her room now. You can follow us. Do you need assistance?" The physician motioned for a nurse to come and help Ellis. He was in bad shape.

The nurses moved Tyana's bed to a private room and got her all set up. Ellis was right behind them. After several minutes, he was left alone with Tyana as she still slept. He held her hand and rubbed it gently, still staring at her beautiful face. His mind was still on the shocking news he had just received. She lost the baby. How long had she been pregnant? When did she know? Was she going to tell him this weekend? Why did she show up so early? Those were a few of the random questions he had in his head. He couldn't help but feel shame and guilt for what he'd done to her and, ultimately, to their relationship. He had never intended to hurt Tyana, but now he wasn't sure how he could not have intentionally set out to hurt her if he had willingly engaged in an affair with someone else. He spent the next hour berating himself for putting her in that position. He knew everything was completely his fault and he was to blame for the miscarriage that she didn't even know about yet. Tears filled his eyes and rolled down his face as he thought of the hurt he had caused her, and of the pain she would yet endure. He sat next to her the entire time that she slept.

Charlotte had left the hotel after the paramedics had taken Ellis and Tyana to the hospital. She went to her beach house, where she waited to hear something from Ellis. She had asked Ellis to call her to let her know if Tyana was going to be all right, but Ellis had barely acknowledged her as he got into the ambulance. Her phone rang and she jumped up to answer it. She glanced at the clock to see that it was seven-thirty. It had to be Ellis, she thought, but it wasn't.

"Hello, Ms. St. Jean?" inquired the voice on the other end.

"Yes," Charlotte answered.

"This is the lab at the hospital. We have your test results." Charlotte was a bit confused, thinking about Ellis and Tyana at the hospital. Why were they calling her with Tyana's test results?

"What are you talking about? What test results?" she asked anxiously.

"From your recent visit. We've given your doctor the information, so you may contact him at your earliest convenience," explained the voice on the other end.

"Oh, I'd forgotten all about that. What are the results? Just go ahead and tell me, I don't have time to call Dr. Miller," she snapped back.

"Well, Ms. St. Jean, your tests are positive. You're pregnant." Charlotte dropped the phone.

Tyana slept through the night and Ellis was right there by her side. He never left her once. He was exhausted as he lay awake most of the night, watching her sleep. He finally drifted off to sleep around five in the morning. It was seven when Tyana awoke. She was understandably disoriented as she scanned the room. Then she saw Ellis sitting in the chair next to her sound asleep. She didn't know where she was or why she was there. She noticed that her wrist was wrapped and she had a headache. She saw the tube coming out of her hand and then realized she was in a hospital. She wasn't wearing her clothes, but a hospital gown instead. Then she noticed a pad between her legs and became instantly hysterical, shouting "No! Oh God, no!" Ellis jumped up from his chair and saw her crying as she clutched her abdomen. She looked at Ellis, panic-stricken, as she cried.

"Tyana, sweetheart, I know, I know. I'm so sorry." He held her and rocked her gently. She continued to sob hysterically.

"I lost the baby. I lost the baby," she kept crying. He couldn't console her, try as he might. He finally called the nurse to help calm her. They gave her another sedative to get her to calm down and to keep her blood pressure down. She quieted after a few moments. Ellis was scared for her. He was shaking and pacing. He didn't know what to expect from her now that she knew what had happened to her baby.

Tyana slept for another four hours as Ellis stayed by her side. It was lunchtime now and her lunch was being brought in. The nurse tried to wake her and she slowly came to. It was important that she eat something. She awoke feeling very groggy. The nurse took her temperature and blood pressure and left her in Ellis' care to see that she ate.

"Tyana, sweetheart, your lunch is here. You have to eat something," he said to her as he helped her sit up and get comfortable. She was becoming more coherent as she watched him through the tears in her eyes and remembering the revolting scene with him and the blonde.

"Ellis, I don't think I want you here. I can't bear to look at you right now."

"Tyana, I know, I know, I am so sorry. There aren't words to describe how sorry I am. I don't know how I could have done that to you, baby. You didn't deserve that; you didn't, please believe me. You need to eat, sweetheart. Please do that and let's talk about this afterwards." Ellis was really afraid for Tyana's health. He felt completely responsible for her, more so than he had ever felt before.

"I can't eat, Ellis. I lost the baby. What difference does anything make now?" She began to cry again.

"Don't say that. You have to eat something." He was worried about her. "Tyana, when did you find out about the baby? How long have you known?" he asked, looking at her with tears in his eyes. He couldn't believe he was almost going to be a father and didn't even know about it.

"I had just found out a few weeks ago, but you were in Madrid…with *her*," she added. His eyes got big. He was sensing that she'd known about his affair before now. "I was going to tell you when I got here this weekend. I didn't want to tell you over the phone, plus you obviously haven't had much time to really talk to me lately." He knew she was right about that. She continued. "I've known about the affair, Ellis."

"What do you mean? How? When? I'm so sorry I've hurt you. It was a stupid, idiotic thing to do and I'm sorry." He felt embarrassed talking to Tyana about this now after her ordeal.

"Little things just kept adding up the last few months. Then I saw you in the coffee shop at the airport with *her* a few weeks ago when I was in town. She was all over you. And I knew she'd been going to Madrid with you. She was the same woman that I told you had approached me in the airport and told me she had just been in Madrid the same time you were there; you were on the same flight. You denied knowing her but then I saw you in the coffee shop with her; she was touching your leg. She was also the same woman that answered your phone in Madrid, I'm guessing, unless you're sleeping around with other women as well."

"No, no, Tyana, don't think that. I know this doesn't make the situation any better or any less wrong, but she's been the only one. Baby, I'm so sorry. I shouldn't have done it, but I know there's nothing that I can say now that'll excuse any of this. I was wrong and I'm sorry." His hands were shaking as he spoke to her. "Tyana, I love only you. I don't love anyone else. It was just a stupid, fucked up thing that I did."

"Ellis, I don't care anymore. All I cared about was the baby. It didn't deserve what happened. I wanted to come here to tell you about the baby and to ask you to your face if you were involved with someone else, but I guess I didn't have to ask you, now did I? I thought you had a right to know about your child. And I had a right to hear it from you that you were cheating on me. What I didn't expect was to actually have to see you in the act. Why were you even with her then, in your suite, when you were supposed to be picking me up at the airport?" she asked, looking confused, hurt, and disgusted.

"Tyana, it shouldn't have happened at all and especially not then. I got your message that you were coming in at eight..." Ellis couldn't finish his explanation. He was too ashamed to even look her in the face.

"But I called your assistant and specifically told her three, not eight! Where the hell did you get eight from? Ellis, does this woman have access to your office? If she knew I was coming in then you might want to ask her about the message." She paused and he said nothing, wondering if Charlotte did have something to do with it. "How involved are you two; how long has this been going on between you?" she asked, felling a large lump in her throat. She winced in pain. He responded to her body language.

"Tyana, are you all right? What's the matter?" He was on edge with worry over her.

"I'm fine, it's just painful losing a baby, I guess...in many ways." She lay back and looked at him, waiting impatiently for an answer.

"She's someone I work with here in San Diego and I've known her for several years, but we have only recently been lovers." It was very difficult for him to refer to Charlotte as his lover in front of Tyana. He felt sick. He looked at her and the look on her face tore him up inside. His voice started to crack. "It started when I was trying to attain this region and she was instrumental in my promotion here, and in Madrid. She's made it all happen for me..." He was interrupted.

"So, you felt you owed her a blow job? Fuck you, Ellis! Was it that important to you that you had to sleep with her to get promoted? That's despicable. We were doing just fine financially." She turned her head away. He was speechless. "I thought we had something special. I trusted you. I loved you with everything I had. This is a nightmare come true for me and now I've lost the baby because of all your brilliant decisions, starting with the one that gave me a front row view of you enjoying her *goods*! When can I get out of here?"

"Tyana, I do love you—only you. She doesn't mean anything to me like you do. I said it was a stupid thing that just happened, then I couldn't stop it. I didn't know you were pregnant."

"What? And knowing that I was pregnant was going to cure you of your wandering penis?" Just then the nurse came in and caught the last part of their conversation. She looked at Ellis with a surprised look on her face. She encouraged Tyana to eat, but inside could understand why Tyana had lost her appetite. She left the room.

"I don't know but yes, it would have changed things knowing. Tyana, I don't know how I could ever explain any of this. I don't know myself how I got in this situation. It wasn't planned; I was drunk—then she was threatening my job..." He was reaching for any kind of explanation that could ease her pain, but he wasn't making much progress.

"Ellis, the baby is gone. I lost the baby. I shouldn't have been running, then I fell. I lost our baby." She had suddenly realized her miscarriage again and was becoming hysterical again. He grabbed her and hugged her tightly.

"No, baby, you did nothing wrong. It's all my fault; you were perfect. Please try and relax. It'll be all right. Shhh…baby, you'll be fine. I'm so sorry, Tyana, please know that. I'll do anything to make this up to you. Please calm down." Ellis wasn't having much of an effect on her. She continued to cry and he held her until she fell asleep.

Ellis left the hospital while Tyana slept to go back to the hotel to shower and change. He also wanted to bring Tyana's things to her. When he walked into his suite, he just stood in place and looked around, imagining what Tyana must have gone through as she stood in that exact spot watching him perform oral sex on Charlotte. He began to get emotional. A thousand thoughts flew through his head and they all were thoughts of her having been pregnant with his baby only twenty-four hours ago. He couldn't believe he was responsible for her losing the baby, his baby. Tears fell from his eyes and onto her luggage. He quickly showered and changed. He wanted to get back to her as soon as possible. While he was changing his clothes he noticed his message light was on. He listened to the message. It was from Charlotte. He didn't call her back, but instead rushed back out to the hospital.

Ellis stayed with Tyana the entire weekend. She was released Sunday afternoon. Because of her concussion, the doctors wanted to

255

monitor her another day just to make sure there wasn't anything more serious going on. When she was cleared to leave, Ellis took her back to the hotel suite where he put her to bed immediately. She was still traumatized from losing the baby. The doctor told Ellis that it would come and go for a period of time, depending on her emotional state. Ellis didn't divulge their problems to him, but he knew that Tyana wouldn't heal from this tragedy for a long while. She ate some soup and fell asleep right away. Her eyes were swollen and red from crying for two days. He slept next to her, holding on to her tightly while she slept.

It was two in the morning when Tyana got up to go to the bathroom. As she walked by the door, she turned and thought she saw Ellis on the couch with Charlotte and she screamed. Ellis leaped out of the bed and ran to her, nearly tripping over the chair in the process.

"Tyana! What is it? What are you doing out of bed?" He was half asleep as he fumbled for the light switch. He found her and ran to her. She was sobbing uncontrollably.

"I can't stay here. You've been with her here and I can be here. Ellis, I hate you! Please take me home now!" He couldn't get her to calm down until he promised to get her out of the room.

"Tyana, we can catch a flight out in the morning, but I don't think you should fly just yet. How about we go home on Tuesday? You might be feeling better by then." He was trying to reason with her, considering her condition.

"I want out of here—now! I can see you with her here. I can smell the sex; it's everywhere. Please get me out of here!" She was very upset. He had to make her take a sleeping pill prescribed by the hospital doctor to get her to calm down. He helped her to the bathroom, then back to bed. She slept for the next nine hours. He never left her.

Ellis had to phone his office and let his assistant know that he had an emergency and couldn't get to his office until later that afternoon. She was to dial him in his room if she needed him. He would work from there after his laptop was brought to him. The news about Ellis' girlfriend falling in the stairwell was getting around the hotel. His assistant was made aware of it that morning. She didn't discuss it with Ellis out of respect for his privacy. No one, at that point, had heard anything about her miscarriage. Ellis set up camp in his suite to be near Tyana. He wasn't going to let her out of his sight. He had already caused enough pain and harm to her, and he wasn't going to let anything else happen to her now.

He had ordered room service for Tyana when she awoke. She was upset that she was still in his suite, but she wasn't feeling up to flying just yet. She called Trevor to let him know that she wouldn't be home for a few days. She didn't go into much detail with him over the phone, but he sensed that something was wrong. She didn't sound too good, which made Trevor worry and wonder if she had told Ellis yet about the baby. He wondered whether her detainment was because things had gone well or because things weren't going so well and they needed more time to sort it all out. It was killing him not knowing what was happening. She put him off by telling him that she would tell him everything once she got back home. She needed her friend especially now, but didn't want to upset him over the phone. She knew he would get angry and upset and would threaten to fly out immediately. She didn't need a situation between him and Ellis on her hands at that moment in addition to everything else she was dealing with.

Her head was still hurting and her wrist throbbed occasionally. Ellis sat with her when she was in pain to comfort her. She let him take care of her. She had no choice, considering she was away from home and her friends. She needed someone to care for her; she was still grieving for her lost baby. She watched him fuss over her and she couldn't help but feel that he did still love her. She no longer felt the same about him though, especially now. She knew in her heart that they were finished as a couple. It hurt her to think that, because they had had so many good years together in the beginning. She wasn't sure when they started to change and grow apart, but something had to have happened to allow strangers to come into their lives and separate them from each other. She then thought of Antonio. She missed him so much.

Charlotte was still leaving messages for Ellis but he was unavailable to her. He thought she had a lot of nerve trying to contact him in light of the recent developments. He would contact her when Tyana was safe at home and not before.

The next day, Tyana was feeling better and insisted on going home. They caught the first plane out of San Diego to Phoenix the following day. They were both very quiet on the flight home. Tyana slept most of the way.

When they arrived back at their home, they entered the house and just stood looking around at all the boxes. She was in the midst of packing their things. This was their home together, the home they had created out of love. It brought tears to Tyana's eyes knowing that they would not share their home again the way they used to. It was all in the past. They were different people now. Tyana would never be the same after losing her baby. And no longer was she packing for their future together in San Diego, because they would no longer share a home together.

Tyana had phoned Kellie before leaving San Diego and told her about the miscarriage and that Ellis would be escorting her home. They didn't talk too much about her fall; Tyana didn't want to go into the details over the phone. They would catch up later at home. Kellie phoned Trevor and alerted him that Ellis would be coming home with Tyana. He didn't know what to make of that change of plans.

Ellis had planned to stay with Tyana for a few days, just until he was assured that she was going to be all right alone. She had insisted that he not stay, but he won that battle.

"Ellis, I've decided that I won't be moving to San Diego with you after all. I'm sure you've figured that one out yourself. I'll stay here in Scottsdale and keep my business. Of course, I'll have to buy my own house. I guess it's a good thing that we sold this house. I don't think I would want to stay here with all our memories."

"No, I didn't think you would be staying here alone. I mean, I thought we could try and work this out." He knew as soon as he said those words how ridiculous they sounded, knowing how much he had hurt Tyana.

"No, Ellis. It's not going to work, not ever. I need to live my life for me now. I'll always be reminded of that dreadful day that I lost my baby. You may not have planned to hurt me by sleeping with someone else, but you did and I can't excuse that. The image in my head will stay with me forever, and it'll haunt me to the point where I wouldn't be able to trust you again. I'll always see you with her in that way. You work together, for God's sake. Do you think I can live with that?" She began to walk around the room. She suddenly had an incredible flashback as if she'd had this conversation with Ellis before. She stood dazed for awhile with her hand touching her forehead. Why was she feeling this—like she'd been here with him like this before? It was eerie, and she had a look of terror on her face momentarily. Ellis was alarmed by this. He thought she was experiencing some trauma from her fall or the miscarriage. He started to go to her, but she stopped him and continued. She shook off the weird feeling.

"I'll pack your things and have them shipped out to you in San Diego. I'll move out of the house as soon as I can get everything finalized. I'll take care of everything. If I need you for anything, I'll call you. Please don't call me. I'll be all right here now so I want you to leave. If I need anything, I'll call Kellie or Trevor." She walked away, leaving him standing alone. He walked after her.

"Tyana, I'll transfer back if you want me to. I'll do anything to make this up to you. Please reconsider. I love you. I screwed up. Can you give me another chance? I promise it'll never happen again." He had to take a shot at it; he had nothing to lose. He wanted her desperately and was willing to do anything to get her to change her mind about severing their ties, their life together. He hadn't even thought about Charlotte the whole time he had been focused on Tyana. He was certain that he didn't want to lose Tyana. He was even willing to adjust his career to make it possible to keep her in his life.

They talked for a few hours more, but nothing that he said would change her mind about staying with him. She was moving on, but first she wanted to mourn her loss. She couldn't forgive Ellis right now for creating a terrible situation that would ultimately change her life forever. Ellis returned to San Diego the next morning.

Charlotte met up with Ellis almost immediately, having been told he would be returning to work that day. He looked weary and depressed. He wasn't in any mood to contend with her. He was wounded and he had just realized the consequences of his decision to pair with Charlotte physically. Charlotte entered Ellis' office and closed the door.

"Ellis, how are you? What's happened?" Charlotte hadn't heard about Tyana since she saw her being taken away in the ambulance and she hadn't seen Ellis since. She did get word that he had left for Phoenix with Tyana.

"I don't want to talk about it, Charlotte. Everything's fine. What's going on here?" He was clearly depressed and was trying to focus on his work again.

"Things are fine here. What happened in Phoenix?" She wanted to know the status of his relationship. Had she been successful at getting Tyana out of the picture?

"Charlotte, I said I don't want to talk about it. What do you think happened? My girlfriend walked in on me performing oral sex on you! And did you have anything to do with me getting the wrong information about her flight time?" He was bitter and didn't care about anything but Tyana. "She left a message that she was getting in at three, not eight! And somehow I think you had something to do with it. Like you talking to her in the airport when we were connecting here to Hawaii. What is wrong with you?" He walked to his chair to sit down.

"I don't know what you're talking about, you're not making sense," she replied, knowing that they must have had extensive conversations during this time. Apparently Tyana was aware of her presence in his life. That can't be a good sign for the survival of their relationship. By the looks of Ellis, her guess was that he and Tyana were no longer together.

"Cut the bullshit, Charlotte, she knows everything! Are you happy? She knows everything. She's known for a while and I've hurt her beyond comprehension." He slammed the files in his hand down hard on his desk. "Her walking in on us was the icing on the cake. I might as well have pushed her down those stairs myself. And she lost our baby." As he said those words, he began to get tears in his eyes and was getting choked up. He turned away from Charlotte. She stood shocked by his words. Charlotte had had no idea that Tyana was pregnant. And now that Tyana had lost his baby, she herself was sitting pretty, she thought, being pregnant with his child. He obviously wanted that baby badly. If Tyana couldn't give him a baby, she would. She wasn't sure at first what she was going to do with her own unexpected news, but now she thought that maybe she should keep the baby, to have a permanent connection to Ellis and his money. She would get it one way or another.

"Ellis, I'm sorry to hear about all that, you must be very distraught. Is there anything I can do for you? Would you like to go back to your suite and I can give you a massage? Come on." She was trying to get him to go with her.

"I have a lot of work to do. I'm not interested." He was numb. She left and went down to the lounge and ordered a strong Bloody Mary for Ellis. She returned moments later and Ellis was still sitting in the same position. He hadn't moved an inch. He was staring blankly out the window at the ocean. He could only think of Tyana. He didn't hear Charlotte enter with the drink in her hand. She approached him slowly and put the drink on his desk. She then went around the back of his chair and began to rub his head at his temples. He continued to just sit quietly. Tears fell from his face. Charlotte leaned around and kissed him on his lips.

"Ellis, I need to tell you something." He wasn't responding. She began to rub her hands over his chest then his face. She continued to kiss him with more passion. He jumped up in fury.

"What do you want, Charlotte? What?! Do you want me to fuck you right here so someone else can walk in on us? Do you even know what this means? I'm fucked if this gets out. I'm already fucked with Tyana. I've lost her. I know this means nothing to you but it means a hell of a lot to me! Do you think you can just go and leave me alone for a while?"

"Just a fuckin' minute, Ellis! You don't talk to me like that! What the hell do you take me for, a piece of meat? What do you think you've been doing with me all this time? And now you're going to make me believe you had special feelings for her? Get real. You've fucked me every chance you got for months and you liked it. Hell, you loved it! You wanted it. You wanted me, not her. You were with me most of the time, not her, so don't give me that shit! And because you got caught and she saw you with me, where you chose to be, enjoying the hell out of me, you're going to turn on me? Uh-uh...think again. I ought to sue your ass for sexual harassment. The only reason I won't is because I'm carrying your child. Yeah, your baby, Ellis. You dwell on that!" She stormed out of his office, making certain not to create a scene in front of his assistant as she left. Ellis gasped in total shock at her words. He couldn't breathe.

Chapter Nineteen

Once Tyana returned home, she saw her doctor and had a thorough examination regarding the miscarriage. There didn't seem to be any additional concerns in that regard; she was healthy otherwise. Her doctor recommended that she remain home for a few days to rest her body, especially in light of her concussion and minor injuries. Her doctor was especially concerned about her emotional state at this point because of the trauma of losing her baby and the situation with Ellis. She had explained some of the ordeal leading up to what happened, leaving out the sordid details. Something like that was sure to have a lasting effect on her for some time to come. The doctor wanted to make sure she had an ample support system available to her. With her separation from Ellis at the same time, her doctor was afraid that the additional emotional stress might slow her healing process. She had assured the doctor that she would be all right, in time. Trevor was waiting for her at her house when she returned from her doctor visit.

Trevor got out of his car and went to Tyana when she pulled up. He opened the car door for her and immediately hugged her when she got out.

"Trevor." She broke down and cried in Trevor's arms. He helped her into the house.

"I know, sweetheart, I'm so sorry. I'm glad you're back home. You'll be fine now." They sat down out back by the pool. "Just sit back and put your feet up. Tell me what you need and I'll get it." He was eager to do what he could to make her comfortable.

"I'm fine for now. I'll get something in a little bit. I'm just so tired right now. Mostly mentally drained."

"Tyana, I'm really sorry. Maybe it wasn't such a good idea to go to San Diego to tell Ellis."

"Trevor, don't. Don't think that any of this was your fault at all. I was going anyway. And I didn't get to tell him about the baby, before…" Tyana got a lump in her throat and began to choke on her words when she thought about Ellis and Charlotte again.

"What is it Tyana? What actually happened? Can you talk about it?" he asked as he stared at her with bated breath. She took her time preparing to relive that eventful day.

"I got to the airport and waited for Ellis to pick me up, except that he didn't come. I found out later that someone had given him the wrong information about my flight arrival time and he didn't know I was there waiting. So, eventually, I left and took a cab to the hotel. I went up to the suite to put my things down and relax while I waited for him. I just figured he was tied up in some meeting or something." She paused for a moment, then continued.

"When I got to the suite, I used my keycard that I still had from the last time I was there so I just walked in." Tears filled her eyes as she looked away. "I walked in to find him with her, giving her…he was having oral sex with her. They were both naked on the couch. It was shocking and I didn't know what to do."

"What? Are you kidding?!" reacted Trevor.

"She was the same woman I saw him with in the coffee shop at the airport in San Diego when he was flying to Madrid a few weeks ago; the same woman that bumped into me at the same airport when he and I were flying to Hawaii. I couldn't stop staring at them but yet I couldn't move either. It was as if my entire body was paralyzed." She paused again and Trevor comforted her.

"When I finally realized what I was seeing, I turned to run and tripped over my bags on the floor. They both turned and looked at me and he yelled my name or something. I don't remember. I ran out of the room, down the hall as fast as I could and ran into a stairwell. I was running down the stairs so fast, plus I was crying, I couldn't see. I lost my footing and fell down a couple of stairs, hit my head, and passed out. The next thing I knew, I was in the hospital and Ellis was with me. That's when he learned of my pregnancy—when the doctors told him I had a miscarriage."

She started crying again when she thought about her ordeal with losing the baby. "He's been distraught over the whole thing ever since. They think it was the fall that caused me to lose the baby, but when I was running I remembered grabbing at the baby because I felt this incredible pain in my uterus. It was horrible and I knew I was going to be sick. I felt a contracting sensation afterwards. That's all I remember; that's about when I fell. Today, I talked to my doctor and told him the whole story. He told me that my fragile condition from the stress of everything prior to going to San Diego, coupled with the trauma of what I walked into, and then the fall, all of that together probably caused a chain reaction of many physical things that resulted in the miscarriage. All of which now makes me feel worse knowing that Ellis' affair is the indirect cause of me losing the baby." Her voice trailed off into a whimper as she cried a little harder. Trevor held her tighter in his arms.

"I can't believe the asshole was so stupid to have had the woman in your suite—mix-up or no mix-up about the time. What I really can't understand is the fact that he cheated on you in the first place. And why? He had everything with you! It doesn't get any better than you." Trevor was thinking back on the time when he had been in love with Tyana.

"What are your plans now?" he asked, looking at his frail and broken-hearted friend.

"I've left him. He was here with me when I returned and we talked all day and night. He wants me to stay with him desperately and is willing to move mountains to get me to give him another chance, but I can't and told him I needed to move on, without him. I could no longer trust him with her. He works with her and they're involvement seems more than just a casual fling. To me, you can't just turn that off instantly. What I saw them doing would be described as a very personal and intimate act in my opinion. At least I'm sure she's not going to go away easily, even if he did decide to end it. He should have thought about all that, and me, before he did it. For me, losing the baby would also always be a constant reminder of his affair and infidelity. I can't live with that on a daily basis. I'd probably grow to hate him and make him pay for it every day of his life with me. We can't live like that and try to have a loving relationship at the same time. I owe myself much more than living a life like that. There was something missing in our relationship anyway to leave the door ajar for this to happen in the first place. Under normal circumstances, we could probably examine the weak link and try and repair it, but with him having been sexually active with someone else, that makes it a lot harder to get past in order to work on our problems. We're beyond repair at this stage of the game." She took a deep breath.

"So, what are your plans now? Do you know?

"I'll be buying another house, here in Scottsdale. It's best that way anyway. I'll be staying here and keeping my business and starting over on my own, I guess. I'll be OK, Trevor." She hugged him for a long time. He held her until she drifted off to sleep. He carried her inside and put her to bed. He sat with her while she slept. She looked so peaceful, like an angel. He couldn't believe that so much pain could dwell within someone so lovable. He left a few hours later when Kellie arrived.

Ellis decided to meet Charlotte at her beach house that evening after hearing her shocking news. He had already been feeling sick to his stomach all day and could concentrate on very little under the circumstances with Tyana, and now this with Charlotte. He was a basket case to say the least. He arrived at her door at ten p.m. She let him in.

"Charlotte, what happened? You told me you were protected…when did it happen?" Ellis was very weary and was hardly audible. He had been so torn up over Tyana—she wasn't taking any of his calls and he had been very emotionally unstable in the privacy of his suite. He had cancelled all his meetings that afternoon because of lack of concentration and he hadn't eaten in two days now. He just sat and stared at Charlotte, wondering how all this could be happening to him. If he had had any chances of getting Tyana back, they were all but eliminated now. Tyana was sure to find out and he was certain that she would cut all ties to him at that point. She was the only thing that meant anything to him. He didn't even wonder whether or not he was the father. He was certain he was. He knew that Charlotte had been with him exclusively.

"I don't know exactly, I have an appointment to see the doctor in a few days. I just got the lab results the other day. I went in because I was late and wasn't feeling very well, but just thought it was caused by my prescription—it has happened before. But never pregnancy! They insisted that I take the pregnancy test over my objections. I was certain they wouldn't find that to be the problem. I'm just as shocked as you are Ellis, because yes, I used protection. This doesn't exactly fit into my plans or my lifestyle. So, you're not the only one who's inconvenienced over this." She had never seen him look so defeated and despondent. She almost hated to spring all this on him. Almost.

"I'm sorry it happened, Charlotte. When you see the doctor, are you going to make an appointment for an abortion?" He fought through those words. He had never expected that he would ever speak of anyone aborting his child. Of course, the only person he thought would ever be pregnant with his child would be Tyana. That wasn't going to happen now.

270

"Whoa.   What are you talking about, abortion?   Who said anything about that? Although this creates a major cramp in my style, I haven't exactly thought about an alternative.   This is my decision too, you know, and my body!" Charlotte said as she stood straight up. There was no way she was going to get rid of her baby now, not after what happened to Tyana. She had Ellis right where she wanted him. It would mean a tremendous sacrifice to her, but one she was willing to make.

"But Charlotte…what do you plan to do with a baby? This isn't something that I'm ready to deal with. We don't have a relationship, in the traditional sense, I mean. I'm not in a position to accept that kind of responsibility with you. You and I aren't exactly open with our 'arrangement' and the timing isn't good."   He was getting nervous. He couldn't imagine anyone but Tyana being the mother of his child.

"Well, get used to the idea. I'm having the baby. If you think you don't want any part of this now that things have turned serious, too bad. You sure wanted every tasty part of me before, or have you developed amnesia? Ellis, let me put it to you in terms that you can get on board with. If you don't start acting like a good little daddy and cooperate with me better on this little situation that we have, I may be forced to let our secret slip out. And it may get all the way to Spain. You might be thinking that that wouldn't be so terrible, but maybe you will when it gets back to your precious Tyana. Do you think she can handle your news about our little surprise now, and how you're so happy that we're pregnant since you've always wanted a baby, and that you're free to be with me? What do you think she'll do, Ellis? Do you think she can handle hearing that?" Charlotte wasn't going to let Ellis control her and force her to into having an abortion. She was ready to take this charade as far as she could. He stood up and glared at her when she mentioned Tyana. He was getting that sick feeling in the pit of his stomach again. He was going to let her have it about her threats to Tyana, but instead he just walked out.

Charlotte felt she got his attention now. He stood just outside the door for a few moments, feeling his blood pressure rising. He was so angry he felt like doing something drastic. His body was shaking and he knew he had to get away from there immediately. He left and drove back to the hotel.

The next few weeks were rough for Tyana. She had her bouts with depression but managed to get back to work full force. She thought it would help to keep her mind off of things, but her job only distracted her temporarily. When she was home alone in the late evenings, she couldn't get her mind off her baby. Ellis was calling her every day still, trying to get her to reconsider and take him back. She wasn't returning his calls.

Charlotte and her doctor had determined that she had gotten pregnant when she and Ellis were in Madrid the first time. What Charlotte didn't know was that she had become pregnant just before Tyana had gotten pregnant in Hawaii. Charlotte thought about her situation long and hard. She was prepared to keep the baby. She was going to be the mother of Ellis' baby—not Tyana.

Tyana managed to get through her days by working long hours. She spent all of her available time searching for a house for herself. She didn't have much luck at first, but as her time was running out, she found the perfect house. It was ideal for her because it allowed her to incorporate her own unique personality into it. She was able to move in right away, which was convenient for her because now she wouldn't have to move twice. She needed to be out of the old house soon so the new owners could move in. She got to create a space in her new house that reflected her own style and flare and not that of Ellis' as well. She was going to design this house in a way that she desired and she was going to have a great time doing it. Once she moved in and got started redecorating, it became therapy for her. It kept her busy and preoccupied so she thought less about her lost baby and relationship. She thought of Ellis often and even missed him terribly, but she knew she had done the right thing for her. They were no longer the same people they were when they had met over ten years ago.

Theresa E. Liggins

Chapter Twenty

A month had gone by and Tyana was getting settled nicely in her new home. It was a new beginning for her now and she was ready to embrace her new life without Ellis and live on her own. Her business was doing great, she had spent a few days with her parents and Trevor and Kellie made sure she wasn't lonely. She didn't allow herself to think too much anymore about Ellis or the baby she'd lost. They were almost faint memories to her now. At least she wanted them to be. She was focused on looking ahead and keeping busy for her own sanity.

Charlotte was nearly three months pregnant now. She and Ellis were still working together as hard as ever. Ellis had come to terms with her decision to keep the baby, although he had disagreed because of the circumstances. She had decided to not tell Tyana about the baby as long as he cooperated and gave her what she needed when she needed it. He did just that. He would do anything to keep that news from reaching Tyana. He still loved her with all his heart and he longed for her each and every day. Nothing else mattered to him anymore, now that Tyana was no longer a part of his life. He had constant reminders of his foolish mistake every time he saw Charlotte and the subtle signs of her pregnancy. He had eventually moved out of the hotel and into a condo he had bought. Charlotte had requested a key to his condo and would usually show up at odd times of the night or day. He wasn't free to have a social life that didn't include her.

Charlotte particularly didn't like the fact that Ellis was non-responsive to her most of the time. She knew he was still thinking about poor Tyana. Of course, he gave in to her needs, but his coldness was beginning to irritate her. She thought he needed something exciting to happen in his life, something that would give him a reason to be more attentive and happy with her, especially in public. She knew she would be showing soon, so she insisted that they get married—and quickly. They would announce their marriage to one another and then he would have to show his excitement about her. And perhaps he would get used to the idea that this was something that he had to do and he would then begin to accept it and like it. She also considered the fact that once they were married, he could screw up if he wanted, but she would have access to his money whether it would be in the form of blackmail, alimony, or child support. She didn't care; she was actually banking on all three. He initially refused her proposal of marriage until she picked up the phone to invite Tyana to their wedding and baby shower. They left for Vegas the following weekend and got married.

Tyana was at work preparing for a major presentation for a potential client when her phone rang and interrupted her train of thought. She was momentarily flustered by the interruption, which broke her concentration.

"Tatyana speaking," she answered, sounding slightly uptight.

"Tyana, this is Antonio. Did I catch you at a bad time?" Tyana's heart skipped several beats and she dropped everything. Her mind was instantly cleared of any other thought that could distract her. It had been several months since she had seen or spoken to Antonio. She knew she had hurt him, turning him away, but with everything else going on in her life she had decided to leave him out of it. After the miscarriage she hadn't thought about anything else other than trying to pick up the pieces of her own life.

"Antonio…hi. No, you didn't, I mean, this is fine. How are you? It's so good to hear from you." She didn't know what to say to him.

"It's good to hear your voice, Tyana. I've thought about you a lot. I thought of calling but wasn't sure that it was the right thing to do. I'm surprised to find you still here, in Scottsdale, I mean. I took my chances calling. I thought you would be long gone to San Diego. Are you still moving? I was hoping to see you before you go."

"No, I didn't go to San Diego, I'm still here. In fact, I'm staying right here. I'm glad you called. I want to tell you that I'm sorry for everything and for complicating your life."

"You didn't complicate my life—you enhanced it. And, what do you mean, you're staying? Did something happen? Is everything all right?" He was confused by her comment and wanted to find out what it all meant.

"Well, it's a long story."

"I've got time.

"I don't know. It's rather personal. I don't know if I'm ready to talk about it. This isn't the time." Memories were starting to flood Tyana's head and she wasn't ready to open up just then.

"OK. Can I see you then? I'll understand if you don't want to but I would like that very much. We still have the competition in Florida coming up in about six weeks. I would still love to dance with you if that's possible." He didn't want to come across too personal with her just yet. He figured bringing up the competition would ease some of the tension for her and she would agree to see him. He knew how much she loved dancing.

"Well, I don't know...I had forgotten all about it. Time flies." She didn't know what to do.

"Tyana, just agree to see me and we can talk about it. That's all— no pressure. You still have lots of hours on the books and I just want you to take advantage of them. They're yours. Otherwise, we can make arrangements to refund the balance to you." She heard the sadness in his voice just then.

"OK. Sure, we can talk."

"Great, how about tonight? I'm free anytime you want. Just come by the studio and we'll talk. Any time."

"That sounds fine. I can come by around eight-thirty. Will that work?" she asked as she glanced at her schedule.

"Eight-thirty is perfect. I'll be here. Thanks so much, Tyana. I'll see you then." Antonio was prepared to cancel whatever he had scheduled in order to meet with her. He cleared his schedule for the rest of that evening just for her.

They hung up and it took several minutes before she could refocus on what she'd been doing before he called. She was now plagued with thoughts of Antonio and the last words they had spoken to each other when he divulged his attraction to her. How things had changed. Back then she was preparing to move to San Diego to be with Ellis. She was pregnant with Ellis' child. She was selling her business. She was fighting to ignore her own feelings for Antonio in order to concentrate on her relationship and her family.

After they were married, Charlotte moved in with Ellis but still kept her beach house. They would go there on weekends and holidays. Once she found out she was pregnant with Ellis' baby, she got rid of Carlos. She didn't want any distractions at that point. She replaced him with a less desirable housekeeper. When they returned from Las Vegas, they made their announcement to their co-workers, which came as a shock to most. Ellis' assistant was the most surprised by the announcement, having known about Tyana, although she had had her suspicions about Charlotte's interest in Ellis, given the amount of time she spent with him in his office and on trips. She was also the first one to suspect Charlotte's pregnancy and decided in her mind that this was a marriage out of respect for the baby and not love. Ellis' demeanor of late was anything but happy or content. He could usually be found locked up in his office, keeping to himself. His assistant could easily detect his depression and felt sorry for him. She had a feeling that he screwed up and got Charlotte pregnant, and knowing Charlotte the way most did, that he was now paying dearly for his mistake. On the other side of the floor, his new bride was glowing with pregnancy, as she would strut her blossoming figure around the office. Because of her firm body she was barely showing yet, but her naturally well-endowed breasts were definitely showing signs of growth.

Tyana drove up to the familiar dance studio, sat in her car and took a deep breath. She sat for several minutes before going inside. Her heart started to flutter just thinking about seeing Antonio again. What would she say? What would she do? Thoughts and questions were swimming in her head. She was admittedly a little nervous. She got out of her car and proceeded toward the entrance. Once inside, she saw the familiar scenes and felt a tugging at her heart.

"Tyana, it's good to see you again," said Antonio as he greeted her warmly. He had been waiting for her. And she was once again in the familiar arms of one she truly loved. His heart beat wildly for her the moment he saw her. He led her to his office to talk with her in private about her plans to continue to dance. He hadn't had very many opportunities to instruct someone as talented as Tyana. She had such a flair for dancing that it would be a shame if she didn't continue to pursue this art, he thought. Aside from how he felt about her personally, he respected her talent and wanted her to consider developing it further, especially since she was staying now. He had to convince her that he was sincere about her dancing since he had exposed his heart to her.

"How have you been? You look well. We've missed you around here. I've missed you around here. Can I get you something to drink?" He was a little nervous about seeing her again. He wasn't sure what to expect, given their last meeting. Tyana was nervous too, and felt she owed him some explanation but she wasn't sure how much information she was ready to share with him.

"I'm fine, thanks. Things are good; I'm doing well. I missed being here too, actually. I've been rather busy though with my work and buying and redecorating a house—real busy with that."

"Yes, you said you were staying here instead of moving to San Diego. I'm glad to hear that. It sounds like there's been a lot going on with you. Do you think you can manage to fit dancing back in your schedule? I mentioned that the Florida competition is coming up in about six weeks and I would like it very much if you would still consider participating. You've already paid for it and we've started most of your routines. But you can determine if you want to continue to do the number of dances we originally talked about or if you want to do less; it's up to you. I would like it very much if you would seriously think about doing it." He held his breath waiting for her to respond. He also was curious about the fact that she said she bought a new house. Was that for just her?

"Well, I've been away from dancing for a while now and I'm not sure that I can get back into that kind of schedule in time to make that date. Six weeks isn't very long when you're talking about preparing for a competition."

"Tyana, you're such a perfectionist. You're already a great dancer and it wouldn't take you long at all to get up to speed—you'll see. Once I get you back out on that dance floor it'll all come right back to you as if you'd never taken a day off. I would love to see you do it. You've worked so hard and I know you'll be ready for it. I know you'll perform beautifully. You know that yourself. You have to have more faith in yourself when it comes to this. Trust me. You're a natural and you possess so many skills already. Don't decide against it only because of time. We have time. Please consider this."

"I don't know Antonio." She paused and thought of them dancing together. She did miss dancing and especially dancing with him. She missed the excitement of competition and the feeling of accomplishment that it gave her. But most of all, she missed the satisfaction and joy it brought to her life. It fulfilled her. She needed something like that once again.

"OK, I'll consider it. But if I find that the schedule won't work with my work schedule, please respect my decision to change my mind." She knew she had no intentions of backing out on a commitment. She was giving her word to Antonio and she wouldn't think of letting him down. She felt she owed him and herself this dance.

"Great! Fantastic! Oh, you won't regret it. Thank you so much!" Antonio hugged her and felt a tingle up his spine. He was so happy that she would dance with him again. He wouldn't let her leave him this time. "When can we get started? How about tomorrow night? You set the time and we'll do it! Thanks again, Tyana." They made plans to resume practicing right away.

When Tyana left the dance studio after her first lesson since her return, she felt very different than when she'd gone in. All the magic she'd experienced previously had come flooding back. She hadn't realized how much she had missed dancing, not to mention, how much she'd missed being in Antonio's arms. They spent a great deal of time working on routines they had previously choreographed. She hardly missed a step.

After several more lessons, she felt for the first time that this was something she *needed* to do for herself instead of just something she wanted to do. It was more than just a hobby or a pastime. It had more meaning for her now. It was a part of her. It had been the missing piece of her life and now she had found it—for good. She wouldn't let anyone or anything take that away from her now. Although she had a rewarding business, Ellis had been a vital part of her life. But now, she finally felt a sense of purpose in her life again, and Antonio—as well as her dancing—was definitely a part of that purpose.

Ellis had spent a month in Madrid. Charlotte had gone out for only two weeks. Now that she was pregnant and showing, she didn't want to take any chances of overexerting herself or working too many crazy hours. She had cut back considerably, especially by her standards. She was determined to take care of this baby—it was her ticket to Ellis' bank accounts. She hadn't really developed any maternal feelings or instincts yet with her pregnancy. She had never thought that she would ever succumb to this type of lifestyle. It just wasn't for her. She had never understood all the hoopla over it and why women got so giddy about it. She wasn't looking forward to what it was about to do to her shrine of a body. She was very proud of her figure, and the fact that it was about to get all stretched out of shape didn't set well with her. But she would go through it for Ellis' money. She knew that there were other ways to get her mitts on his money, but when she learned that she was pregnant, she figured this would be the easiest means and wouldn't require too much creative deception on her part. He would be committed to her through their child.

Ellis and Charlotte were spending considerably less time together since the marriage. He was clearly depressed and was missing Tyana. He was spending quite a bit of time in Madrid, which was the only time he could get space from Charlotte. When they were together, Charlotte noticed the distance between them, emotionally and physically. Although her motive to secure his money was the driving force behind their union, she was beginning to feel different about their situation. She could sense how much he loved Tyana, which made her look at her life and where she'd come. She had never been in love before. She was used to having men at her disposal that she didn't take the time to fall in love with any of them. It was more of a conquest to her. And when a man would want emotional closeness with her, she would generally push him away. She hadn't thought too much about settling down with one man. But seeing Ellis reject her now gave her a new perspective on her life at her age. She wondered why she had insisted on the marriage. Did she really do it for the access to his money or were there underlying reasons? She was now questioning her motives, especially when she could see evidence of their baby growing inside of her. She thought it might have something to do with her pregnancy hormones because lately she would find herself missing Ellis when he was in Madrid. She wanted to share things about the baby with him. There was no one else she could talk to.

Charlotte was now almost four months pregnant and was scheduled for an ultrasound that morning. Ellis was still in Madrid but she figured it was a routine procedure and so she didn't request his presence. He was due back the following day anyway. Her belly had begun to grow rapidly, and her doctor had become concerned about her size and wanted to see if they were going to be dealing with a large baby. Ellis was six feet three inches tall, and Charlotte was five-nine. Chances were good that their baby would be bigger than the average size of a newborn.

Tyana and Antonio had been working hard for over a month now, preparing for the competition in Florida. Antonio was right; Tyana hadn't lost any of her ability to remember her steps or the techniques. They were both having a great time practicing their routines and choreographing new ones. They often worked late into the evenings until they were satisfied with the results. They were both perfectionists when it came to dancing. They wanted to do their absolute best and it showed. Since they were spending so much time together, they were becoming more comfortable with each other— getting to know more about each other. Tyana rarely talked about her personal life in terms of Ellis, but talked more about her career, her hobbies, her family, and her friends. They were getting closer as friends. Antonio was sharing parts of his personal life with her as well. He could tell she was being very careful with what she allowed him to know about her private life. He wouldn't push her—he'd wait. He still didn't know the whole truth about her staying on in Scottsdale instead of moving to San Diego, but he figured the reason was too difficult for her to talk about. Every time he saw her, he felt something inside that made him want to know more about her. There was no doubt anymore about what he was feeling for her, making his job as her dance instructor that much more difficult—to remain exclusively on a professional level with her.

As the competition got closer, Antonio arranged for special coaching to critique and enhance their routines. Tyana had ordered her custom-made costumes back when she'd agreed to do the competition, and now they were ready. She had become even more excited about the event once the costumes had arrived. They were exquisite. The details on each of them were amazing and labor-intensive. The beadwork and the rhinestones on each costume were strategically positioned, creating even more drama in the dresses. She could hardly believe that she would be dancing in costumes so extravagant. She couldn't wait to show Antonio. They had decided to have a dress rehearsal a few days before leaving for Florida.

Charlotte was stunned by the findings of her ultrasound. She was afraid to give that kind of news to Ellis over the phone. She would wait for him to come home before telling him. She didn't know how she would tell him, or how he would take it. She thought about it all that day and into the evening. The following morning, when she awoke from a restless, sleepless night she was still in shock and decided to stay home from work and wait for Ellis so they could deal with the news together. She told her office that she wasn't feeling well. She hadn't slept much from thinking about what her doctor had told her. She was overcome with emotions, magnified by her hormones, and cried until daybreak. When she looked at the clock it was seven-thirty. Ellis would be home in a few hours. She thought a lot about him as she waited. She knew he didn't love her, but loved only Tyana. She cried harder. She decided she wouldn't tell him of her newfound feelings for him. She knew that he was only going along with everything because of the baby—his baby. He wasn't going to turn his back on his child, even if it wasn't to be born to Tyana. Now she wasn't sure what her news would do to them as a couple, especially since she was coming to terms with wanting more with him.

The nights Ellis spent alone, without Charlotte, were the nights he dreamed of Tyana and their baby. Those nights were painful for him. Most of the time he would wake up in a cold sweat, calling out for Tyana. He would look around and reach for her, but she wouldn't be there. He had given up trying to contact her now that he was about to be the father of Charlotte's baby. He could never have Tyana in his life again the way he wanted her in his life without her finding out about that baby. Charlotte would make sure of that.

Ellis thought about Tyana during most of the flight. He wondered how she was doing and what was she doing. He often thought of just flying to Arizona to see her, but knew it would be too risky. He missed her so much. He also thought about his heavy workload and schedule. He would be back in San Diego for a month before returning to Madrid, but he had to attend a conference in Florida in two weeks, that he couldn't get out of. He was exhausted, mentally and physically, and needed some time to just be alone. But that wasn't possible for him right now. His job was demanding and Charlotte, was demanding, especially now with the pregnancy. She wasn't giving him even a second to think about Tyana.

It was nine a.m. when the plane landed in San Diego. He would go straight home to get some rest—at least he was hoping to, since he knew Charlotte would be at work. He drove directly home, thinking only of relaxing. When he pulled into the garage, he saw Charlotte's car. He didn't understand why she would be home and immediately grew concerned about the baby. He rushed out of the car and ran into the house. He found her resting quietly out on the patio. She looked even more pregnant than the last time he saw her, which had only been a few weeks ago. She had a strange look on her face. He went out to her.

"Hi, I'm finally home. What are you doing here—everything OK? Is the baby OK? What's going on?" Ellis was getting worried from the look on Charlotte's face. She looked as if she were in shock. She had stressed herself out anticipating Ellis' return home and having to give him the same news her doctor had given her. "What is it?" he asked again.

"Welcome home, Ellis. Would you like something to eat? I can have the cook make you something." Charlotte had insisted that they have a full staff, housekeeper/cook and gardener, especially since she was pregnant. She wasn't the domestic type.

"Charlotte, what's the matter? Why are you home? How's the baby? Did you have your appointment yesterday? What did they say?" He was growing impatient with her.

"Ellis, please sit down. I have something to tell you and it may be a little shocking to you; it was to me."

"Charlotte! Is the baby all right?!"

"Yes, yes," she paused, "the babies are fine."

"Babies?"

"We're having twins, Ellis."

Theresa E. Liggins

Chapter Twenty-one

Tyana and Antonio managed to get through all their training without incident. They were too focused on their goal to introduce any of the distractions of their personal lives or feelings. There were many times on the dance floor when they were enticed by the romance of the moment but they stayed focused, as if on a mission. They both knew how important this competition was, especially for Tyana. At the moment, that was all that mattered. They put everything they had into this competition. Antonio knew that it would be a chance to create greater things for the two of them. He would be patient enough to get through the competition without dealing with his emotional and physical attraction to her. He was confident that she still knew how he felt about her; he didn't want conversations about his feelings to disrupt their concentration.

For Tyana, this would be the start of something even greater for her. She wouldn't let anything interfere with her getting to this competition and doing well. She had never worked harder and with more pride and purpose. Throughout her life when she danced as a child, when she dreamed of dancing when she was a college student, and when she affirmed her love for dancing when she met Antonio, she knew she was born to be a dancer. It was in her blood, and this competition would be the cornerstone of her future. Her heart had grown even fonder of Antonio during this time together but she was certain that he knew; their bodies spoke the language of love. She didn't need the words right now. In the process of reaching their dancing goals, they had created a special friendship and bond between each other that only enhanced what they were feeling inside their hearts and on the dance floor.

Since learning that Charlotte was carrying his twins, Ellis had become more attentive toward her. He was now always around to take care of her and his babies no matter what. He was coming to terms with the fact that he was going to be a father instead of looking at the situation as just Charlotte being pregnant. He became more sensitive to her needs as his wife and mother-to-be. It was important to him that she take care of herself every day, and he would do what he could to see that she did.

While preparing to leave for the conference in Florida, Ellis had insisted many times that Charlotte stay at home and rest, but she wanted to go. This conference was important to her as well and neither one of them could really afford to miss it. She felt fine other than adjusting to her rapid growth. She felt uncomfortable a lot of the time, even in her second trimester. Ellis did what he could to help her with her discomfort, whether it would be rubbing her back or treating her to a full body massage at her favorite spa. She noticed the change in his behavior toward her; it was as if he now respected and accepted her as his wife. She found his efforts endearing and began to acknowledge her feelings toward him. Hearing the heartbeats of their babies together for the first time had also brought them closer. They both cried at the miracles growing inside of her. Although his thoughts still weren't far from Tyana, he had accepted responsibility for what he had done to her life and his own, for that matter, and didn't think that hating Charlotte any longer would change any of that. Most of his change of heart was a direct result of her pregnancy. Once he learned that she was carrying his twins and could hear their hearts beat, and could see them growing inside her, it all became very real to him. He was now obsessed with his babies and didn't want to play any part in bringing harm to them. He felt he had already caused one baby's death because of something he had done; he wasn't going to let that happen again. Ellis and Charlotte were on their way to Florida.

Antonio saw Tyana for the first time in her costumes as they prepared for their dress rehearsal. Words couldn't describe what Antonio felt inside when he saw her. She was like a vision from Heaven. Seeing her left him breathless for a moment. He couldn't stop staring at her as she gracefully approached him. She had that air of a dancer about her. Throughout her training she had refined her dance movements, which carried over to her own demeanor. It was as if she had been a dancer her whole life. In her mind, she had. With the completion of her dance school figures required for this competition, she had graduated multiple levels of dance programs in a very short period of time. She had managed to improve her dance skills at a rate most students couldn't imagined to be possible. It was like she had put her entire soul, heart, and spirit into her dancing. It was now a part of her. She had nothing else as far as she was

293

concerned. She had reduced her working hours considerably in order to achieve this accomplishment. It was the one thing she could claim for just herself that no one could destroy like Ellis had destroyed their relationship and their future. She protected this endeavor with everything she had. Antonio composed himself and they proceeded to dance flawless routines—one right after another. They were now ready for Florida.

A few days later, after arriving in Miami, they were ready to take the grand competition by storm. They were now unstoppable. They were existing on sheer excitement and adrenaline. She had a fearless and confident attitude about her, which was natural for her in situations like that. She had come to meet all her challenges with boldness and purpose. This was no different. With her skills, and a talented partner, she had nothing to worry about.

Charlotte and Ellis attended most of the segments of the conference throughout the week. The conference was being held at one of their properties in Miami Beach. It was a perfect setting for romance, although Ellis had never felt that way with Charlotte. But once he knew about her carrying his twins, his heart started to change ever so slightly. Most of that was because of the babies and not necessarily because of his feelings for her, at least at first. But now he was feeling differently about her, too, and was surrendering to the fact that he was married to her.

Once they got settled and relaxed, they decided to stay through the weekend for some much-needed rest and relaxation; sort of a mini-honeymoon. Charlotte was delighted to have some uninterrupted time alone with Ellis. Although she had felt the tension between them ease somewhat in the last weeks, she was hoping that their extended trip together would be what they needed to really get their marriage on track. She wanted them to start behaving more like a couple than like partners or co-workers. She knew that most of Ellis' concern and attention were for the babies and not for her. Under the circumstances, she accepted that.

Ellis had insisted that Charlotte keep her agenda light to avoid tiring herself out. He watched her closely and at the slightest hint of her looking tired, he would escort her back to their suite to rest. There he would stay with her and do what he could to make her comfortable. Those babies were the most important things to him now and everything else came second. The news of their marriage and pregnancy resonated throughout the conference, and everyone, although shocked, congratulated them and wished them well. A lot of Ellis' colleagues knew Tyana, and Ellis sensed their confusion and curiosity. Charlotte had a reputation for getting what she wanted, so most of them figured she had pursued him aggressively. There was gossip about them during their stints in Madrid regarding the amount of time she spent with him. Everyone suspected that she wanted in on his action, even though she was largely responsible for his success. She was experienced at conveniently putting herself in the right places to do just that. Ellis couldn't help but feel a little embarrassed of the innuendos he sensed during the conference. For the first time, Charlotte got a sense of what his relationship with Tyana had meant to him and others. Even now, with Tyana out of the picture, Tyana was still making a huge impact on Ellis' life and career. Not many were too concerned about Charlotte's role as Ellis' wife or the fact that she was pregnant, other than as a topic for gossip. Some of them just left that situation alone as if they didn't really care at all. And although he was still bitter about her manipulative ploys to rattle his relationship with Tyana, he was still married to her and tried to shield her from some of the comments and criticism that came her way about her new position as his wife and mother of his baby. He didn't want anything to upset her now. He was extremely protective of her and the babies. No one at the conference knew about them having twins.

Although Tyana usually had nerves of steel in a situation like that, she was a little nervous about the fact that her big weekend meant staying at one of the hotel properties that Ellis worked for. She knew the chances of running into him there were remote because he would probably either be in San Diego or Madrid, but she still was a little uneasy about being there. It was a reminder for her of what her life was once about. Those feeling of uneasiness wouldn't last long before Antonio would consume her time and occupy her mind with dancing—practicing for the big event.

The first thing they did when they unpacked was head to the restaurant for lunch. They ate outside where they could have an unobstructed view of the beach and ocean. It was calming and beautiful. It was the first opportunity in a long time for Tyana to just sit and relax. Her mind wandered way out into the ocean's horizon. She stayed that way for several minutes, as if she was connecting with something out there.

"Tyana, where did you go?" asked Antonio, watching her and noticing her tranquil expression; she had a kind of solemn cast about her. There was something different about her, he thought, as he watched her carefully. He couldn't put his finger on what it was but it was something he hadn't seen in her before. It was something very profound and almost sad.

"Oh, I'm sorry. I guess my mind wandered, thinking about the competition." That was the best she could come up with. It was the first time in long while that she had thought about her baby. Thinking of her lost unborn baby made her think about Ellis and Charlotte and the day she caught them together. It made her sick to her stomach. Her doctor had often suggested that she seek psychological counseling to deal with her losses—the baby and her relationship— but she never bothered. She just wanted to put it out of her mind. She turned her thoughts back to Antonio. "Well, what should we order?"

"Somehow I didn't get the impression that you were thinking about the competition at all. I know you're not worried about your performance, and the look on your face was not exactly one of excitement. So, what's wrong? We're in this magnificent setting, getting ready to perform in a beautiful grand ballroom of this exquisite hotel. What could be troubling you at this moment? And I want the truth this time," he said as he smiled at her.

297

Just then the waiter approached their table, so Tyana quickly glanced at her menu to give her order. Antonio smiled at her, knowing that she had caught a break—but just for a minute. After they ordered, a woman who recognized Antonio approached their table and they engaged in conversation with her. Tyana thought to herself that she needed to be careful to not let her mind wander like that again. At least she shouldn't get caught doing it.

The dance heats that they were entered in were to begin at eight that evening. They had time to get in some more practice and then they returned to their rooms to change. Antonio reached Tyana's room promptly to escort her down to the ballroom. She was doing her smooth dances that evening and she chose a beautiful black and gold gown to dance the fox trot, tango, waltz, and the quick step. Her dress, hair, makeup, nails, and accessories were impeccable. Antonio felt a fluttering in his stomach when he saw her. He was beaming from ear to ear, proud to be her escort and dance partner. They headed to the magnificent grand ballroom, where they turned heads from the moment they stepped out of the elevator and from the second they stepped onto the dance floor. There they had the attention of the entire audience and the judges. They danced one flawless routine after another. By the end of the evening they were extremely pleased with all their performances. One set down, one to go.

To end the evening of a perfect day, they decided to have a late night cocktail out by the beach. The night air was warm and breezy. The dark sky was full of bright stars sprinkled all over the universe. There was a certain electricity in the air and Tyana was feeling it as

298

she sat across from Antonio with the sound of the ocean waves in the background. She was having that weird familiar feeling once again, as if she had been with him previously in this setting, with the moon, the water, and the sounds of the ocean. She just sat there staring at him, trying to figure out why she was experiencing this again. It was so much stronger this time. Then it vanished.

"What's the matter? Are you feeling OK? Is it your drink?" Antonio wasn't sure what to ask her based on the far-off, strange look he saw on her face. He was now convinced that she was holding something back that was significant enough to absorb and divert her mind even at this moment. He wanted to know what it was. "Let's go take a walk on the beach." He got up and took her hand. He paid for their drinks and then led her out to the beach, where they began to walk in the sand. He was still in his tux, she in her ballroom gown. They looked like Cinderella and Prince Charming. Antonio was practicing great restraint with her, knowing that they still had another evening of competition dancing and not wanting to compromise her trust in him as her instructor and dance partner. They'd worked too hard to blow their concentration now. He wasn't sure what her plans were after the competition; they had been too busy working toward this event to even talk about it. He was still hoping to talk her into an instructor position at his studio. Once she was properly trained, he was convinced she would be an excellent dance teacher. Personality-wise, she was of the caliber he could only dream of having in his studio. He also wanted more with her. He wanted much more.

Theresa E. Liggins

"Tyana, you danced so beautifully tonight. I have never been more proud. Everyone was focused solely on you tonight out there on that dance floor. And it's very obvious why." He put her arm in his as they continued to walk along the sandy beach.

"You're too kind, Antonio. But I did feel I did well tonight—it was a good night. We danced well." Her mind was going a thousand miles a minute. Then suddenly she began feeling anxious about something. She didn't know what it was but she just had a strong feeling that something was wrong. The feeling was all around her. She was beginning to shiver in the warm ocean air.

"What is it? Are you all right? Do you want to go back?" asked Antonio, stopping to face her. She nodded her head. He saw tears in her eyes.

"I'm not sure what's the matter with me. I just feel overwhelmed by something—I'm just not sure what. I should go back to my room and go to bed. I need to be rested for tomorrow. We have a big day ahead of us tomorrow. The Latin heats take a lot of energy and I plan to do well." They turned back and headed toward the hotel.

"You're an amazing dancer, Tyana; of course you'll do better than just well. Right now you are the envy of just about everyone else out there on that floor. I'm walking on a cloud because I get to dance with you. You make me excited about dancing and especially competition dancing. I don't have to hold back with you. You're a strong dance partner and you allow me to dance at the level where I'm most comfortable. It's just so easy with you, Tyana. Thank you for

300

coming here and dancing with me." Antonio looked deep in her eyes when he said that. They walked on.

When they reached the hotel, he escorted her back to her room, where he left her with a warm embrace. He walked slowly back to his own room, thinking only of her. He knew something was troubling her and he was hoping she would let him in on whatever it was. He wanted only happiness for her. She was definitely a special woman to him and he wanted to be part of her life—in many ways.

Ellis and Charlotte left one of the other ballrooms where they were attending the conference. The hotel was catering a formal dinner and dance for the conference attendees and their guests. It was the last night of the conference, but they were staying over the weekend to relax and enjoy the sights in Miami Beach. They returned to their room after saying goodnight to their colleagues. It had been a long day for Charlotte and she was ready to go to bed. Ellis left her momentarily to fill their ice bucket. He knew she would get thirsty in the middle of the night.

Antonio turned the corner to the corridor that led to his room. He was so deep in thought about his evening with Tyana that he didn't see the gentleman he almost bumped into. "Oh, excuse me," said Antonio, moving slightly out of the way.

"Pardon me," said Ellis, giving Antonio a courteous nod.

Theresa E. Liggins

Chapter Twenty-two

Tyana awoke still feeling strange about being in that hotel. She wanted nothing more than to get the competition over with so she could get out of there. She had gotten through many weeks and months of not thinking about Ellis but that weekend he was all she could think about. At times she thought she could even smell his scent. These thoughts were starting to make her feel extremely unsettled. She needed to remain fully focused in order to get through her dances with her usual intensity. She lay in bed pondering her paranoia until she realized the late hour of the morning. She was supposed to meet Antonio for breakfast in forty-five minutes. She needed to get herself together and concentrate on performing well. It was her final night of competition and her final days in an opulent atmosphere, dancing with the man she secretly loved.

Charlotte woke up before Ellis; she felt restless. She got out of bed and walked to the balcony, where she looked out onto the sandy beach as the warm coastal breeze filled their room. It was a remarkable view of the ocean and beach below. She stood there taking in the marvelous view, feeling the tepid sun rays on her body. All of a sudden she felt a weird stirring inside her, which quickly turned into a fluttering. It continued for several seconds before she realized she was feeling her babies move inside her body for the first time. She gasped. She held her modestly swollen belly with one hand as she cupped her mouth with the other hand in astonishment. She began to get emotional when she felt Ellis' hand on her shoulder behind her.

"What's wrong, Charlotte? Is there a problem?" he asked, not knowing why she was standing like that. Tears fell from her eyes and her bottom lip quivered slightly as she turned to face Ellis.

"It's the babies. I felt them move for the first time. It was so amazing and precious. I never knew it would be like this. It's such a wonderful feeling." Charlotte was so caught up in the miracle moment that she could hardly compose herself. She also couldn't believe that she was reacting so emotionally to pregnancy. Her entire life she had only viewed pregnancy as a nuisance and inconvenience. She had never thought she would ever burden herself with it, but here she was in the middle of a miracle.

"Really? Oh, Charlotte, that's wonderful. How do you feel? Are they moving right now?" Ellis was becoming excited.

"There they go again. Put your hand here," she said, taking his hand and placing it gently on her belly at the point of the movement. "There! Did you feel that?"

"Yes! Yes, I did! Wow! That's amazing. I feel it again! Oh my God, this is so beautiful, sweetheart." He didn't realize what he had said at first. This was the first time he had acknowledged her by any endearing name. They were both surprised by it, but more surprised by the moment they were sharing, feeling her protruding belly move about. Ellis looked lovingly into Charlotte's eyes and kissed her softly on her lips. She had longed to touch his lips with hers. It had been so long since they had been intimate. Sure, they'd had sex at her request, but it was far from being intimate. They were now sharing an intimate moment and her body was feeling the effects of his kiss. He began to kiss her more passionately after a few moments. He slowly lured her back to the king-sized bed they shared and gently made love to her as the warm breeze continued to fill their room.

"Did you sleep well last night?" inquired Antonio, thinking about Tyana's preoccupation when they had been strolling along the beach the night before.

"Yes, I did. How about yourself? It's such a beautiful morning," she said as she looked out at the blue sky, white sands, and turquoise water.

"I slept well and yes, it is a beautiful morning, now." He wasn't shy about letting her know that he meant her. "Are you ready to do it this afternoon? We have ten heats, then the awards ceremony and banquet this evening. That's usually a very spectacular event at these more prestigious competitions. Tomorrow is our day for recuperating from the late-night celebration parties and we can either do some sightseeing or get in some beach time. It's up to you what you prefer." They were scheduled to fly out early Monday morning. "So far, this has been an enjoyable trip, and I thank you for making it possible."

"Yes, it has. I'm happy to be here and doing what I love. I'm having a great time. Thank you. And yes, I'm looking forward to tonight. I'm ready. But right now, I'm ready for a light breakfast."

They ordered their breakfast and continued to talk about the competition and the people they'd met. Tyana was surprised, however, that Heather wasn't participating in this event. She hadn't seen her around the studio lately and wondered what had happened to her. It didn't matter. She was just relieved that she was no longer around to latch herself onto Antonio.

Ellis and Charlotte didn't leave the room until several hours later. They lay in bed making love most of the morning, creating a new bond between them, which included their babies now. It was the first time in a long time—since Tyana had left him, in fact—that he had felt happy about something, and he felt alive inside once again. He had never told Charlotte that he loved her, but she knew he loved their babies and she would give him time to fall in love with her. That didn't matter to her right now. He was her husband and the father of her babies. She was happy about that.

Charlotte and Ellis took in the sights, did some shopping, and lay on the beach that afternoon.

Tyana and Antonio prepared for their final heats, which were ten Latin dances. They would dance the cha-cha, samba, pasa doble, bolero, and rumba. They would dance each dance twice; they had created two separate routines for each dance. They had worked extremely hard in a short period of time to get ready for this competition at the level she was competing in. The routines they chose weren't particularly difficult but would focus on the more advanced steps associated with each dance. Tyana was a whiz at mastering those steps. That's what made working with her a joy for Antonio. Usually he had to create a more cumbersome routine in order to compensate for the lack of the level of skills in the students he had to work with. She was indeed a treasure to him. He wouldn't let her get away from him again. The heats were about to begin.

Antonio's mouth dropped open when he saw Tyana in her Latin dance costume and in full makeup. Her body complimented the form-fitting, sexy costume perfectly. The dress accentuated the sensual curves of her body in an alluring, yet modest way. He was certain he hadn't seen a sexier woman in his life. This was becoming a night to remember for him.

The competition that night was grueling. The energy level was high and the excitement contagious. The judges had a tough job before them evaluating the dancers as they exhibited their best performances for them as well as for the spectators. Although the competition was quite nerve-racking and strenuous, everyone was having a great time on the floor. Tyana and Antonio were quickly becoming the crowd's favorite. They were dancing with precision, they were exotic, expressive, sexy, and seemed to be in perfect synchronization with each other as if they had been dancing together for years. They looked so natural together that many thought they must have had a long-standing dancing relationship. Antonio felt the same way when he danced with her. It was as if he had been dancing with her for a lifetime. She was the dancer of his dreams. They were approaching their last few heats.

Charlotte and Ellis had cleaned up after the full afternoon of lounging on the beach and shopping in the many nearby upscale shops. Even being pregnant, Charlotte was still one of the sexiest women on the beach. Her golden tan only enhanced the pregnancy glow, which was now a part of her aura. Ellis also thought she was just as sexy as ever. They ate dinner at an exclusive restaurant, then headed back to the hotel because she had become tired. As they strolled through the hotel lobby they noticed all the people in elaborate gowns and tuxes going in and out of the grand ballroom. They learned that there was a dance competition taking place, and Charlotte thought it would be fun to go inside and see a real live dance competition. It was amazing to see all the beautiful costumes that were being worn by these dancers. The sparkle from all the rhinestones, beads, sequins, and glitter was almost blinding. A person was drawn in just by the ambience alone. Ellis was hesitant at first, thinking about Tyana and her dance lessons. He was thinking about how he never paid any attention to her when she would try to tell him about her new hobby. He was always too busy to hear about it or to see what she was doing. He remembered how excited she had seemed about this dancing thing, but it didn't interest him; therefore, he had ignored her on many occasions. He was now wondering if she was still dancing. He was also wondering if she ever thought about him.

Ellis finally gave in to Charlotte's curiosity and purchased two tickets to watch the event. He was worried about Charlotte getting too worn out but she assured him that if she felt tired, they would leave. They didn't have far to go anyway, so she didn't see the harm in sitting and watching the competition for a while. They went in.

It was Tyana and Antonio's last dance of the competition. After the pro/am division, the professionals would dance. There was so much talent in that ballroom it was mind-boggling. Tyana and Antonio took to the floor for their rumba dance. They were accompanied by five other couples. They were all in their positions before the music started, and soon the dancing began.

The first rumba routine they had done earlier created a mood between them that was hard to defy. They were being pulled into each other's souls, feeling the constant tugging at their hearts. At times it was difficult to concentrate on their routine and they almost forgot about the judges and the other dancers. They caught themselves several times taking the routine beyond just dancing the steps. Of course, she scored extremely high because their performance was so convincing and appeared so natural. No one knew that these two were really in love and together were dancing the real dance of love.

This sensual dance routine would again pose the same challenges for them and they knew it as they looked into each other's eyes before taking the first step. Antonio squeezed Tyana's hand tighter and looked at her with love in his eyes, and she smiled back at him in the same way. They stepped closer in to each other until their bodies touched, and they stared hard into each other's eyes with an alluring look of fiery intensity. There was such incredible sexual tension between them that it only made them dance with more of the same fire that had been building inside them. At that point, it was hard to know where their dancing ended and their sexual desire for each other began.

Because of Tyana's dramatic costume and her accentuated makeup, Charlotte didn't recognize her on the floor, nor did she recognize Antonio from the pictures she had received from her private investigator. There was so much going on, and she wasn't paying close attention to any one particular person. But Ellis was. He almost leaped out of his chair when he spotted her. He was instantly very nervous and uncomfortable. And there he was with a very pregnant Charlotte, knowing what he had done to Tyana and their baby. He knew he had to get out of there. He tried to talk Charlotte into leaving but she was persistent about staying. She really wanted to see the professionals dance. Ellis finally calmed down and decided they would stay. He figured he was safe in the audience of thousands, and the chances of Tyana seeing him were practically nil; but all the while, he was shaking inside. Seeing her brought to the surface how much he loved her and how much he had hurt her. He was ashamed of himself. He wanted to hold her again; he wanted to make love to her again; he wanted to marry her.

When the music stopped and the dancers slowed their movements to a halt, Tyana and Antonio held each other in a loving embrace that was designed for the routine. Little did they know that when they choreographed this routine it would become the most natural routine for them to perform. It was real for them—too real. When they broke their stance they were breathing very heavily. It was their last dance and it was all over—for them the competition had ended. They knew they had done well and they were partly relieved that it was now behind them. Antonio leaned into Tyana and kissed her gingerly on her forehead as they continued to hold their embrace. Ellis watched with heightened curiosity and instantly felt an ache in the center of his heart. Not only was he curious about her relationship with the man she was dancing with, but he was astounded by her dancing—the skill with which she danced and her ability to show that she owned the floor. He had no idea that she could do that. He was saddened further by not knowing that this talent existed in her. How could he have ignored her to that degree? He could only hate himself more. They continued to watch as the professionals took to the floor. Antonio and Tyana would wait now for their results, which would be announced during the banquet. They would leave the ballroom to change and return afterwards to watch some of the other performances before attending the banquet.

The performances were over around nine, and Ellis and Charlotte decided to head back to their room to relax. Antonio had reached Tyana's room to escort her to the banquet. He was still basking in their moment on the dance floor. When she opened the door she appeared before him dressed in a breathtaking after-five beaded cocktail gown that complimented her shape and showed off her long legs through the slit in the side that traveled up to her thigh. She allowed her long, dark hair to flow down her back like a cascading waterfall. She was a vision of beauty. He couldn't be more excited to

311

be her escort for their entire weekend in Miami—but particularly because she was the love of his life. Antonio was in his tux, which always set off his dark eyes. He was an extremely handsome and sexy man with striking and intimidating looks. She felt especially honored to be escorted by him, aside from the fact that she was in love with him. They headed down to the banquet.

Charlotte and Ellis were headed to the elevator to return to their room. As they stood in the lobby waiting for the elevator, Ellis continued to look in all directions for any sight of Tyana. He wanted to get Charlotte back to their room as quickly as possible before they would run into her. He looked very nervous as they waited.

"Ellis, what's the matter? Why are you acting like you're looking for or hiding from someone? You seem so anxious about something. Did you forget something?" Charlotte noticed him acting fidgety.

"No, nothing's wrong. I just can't wait until this elevator gets here so we can get back to the room. All of a sudden, I feel so tired. I just want to lie down." He wasn't sure how convincing he was but he had to get himself together and back to their room before he had a heart attack. The elevator doors opened and they were just about to step in when Tyana and Antonio stepped out.

"Ellis? What are you…" Just then Tyana saw Charlotte standing next to him holding his hand; she saw the familiar expensive bracelet on her wrist. There was silence as her eyes widened when they traveled down to Charlotte's swollen belly and stopped. Tyana stood frozen, still clinging onto Antonio in the elevator. She was stunned and she felt as if her heart had stopped. She cupped her hand to her mouth and started shaking violently. She looked as if all the blood had drained from her body. Antonio couldn't quite understand what was happening as he looked at Ellis, the same man he had bumped into a little while ago, then looked back at Tyana, seeing the look of horror on her face. As the elevator doors were beginning to close, Ellis stopped them and Tyana was jolted from her trance and ran out of the elevator with tears streaming down her face. She just ran and ran.

"Tyana, wait!" shouted Ellis, turning sharply to look at Charlotte then back toward Tyana. Charlotte couldn't believe what was happening. It was all so fast and she began to feel sick herself. The last time Tyana had seen her was when she was in a compromising position with Ellis in his hotel suite and Tyana had walked in on them. And now she had just been standing right in front of them both, with Charlotte looking obviously pregnant with Ellis' baby. Charlotte hadn't expected anything like that to happen. She had not recently thought of seeing Tyana again and especially not while standing with Ellis and pregnant! In the past, she would have probably orchestrated a moment like that, but things were different with her now. The pregnancy had changed her and given her a new perspective on her life, especially her life with Ellis.

Ellis started to run after Tyana, but Antonio, not quite sure what was going on, stopped him and he ran after her himself. She bolted out the doors that led out to the back patio and beach. She ran as fast as she could in her heels, holding her gown up and still crying.

Antonio was right behind her. Ellis started to follow them but Charlotte stopped him.

"Don't Ellis. Not now. Let him go after her. You can talk to her later but right now I don't think it's a good idea. She's really shaken up. She just saw us together and she saw that I'm pregnant. Give her some space right now. This was too much for her to absorb all at once." Charlotte rubbed his arm and guided him back to the elevator. He knew she was right but he felt completely responsible.

"Tyana, wait. Tyana, please stop, please talk to me." Antonio had caught up to her and stopped her. He turned her around to face him. She looked as if she had seen a ghost. She was still shaking. Antonio quickly took off his jacket and placed it around her shoulders and put his arm around her as well. There were a few couples in love walking along the beach, passing by them. "Let's sit down over there." Antonio pointed to a private area of the beach. He was still trying to determine what had just happened, but could figure out that the man at the elevator was Ellis. He wasn't sure of the status of their relationship but knew she hadn't moved to San Diego with him. He wondered, though, why he was in Florida. It was killing him to see her like that and he was going to get the truth out of her this time. He wasn't leaving Miami until he did. He wasn't leaving that beach until he did.

He helped her sit down and he sat down very close to her and held her as she continued to sob into his chest. He rocked her slowly and waited for her to catch her breath. He spoke softly to her.

"Tyana, I'm sorry about whatever it is that has upset you. I take it that the man we saw in there was Ellis. You weren't expecting to see him, obviously. I'm here as your friend. Please consider telling me what he did and why he's here. I have all night—I'm not leaving you for one second." He took his handkerchief from his pocket and wiped the tears from her face. Seeing her like that only intensified his love for her. He was hurting inside just knowing how much she was hurting. He pulled her closer into him so he could wrap his arms around her securely. From that moment on, he was going to protect her from as much pain as he could. He was certain of that. Tyana began to speak but was barely audible. She took a deep breath and looked down at the sand.

"We broke up several months ago after he moved to San Diego. I was preparing to move there with him, as you know. I showed up one weekend so we could look for a house and I caught him having sex, with that woman he was with, in our hotel suite. He got my arrival time mixed up and apparently wasn't expecting me until later." She cried some more over the pain of that moment seared into her memory. After a few moments she regained her composure and continued. Antonio held her tighter after hearing her nightmare.

"I was pregnant at the time." Antonio's body stiffened when he heard her say she was pregnant. He was shocked to learn that. "But when I walked in on them, I was so stunned, I just ran out and ran down the stairs to escape that horrible scene. As I was running down the stairs I lost my footing and fell down about six stairs, hit my head and passed out. When I awoke, I was in the hospital. I had..." She paused again then spoke this time through her pain while crying out loud. "I had lost our baby." Her voice trailed off and she cried from her heart. She hadn't gotten over that loss. It was just as painful at that moment for her as it was when it happened. She had just realized that fact. Antonio cried with her.

"Oh, Tyana, honey, I'm so sorry. I had no idea you've been through so much. I'm truly sorry. Everything's going to be all right. I promise you." He stroked her hair as he held her tighter. He wanted to protect her from anything like that ever happening to her again.

"I left him and decided to stay in Scottsdale and make a life for myself without him. I haven't spoken to him since, although he's tried to contact me to apologize and beg for me to take him back. We have nothing left. I would never be able to trust him again, nor would I be able to get that image of the two of them out of my head. It was awful and so painful." She paused. "And they're here. I had a bad feeling when I got here that something was going to happen—I could feel it. And now I see him here, with her. And she's obviously pregnant—with his baby, I'm sure. She looks as if she's as far along as I would have been." She continued to cry over the situation that had caused the demise of her relationship with Ellis.

"Antonio, it hurts so much. It hurts so much." She hugged Antonio back.

"I know, sweetheart. I know." He didn't want to complicate her life any further, but he could no longer hold back what was in his heart.

"Tyana, I want to help you through this. You don't need this kind of pain in your life. You're an exceptional woman with a beautiful heart and soul—I see that in your dancing and from our developing friendship. You didn't deserve what happened to you. I don't know all the details, but I do know he was a fool to have done that to you. I can't imagine anyone doing that to you. You're so beautiful, warm, sexy, intelligent, passionate..." he pulled her face toward his so he could look at her eyes. "Tyana, I don't want to make this emotional time in your life any more complicated for you but I can't stand by to see you hurt like this and do nothing. I don't know if this is the appropriate time but..." He wiped the tears from her face as well as his own and took a deep breath. She looked at him and she knew. "I love you, Tyana. I love you. I have fallen in love with you and have known for a long time now and I can't hold it in any longer. I want to comfort you in the way my heart guides me to but I needed you to know how I feel about you first. I love you." Antonio looked out toward the ocean sounds. He held his breath. He was so relieved that it was out but he was so scared at the same time.

"I love you too, Antonio. I've always felt it." Antonio couldn't believe what she had just said to him. She could hardly believe, herself, what was happening, but she could no longer hold back her feelings either. It had been a long time coming. He looked back into her eyes again and she repeated it. "I love you, Antonio." He leaned down and kissed her softly on her moist lips. She kissed him back. Tears streamed down her cheeks again but this time they were tears of joy. He had tears of happiness as well. He pulled her closer to his body and kissed her more passionately. She instantly forgot about Ellis and Charlotte and followed her heart right to Antonio where she was happy to stay. They clung to each other for a very long time, hearing the ocean waves in the distance. Not another word was said. They just hung onto each other and kissed while the full moon shone down on them like a spotlight, as the sensual sounds of the ocean created music and their hearts began to dance to its rhythm. Then, instinctively and slowly, they danced under the stars, still kissing each other passionately, until Antonio picked her up and carried her back to the hotel—to his room.

Ellis couldn't just stand by and not do or say something. He left the room and went down to the lobby to look for her. He needed to apologize to her and let her know that he still loved her and was sorry for his mistakes. Charlotte knew she couldn't stop him, so she didn't try. She stayed behind and waited for him to return. He reached the lobby and waited. After a few moments, he saw Antonio carrying her back into the hotel. He stood back out of sight to see what was happening. When Antonio reached the elevator doors, Ellis started to approach them to see if Tyana was OK, but he saw Antonio give her a kiss on her lips and she willingly and lovingly kissed him back. Ellis backed away and just watched them as they got onto the elevator. He couldn't take his eyes off of the two of them as the doors closed. He couldn't help but see that they were in love. He turned away, knowing he had lost the best thing that had ever happened to him. He had a great thing with her and he blew it. He sat in the bar and had a few drinks, thinking about Tyana and their life together—how she had stolen his heart the moment he had laid eyes on her. He thought of their many adventures—how happy they had been together. He couldn't believe he had destroyed all that. He then thought of his marriage to Charlotte and the impending birth of their twins. He knew he now had to release Tyana from his heart but he needed to tell her what was in his heart. He needed to let her know that he still loved her and cared about her. He went to the front desk and got some paper, returned to the bar and began to write Tyana a letter.

Antonio reached his door and eased Tyana down onto her feet. He looked seriously into her eyes as he spoke to her. "Tyana, I love you and I want to open my heart, my soul, and my life to you. I don't want you to go through that door with me without you knowing that, and only if you're ready." He was sincere with his words.

"I know. I love you too and want to open my heart, my soul, and my life to you too. I am ready." She smiled up at him. He unlocked the door, picked her up, and carried her into the room.

He placed her carefully on his bed and laid her back against the pillows. He removed his tie, then his shirt; she removed her dress as he removed his pants. Just seconds later they lay naked against each other as they continued to kiss passionately while exploring each other's bodies. Soon they were hungry for more as their bodies were responding to all the very sensual touching. He explored her body with his mouth, causing her to writhe from the sensation of his tongue. She had never wanted another man the way she desired him at that moment. She explored his body as well, kissing him all over. She fondled him while he fondled her. Their loins were burning from the anticipation of sharing their love for one another, from the sexual tension that had been mounting between them for a very long time. Antonio, no longer wanting to wait another minute to connect with Tyana's soul, kissed her lips, then looked into her eyes and spoke quietly to her.

"Tyana, I adore you; I love you. I want only you and all of you." With that, he entered her slowly as he kissed her eyes, her nose, her chin, then her lips. She moaned with pleasure as she received him, simultaneously opening her heart. She hadn't opened her heart to any man since Ellis, and now she would let Antonio in. While the post-competition celebration was underway downstairs in the hotel ballroom, Antonio and Tyana were engaging in their own private celebration of their love for one another upstairs in the sanctuary of their hearts.

"I love you too, Antonio." She could say nothing further before he kissed her hard on her lips. They made love like neither had made love with anyone before. The moment was magical and so full of love. They felt the magic and knew they had something very special. They had something that no one could ever take from them. They held each other tightly as they indulged themselves in their love. They made love all night and into the early morning until they fell asleep with their bodies entwined.

Ellis had finished his letter to Tyana and slipped it under her hotel room door. He then returned to his pregnant wife and slipped into bed as she slept. He lay awake most of the night thinking about Tyana. He would occasionally watch Charlotte as she slept, placing his hand gently on her belly. At one point the babies moved and he leaned over and kissed her gently on her forehead and whispered, "I love you." Tyana was no longer his to love. He had to let her go from his heart, but never from his spirit. His place was with his family now. He fell asleep with his hand on Charlotte's belly, close to his babies.

Tyana and Antonio awoke a few hours later. She now had a feeling of serenity despite the rocky start to the previous evening. She looked at Antonio without saying a word and smiled. She was home. He smiled back at her as he held her. Although they had satisfied one another several times throughout the night, he desired her once again. And she was more than willing to express her love to him. They engaged in a morning of eternal passion until they both echoed the sounds of love from the depths of their souls. Their lust was quickly transforming into a profound and undeniable passion unknown to either before now. They were developing a bond that couldn't be severed by any mortal. Antonio closed his eyes as a single tear fell onto Tyana beneath him. She had been crying, herself, because she was feeling completely safe and truly loved now. It felt so right. She was having no doubts whatsoever. She couldn't believe that she could fall in love again and so completely. Being with Antonio felt comfortable, in the same way she felt comfortable with him on the dance floor. It was as if her dream had come true. In fact, she felt completely connected to Antonio, as if he were meant for only her. She cried tears of joy.

"Tyana, this is amazing. I've never known love to be like this before. What we have between us is very special and I want you to know that I'll always be right here for you. I'm not going anywhere. Having you in my life is like a dream come true for me. I've looked all my life for you and I'm glad that you walked into it when you did. I need you, Tyana. I love you." She started to say something but he interrupted her with a kiss on her lips. They lay in bed for a long while just kissing.

It was nearly noon when Tyana and Antonio decided that they should get up and get out and share their first day as a couple together, and the last day of their weekend in Florida, seeing Miami Beach. They were both so excited about their new relationship they could barely contain their enthusiasm. Tyana reluctantly left Antonio's room to return to her room to take a shower, change, and get ready to embark on a new life with him.

While Tyana was gone, the competition results were delivered to Antonio's room. He wasn't surprised that Tyana had received first place standings in all her heats. He was overjoyed and couldn't wait to tell her. He was grinning from ear to ear, reminiscing about the whole evening that had led to their union.

When Tyana returned to her room she found a folded piece of paper on the floor just inside the door. She picked it up slowly, wondering what it was and who could have put it there. She unfolded it and recognized the handwriting. It was a letter from Ellis. She slowly sat down on her bed and began to read:

My Dear Tyana,

I can't begin to tell you how sorry I am that I hurt you like this. Please believe me when I say that I never intended to break your heart but I know I have. When I saw you last night on the elevator I saw the pain in your eyes when you looked at me. You have no idea how much I wanted to hold you and pray to God that I could do something to take that pain away. But I couldn't. I knew right then that you could no longer love me after what I did to you. Tyana, I have thought about you every single day since we last saw each other.

You probably don't want to know any of this but I feel I need to tell you the whole truth. I've lied to you for so long and I hate myself for doing it. You did nothing but love me and trust me and I destroyed that. You did nothing wrong in our relationship. It was my greed that came between us. I did a stupid thing and I am truly sorry. I'll be sorry for it for the rest of my life.

I got involved with Charlotte in the process of wanting more power, fame, and money. I didn't realize at the time what I was getting myself into and it just got out of hand. Oh, baby, I can't tell you how sorry I am that it happened.

Charlotte became pregnant. When you saw her last night at the elevator, I know that it must have come as a shock to you seeing her like that and seeing me with her. I should have told you a long time ago but I didn't want to hurt you further, but yet I did anyway. We got married about a month ago. I didn't love her or want to get married but she insisted and threatened to tell you about the pregnancy if I didn't marry her and acknowledge her pregnancy. I couldn't let her do that. I didn't want you to know after what I did to you and our baby. I thought I could hide everything from you because I loved you so much and didn't want to hurt you any more than I had. Tyana, I am sorry. I am so sorry.

After seeing you with that guy last night, when he carried you back into the hotel, I saw the love in your eyes for him and in his for you. I'm happy for you, Tyana. You deserve to have all the happiness in the world. I don't expect you'll ever forgive me for what I did to you, our baby, and our relationship. I'll live

with that pain for the rest of my life. I just hope that
now you'll be happy once again.
I love you, Tyana. I always will.
Forever, Ellis

She put the letter down and just sat on the bed for a few moments. She read it again and lost track of time. When she got in the shower she cried for the love she had lost and cried new tears for the love she had now found.

A few moments later, there was a knock on her door. Still in her robe, she opened it and saw Antonio standing before her.

"Hi, I'm sorry I'm not quite dressed yet. I'll be ready in just a few moments. Come in and have a seat." After letting him in, she started to excuse herself to go get dressed.

Taken aback by her beauty and his abiding love for her, he stopped her. "Tyana, wait. Don't move." He approached her slowly, took her in his arms, picked her up, and placed her on the bed.

"You're the most beautiful woman I have ever had the pleasure of loving so completely." He placed his lips on hers and they continued to kiss until they couldn't resist the temptation to have each other. He placed her down on the bed. They knew at that moment that nothing could ever come between them—ever. He stopped before they went any further.

"I had been thinking for a long time how much I've wanted to share my life with you—my whole life. I love dancing with you and now I love making love with you. Would you please consider sharing my world with me? I had always wanted to ask you to consider being an instructor at the studio, but now I would like you to be my partner. It would be great and it would make me so happy to have you as part of my world. You don't have to give me an answer right now, but please think about it. I know this is rather sudden, but I want to be with you every minute of the day. I know how much you love dancing and I would love it if you would want to run the studio with me."

"Antonio, that is such a generous offer and sentiment." She was nervous, having thought at first that Antonio was going to propose. "I do love dancing with you, and I love you, but I also have my career to consider. I don't know..." He stopped her before she could continue her thought.

"Tyana, what I was trying to ask you was, will you marry me?" He didn't hesitate to ask her. He had prepared himself all night to ask her. He had known the moment he saw her in his studio that she would be the one to change his life forever.

"What?" She sat straight up and looked at him, not sure she had heard him correctly.

In a soft voice he said, "Tatyana Dominique, I love you. I desire you. Will you share forever with me? Will you marry me? I want to dance you to the end of love."

"Oh my God..." she responded, placing her hand on her chest. She was emotionally touched by his words. She looked over at Ellis' letter that had fallen onto the floor, then back at Antonio and smiled as she replied. "They say some meetings are destined by chance, but I believe ours was a gift of fate. Antonio, you take my breath away and I love you with all of my heart. You're the only one I long to share forever with. Yes, I will marry you. I will be happy if you will dance me to the end of love."

About the Author

Theresa Liggins continues Tyana Dominique's journey, which began with her first novel, *Life Is But A Dream*. This compelling sequel once again evokes the powerful spirit of ballroom dancing. Enchanted by this graceful art and sport, Liggins found her inspiration for this gripping love story in her own passion for dancing at the Fred Astaire Dance Studio in Columbus, Ohio, where she trained and enjoys dancing as a hobby.

Writing *Dance Me to the End of Love* and its predecessor, *Life is But a Dream,* has allowed Liggins to expose her readers to the magic of partner dancing, or ballroom dancing, as it's known. She wrote both novels to garner the recognition for the art and sport of ballroom dancing.

Printed in the United States
1054500001B/76-201